Unsung

By Marc Young

To Mum and Dad, with love from Your son Marc

© 2013 Marc Young. All rights reserved. No part of this publication may be reproduced, stored in a retrieval system, or transmitted, in any form or by any means, electronic, mechanical, photocopying, recording or otherwise, without the prior permission of the Copyright owner.
ISBN 978-1-291-56936-0

Cover by Emily Young © 2013

This book can be purchased via the internet.

I set out on this journey of words for myself

But, I am blessed

I finished it for my children

And

For my wife, Kate,

Whom I love more

Than life itself

Are you awake?

If so, come, take time

Today

To dwell and smile

By this lake

Try not to skim or to sink

Take a break

Persist

Through any mist

Stay a while

To reflect, swim and drink

Before you rush

Again

To let tomorrow

Push

And

Pour back in

Contents

0	Porthalloe	Page 6
1	Mother	Page 8
2	Father	Page 21
3	The Early Years	Page 30
4	Hannah	Page 53
5	Penare	Page 65
6	Mary Ann	Page 77
7	Leaving Porthalloe	Page 95
8	The Railway is Coming	Page 109
9	Prosperity & Hardship	Page 127
10	Mr Smith	Page 151
11	Mr Burgess	Page 166
12	A New Life	Page 188
13	Africa	Page 204
14	News from Home	Page 218
15	A Great Force	Page 232
16	Copper	Page 248
17	Elizabeth Ann	Page 265
18	Dolcoath	Page 287
19	Epilogue	Page 302
Acknowledgements		Page 308

Porthalloe ("P'raller")

It is May. Cornwall at this time of year is fresh and green. I love it. The butters are flicking in and out of the cups and dandy's as they lie open to embrace the sunshine. Their tiny yellow faces, all stretched toward the sky, sway in an undemanding breeze. I drink it all in, like a smooth, crisp, golden cider.

It all looks new and promising at this time of year. Up on the hill, overlooking the bay, everything is bubbling up nicely. Everybody is busy going about their business under their cottage rooftops and in their salty back yards.

I can hear Mrs Nicholls cussing her chickens. They cluck in panic and scatter in all directions. Scrambled eggs for breakfast again.

Today the grass is damp but the air is warm, fresh on the face, as I look seaward over Falmouth way where the fishing has already begun. Hungry gulls squawk and swoop over the breakers, tearing the silence with demanding cries for tit bits and attention from the working men in their coloured, bobbing boats.

Yes. It is a beautiful spot. One where I was born and grown. One where if you want nothing for it, there will be no demand on you. A place where I know I can return and be idle. Idle as a cow hand skipping a chore list as long as a horse's tail swishing flies.

Porthalloe, my dear trusty, earthy friend. I am back here to visit. It is a reflective mood, egged by the whisk of hasty time. I can find no better place in the world for a pause.

It is true that there is less care here now for the pilchard. Most boats are gone and with them the scattered families of the bay. What held them here has gently loosened its knuckled grip and released them to a madder world.

At one time all here were known to me, but now, just the odd acquaintance survives, and Mrs Nicholls. Mostly I am looked upon with suspicious eyes. But, so be it. These hills and woods, these sheltered coves, cliffs and pastured fields, amongst the forget-me-nots and skaws, used to be my kingdom.

I may never be able to come again.

1. Mother (Mamm)

My mother was Margery.

She was born in Porthalloe, inconveniently, at the height of the summer harvest, in the year 1800. She was the second child of Zebulon Saunders and Margery Williams.

And a younger sister for Mary.

It was accepted, without questioning, that the second child would be named after the mother's family, unless the child was a first son. So, she was named after her own mother and a long standing tradition, stretching back further than memory allowed, was dutifully maintained.

A baptism was also traditional, and it was hoped a passage, in those times, to some later salvation. For almost a full season after the birth, her father had been reluctant to have anything to do with the Church. Zebulon Saunders' own salvation had always been in work and drink. Sometimes his mood was harsh and he could be as stubborn as an ill-fitting gate, or the granite rock from which it swung. But, during the steady drop of autumn's russet leaves, and after withholding other pleasures, his wife, her mother, had been able to persuade him that there should be a blessing.

So, common ground was thus occupied and an uneasy peace descended. During this lull, a slippery two mile

You have to start a journey somewhere and, at its source, you may not expect very much. Everything may just remain in a pond nearby. But, what if your waters nudge the bank and create a new stream, slipping a seeping vein into virgin soil, and carving out a fresh direction? It may be a turbulent flow, muddy, curling, curving and twisting but, somewhere in amongst, it discovers purpose and direction. It is vibrant, picking up a pebble as it passes the silent swishing tails of sipping cows and rides the current of Father Time's gathering speed. Make the most of the life force, before enjoying the lazy meander as your journey embraces the wide mouthed silver shine of the vast reflecting ocean beyond. There, on the beach, your pebble comes to rest. It forms part of a beautiful view whilst its journey there lies untold. Until this moment. This is a long forgotten old Cornish tale.

journey on foot up the hill to the Church at St. Keverne was made. It was on the Sunday, squeezed between a cold Michelmas and a blustery New Year. There was a sufficient pause then, even for an obstinate, suspicious labourer to cast his eyes fleetingly toward a loftier cause up there on the crescent of the mount.

The baptism ceremony had been shared with two other families.

Dinah, the seventh child in eight years for the noisy Roberts family, and William, the first for the Chings, were the other babes to startle at the bracing waters of the font that day. Such mixed fortune God bestows. Dinah lived until she was seventy three, dying when she reached the same age as her mother had. William Ching was not so lucky and he died peacefully in his sleep, within a year of his baptism ceremony.

And so my mother settled into life, there in the small cottage near Roskerwell Manor Farm, a place she then never left for long. Her very early years were amongst apron strings and butter churns, and she often pierced the air crying for attention until, aged three, she and her sister Mary were joined by a brother, Peter. Her father was, at last, overjoyed. He had a son and heir. An heir to what, no one knew, for there was little, if anything, on that lonely shelf. It did, however, mean a heady summer Baptism and rough scrumpy choruses amongst the freshly stacked hay ricks.

Life then changed for a short while and the mood in their gladed cottage was of sun and song.

Until that day when his son Peter was born, Margery's father Zebulon Saunders' past had been one of scattered ties and abandoned lives. Yet another move to a new Parish and a new farm had been his way of solving problems he alone had created. Folk seemed pleased to see him then happy to see the back of him.

In Budock, where he had been living back in 1785, he had been named as the father of a new born baby boy, called Absalom Trevena. The shamed mother was a young single woman, Mary Trevena, and the Parish had pointed its crooked finger at my grandfather and made him the subject of a £40 bastards bond. This was not surprising, as Mary Trevena's father was the long standing Parish clerk and his quill must have been shaking with rage between his agitated fingers long before it settled on the ledger to ensure the disgrace was recorded, and the culprit named.

No love was given to the little boy either, from any quarter. He served only as a daily reminder of the indiscretions of lust so frowned upon from all the high and holy church spires of the land. He had been named Absalom after the third son of David, King of Israel. How sad it must have been that whilst that third son of David had been a great favourite of his father, and all his people, this mite from Budock remained an uncared for burden, dying unnoticed after only four months.

Both father and mother resumed their uncorrected ways. Whilst Mary Trevena had another child called John, who also died quickly, Margery's father, (my grandfather), married another woman.

Ann, his first wife in the eyes of God, was by then already pregnant. Their daughter, Mary, was born at the start of 1789, five months after they had married. To avoid the whispers and yet more gargoyle gazes from the population of Budock, they moved on to St Anthony. There, soon after, Ann died giving birth to their second child.

The child was said to be a stillborn boy, but none of us ever really knew. We did not know, either, what had become of Zebulon Saunders' innocent little daughter, Mary, from that first marriage. If my grandfather was not for telling then he was not for telling. No one had ever dared venture into asking too much. All those who might have known lay buried, and behind him, like the past.

The death of his first wife Ann was to be another new beginning for Zebulon Saunders.

What brought him to Porthalloe rather than any other village was a younger brother, called Peter. He was a steady person whose good nature was taken advantage of by many over the years. Despite a cost to his own hard earned reputation, Peter helped his elder brother to find work and to settle in the village, with its sea mists and its trickling streams. For my grandfather it was a refuge, a better prospect, and an escape, from a scowling, moody and unfortunate past.

My mother's mother, on the other hand, was from an old Porthalloe family which had remained steadfast in Porthalloe, for centuries, like a cluster of blue mussels on a sturdy rock in the force of a crashing wave, or like Peter, her new born son, who clung mightily to her bosom as she busied about the cot.

Whilst suckling her baby son Peter, my grandmother Margery had kept the fire, baked the bread and tended to the ducks, chickens, vegetables and her two young girls. She was a strong, determined woman, used to the why's and the wherefore's of the area and its people. Having lived in the same house in the same village all her life you could reliably say that she knew everyone. Well enough, anyways, to form a firm opinion from which she was unlikely to then waver.

Margery's mother, my grandmother, had first seen Zebulon Saunders over harvest time in 1796. She was suspicious, but not hostile. He had recently arrived from St Anthony and so she was of no formed opinion. But, as pasture after pasture was mown, his smile and twinkling eyes fanned an interest. She noticed the glistening sweat on the hairs of his bronzed arms. It mixed with the flakes and husks of scythed corn. As the sun shone off a calm sea, he paused in a lower meadow to correct his cap which he used to shield his eyes. At that moment he had drawn her attention, like a smouldering coal that had leapt mischievously from the hearth. As he sucked in a light breeze and steadied his fork, she noted he was taller and stronger than his brother, and glowed with a youthful energy. She was twenty two and he was twenty seven.

After their eyes had met a few times, her moods were caressed by everything he did and soothed by every movement he made. Although he said little, his words were cherished as though the golden flutters of an angel's wings. He was the one, no matter what wise counsel might have said were it ever to have been consulted. His past was swiftly overlooked and, within the year, their wedding was set.

Companionship had to be strong, for life was certainly a bitter and daily struggle. All around them were family but, at the sweep of a witch's broom, you could be cast out like dust into a brisk cold wind. If this happened, perhaps because of something you had said out of turn, all you'd see when looking around would be the shuttered windows of the shunners. It was not advised to be contrary in Porthalloe, or other parts. However, sometimes my mother's father Zebulon's mood would gather like a great dark shoal of pilchards off Nare Point, surging with a force no fisher's net could hold. He could cloud up a storm all on his own and he would care not what others thought of it. 'Tie down your boats and run. Seek shelter' they must have cried.

Bringing back his sunny smile would take a patient watch and an even keel from all in his family. My grandmother became good at it. She accepted his black moods would happen but also that they would blow over. Underneath each tempest there was always a dove. Forgiveness from the village would always take a little longer and, for some, no amount of sugar would ever dampen the resulting bitterness.

In April 1806, Bessie was born. Margery, my mother, was five. Oh dear, yet another sister and another daughter. Hold your breath and hide the hard objects. Although so young herself, she remembered the sallow complexion of the new baby, her father's disappointment with another girl and the difficulties it all caused. Why was her father not pleased with such a fresh bundle? Were boys better than girls? A strong independent spirit from her father but a fierce loyalty toward her mother fused under that five year old head of brown curls.

So, my mother, as a child, again set about her chores and there were many. From first light to fading dusk she learnt, in those months and years, to tend to the chickens, to prepare the turnips, to bake, and to gather wood, or picking sticks as she would say, for the fire. All manner of tasks not so evenly required of Peter, her brother. Keep to the grind, for otherwise the devil might catch you, her mother would proclaim whenever she caught one of the girls lingering a little too long over a task or distracted by something she considered unimportant.

Then, in 1809, it all happened at once.

Two vessels engaged for transport to the far off Napoleonic wars, called the Primrose and the Dispatch, ran aground nearby on the jagged Manacles rocks, both on the same night and with the loss of more than two hundred weary fighting men. Those poor storm tossed souls. They had expected to duck a French man's slashing blade, in a skirmish many miles from home, but not to be undone by the wrath of nature on their own shores and within sight of their loved ones.

Margery's mother, my grandmother, was also once more with child, and her father, Zebulon, fell upon illness.

As her belly swelled, his work in the pastures and meadows, and his general labouring, all ebbed away.

Her father tried hard, determined to succeed, despite a constant pain in his body and a creeping wastage in his limbs. His youthful strength declined, and his efforts to fight back gradually became weaker. After severe and worried consideration, the family eventually took to St Keverne for help. There they knelt 'cap in hand' before the Vestry, whose authority her father had always cursed so much.

A stubborn endurance over thirty nine years of life had forged a fierce independence in Zebulon Saunders. He relied on nobody. He trusted nobody. He owed nobody anything. He did not even care for another opinion if the truth be known. He had loved and lived his way and it had suited him fine whilst he was carrying every sail he had. He knew the land, and sea. He had taken the power of his brawn and had harnessed nature to his own ends, like a tethered orchard sapling. At times his method would bear fruit but this time the illness was unleashed, whipping back at him with a coiled anger. It ripped him from all he had strived manfully to control and cast him into a creeping shadow.

It was May, and Zebulon Saunders was quickly gone, buried beneath a freshly cut sod at the far end of the church yard, in the shade of the grey stone boundary wall. The sharp blade of the grave digger's shovel had barely been wiped clean before Zebulon Saunders' place at home was filled when another daughter was born. Her name was Alice, unknown to her father, and ignored by her tear swept mother.

My mother was eight when her father died on the cusp of forty. She did miss his strong presence and his stories of Barbary's along the coast, doing the devil's work in the dark of night, flashing cutlasses of cold metal that could slice a man in two. She missed his seasonal provision, unwrapped in front of small excited faces when he returned home each day at twilight. His drunken carousing was no different to any other man but she felt that his fierce independence, in spite of others, was something to be admired and carried forth.

She stood by his name, sometimes with overwhelming odds against, like the drowned Manacles rock Dragoons must have done when fighting to protect the pitched regimental standard at Corunna in those far away Bonaparte wars. What good was it all, though, when nature could take you away in one angry swipe?

Baby Alice became my mother's charge. She was a baby doll to care for whilst their own mother, a young widow, cast her life upon the rocks of grief and misery. There she smashed, like the ship Dispatch did, spewing returning Dragoons in their crimson tunics into the angry foams. Was her mother to go under as they and her husband Zebulon had done? Was she to finish forgotten and buried, too, under a poisonous yew in that silent church yard?

The flotsam of this wreck had to be gathered, repaired and renewed. Hope had to be tethered and fed. A pauper's allowance agreed through the Parish brought relief and mercy before God for a mother and her five hungry young children. The family and village came together and, in time, all resolved to move forward for the sake of the living left behind.

Mary, Peter and my mother Margery were thus young siblings engaged in all manner of pastimes, earning a penny here and a penny there. Net mending, pilchards, salvage, milking, churning and milling all helped to turn time into a healer as well as put food on the table. As soon as they were old enough, they were joined by Bessie and Alice. For some of them this life made them stronger, for others it was to make them weaker, piercing their souls with doubt and insecurity, burdens they would never be able to escape.

Yes, my mother was strong and determined. She did not give in and would not be overcome. Work was with the light, from morning to night, with no ambition beyond survival. Her life was amongst beautiful steep green pastures and the sound of the sea. She woke up with the cockerel and the gull, joined in chorus by the lark and the chough. Serene it may sound but, if you did not play the part required of you, life and nature would show you no respect and it would have you for a meal and soon swallow you down.

By the age of ten she was a dairy maid at a nearby farm, the subject of an agreement with the farmer to ease the burden at home for her mother. Lodgings above the animal sheds were provided so it was only on a Sunday that she would walk the three miles home to see her mother and to attend Church with her. The far off war with Napoleon was still raging but its gory glory touched her infrequently. The mud she knew was from the farm and the cliff path. That was her beautiful battlefield. News of a bloody encounter at Waterloo seeped through, lapping like quiet, exhausted seas on the shore, stirring few to any great concern. Someone from Porthalloe had gone to fight. Had he survived? No one knew and the farmer growled that 'Them cows still has to be milked. You'd better get them teats working my 'ansum'.

During this period there were some thin harvests and even leaner bellies, perhaps partly due to the demands of the war and those that made the laws. Nature also always played a part. One year there was no summer at all. Was God so displeased with what he saw that he sought to punish them?

Around this time she met her first and only love, Thomas Pearce, my father.

He worked at the same farm, already an experienced farm hand at the age of fifteen. He had left home in the same circumstances as her, when he had reached ten years of age. He was three years older, full of humour and breeze. To her he was assured and bright, carrying no weight on his shoulders. She had been so matter of fact about everything that it was a relief to be swept along without a care in the short interludes between all the work. His presence broke the routine of cow's udders, water carrying, flour making and parlour sweeping and he made her laugh deep inside and out loud. He became someone she looked forward to seeing and she began to dream about what they would say to each other.

As the years passed they had gradually become friends. Then, one Sunday, he asked if he could walk with her to Porthalloe. He wanted to spend some time with her and see where she lived. Glances and smiles across the farmyard were followed, in time, by lingering walks down into the shrouded folds of the hills, amongst the ancient oaks and wild garlic. Off the beaten track they discovered the magic of blossom in spring, and each other.

For a while nothing else mattered.

But, like her mother before her, she fell pregnant. It was no wonder for at every opportunity Thomas had sought her out around the farm, in the fields and under the shelter of the hedgerows. He was most persuasive, and easily encouraged. Once she realised that there were changes in her body, she told Thomas. He seemed pleased and felt the obligation to marry before too many more days passed. For the first time there was a future, beyond the next day, for them both.

On Thursday, the 4th October, 1821, after her 21st birthday, she and Thomas were married in a simple and straight service at St. Keverne. Their marriage was witnessed only by her mother, who never married again, and some of her family. It was the end of harvest, and a more convenient time.

The last standing corn, the neck, from the crying ceremony to celebrate the end of the harvest, was hung by the ears in the doorway of their new cot, for good luck.

2. Father (Tas)

My father was Thomas.

He was born in 1797 within the boundary of the Church bell peal in the village of Manaccan, Cornwall.

His father was Nicholas and his mother was Eliza. They carried on a family tradition, which is at odds with all the Gospel teachings, of getting pregnant first and marrying second. So, Thomas, their first born, slipped painfully into the world well before his parents first year together was out.

Nicholas worked on the land and there was no part of that land he did not know. He knew all the lanes and bridleways, the fields and their farms. He could look to the skies and tell how the weather would be from the cut and hue of the clouds. He may not have had the legal parchments to wave about that decreed who was the master of the soil on which they all stood but he did not need a waxy seal or an inky flourish of words on a tattered and yellow document to declare that he, in nature's true eye, was the rightful keeper of this bountiful green domain. There, on the slopes above the sea, he would sweat, whilst sails full blown on the crisp blue waters below, clipped by, carrying the fruits of his labour off to feed hungry unseen mouths. Here, whilst the world busied on the horizon, was his quiet and fertile kingdom.

But it was an exchange. He was never short of hard work, was always poor, and, in truth, a victim of commerce. The parchment wavers struck their fortunes from bartering the harvests in places he would never know, whilst he toiled for the pennies which lay forgotten at the bottom of their deep velvet pockets.

To restore the balance of his power and purpose he was wickedly cruel to his family. He saw them as nothing more than useless grubs to feed and that was a chore he was glad to leave for a stupid wife. She had been a drunken side trade with an amorous local butcher. The butcher's young, unwanted daughter, born to his now deceased wife, was passed to Nicholas like a side of beef. It left the butcher free to set about wooing his next plump fancy with seductive offers of free liver and calves tongues.

These wretched people had all now fastened Nicholas there, he thought, in that small damp cottage with its gloomy walls, low ceilings and tiny suffocating rooms. He hated the stagnant stale air. He wanted to be out, and he wanted to be free, to smell and feel the ripening grain, cupped beneath his nostrils. Cows and crops he could handle and understand. Weeping women and sickly babies he could not, and would not.

Nicholas's frustration brought suffering for Thomas, his son, and my father. It also brought fear for Eliza. Nicholas was never minded to ever be kind, even for the duration of a church service. She was young, innocent and flapping, like a fish washed ashore after a violent storm. She struggled to meet the demands of her babies, the chores that were flung her way, and a raging husband. He gave her almost no money. How could she weave a coat with no thread? But, try she did for she would not even dare to suggest that Nicholas was cruel or mean to her. She learnt to never answer back for, when she had done so in her younger days, it brought a heavy swipe from the back of his hand across her bow. If his blow had drawn blood, so much the better, it seemed. Argument excited him and her pain became his easy pleasure.

Through all this Eliza remained physically weak. Her body struggled with any passing illness and her fragile soul was lost serving a man for whom she soon had no love. She was small and he was powerful and she found herself bound like a slave to his persuasive and persistent lust. When he had a lusty mood she longed for that last grunt to come quickly and for the pain to be over. All she wanted was to sit by the river and run her fingers through the clear cold waters. She would dream of its gentle gurgle and the calm peace of the silent surrounding glades.

Soon, however, she was unable to keep up and some chores were being left undone. When Nicholas returned at the end of another day he would sometimes boil up into a fury. How could she be so lazy when he had toiled so hard? He would growl, full of heavy thunder. Why was she not like other women? It was just his damned bad luck that he had been pinned there by her.

Their young family suffered daily for it.

But, the children kept coming after Thomas and another five were born by 1808. Three were boys and two were girls but they were all as good as abandoned to chance once they entered this world.

As her oldest son, my father Thomas tried to protect his mother, but could not and, eventually, abandoned all will to do so. Instead he sought preservation for himself. He escaped, losing himself along the holloway's and under the curly trees of the lush valleys and tangled creeks of Gillan and the Helford river. He trapped birds and fish, ate berries and nuts and scrumped amongst the orchards. He passed, unseen, between the tracks and cuts as far up as Treverry, carving a wild existence, watching the horses being led to water and the oyster smacks hauling their slimy catches aboard. This was to be his schooling.

The time came for him to leave and, at the age of ten, he found himself doing the bidding of a local farmer. Cows became his living with their smell of milk and pasture, in all its glorious forms. My grandfather, Nicholas, was paid sufficient in cider from the farmer's own barn for the trade. For Nicholas it meant one less mouth to feed and a week of hazy headaches. For Thomas there was a release from any obligation at home so he felt that the arrangement was of benefit to him, too.

After this, if Thomas ever returned to the family, his mother always looked a little more downtrodden, pale, and sad than he had seen at any time before. His father simply wanted to relieve him of what little money he might have earned whilst he had been away. His long fingers would reach into Thomas's pockets, fishing for the ghosts of farthings. Home was a dark, dangerous world that lay over the brow of the hill and he sought fresh light with his new independence.

So, in time, he stopped going home and lost contact with them all.

As the crow flies, he lived and worked no more than a few miles walk from what had been home but he could not bear to go back, for he was at odds with the mix of hate and dependence on him. In its stead, he worked on, moved on, stirred in with other people, lads and lasses, all of the same complaint. They shared the bond of unhappy pasts, hopeful beyond reason of a better future. He grew and developed a stocky frame, suitable for wrestling, if he had wished it to be so. Food was not plentiful, especially in some of the very cold winters and the summer that never was, but he had sufficient, for he knew where to look and when. No ripened fruit, from the wild or orchard, hung unthreatened for long, and no coney or culver could rest safe from capture.

It was around 1812 when he met Margery, my mother, for the first time. He was working on an estate no more than three miles from St. Keverne, at Tregidden. She arrived from Porthalloe, young but quick to learn and not afraid of hard work. She had brown eyes, long hair the colour of hazel nuts, and under the sun her skin freckled and went red. She had no interest in him but he kept a watchful eye.

His other eye was on Mary Jewel. She was confident, full of song and could swing a pail without spilling the creamy contents. At milking time more than the udders of cows would be on show, even when she knew all the farm boys were loitering a little too long. She was a tease, able to draw a crowd, and not too shy to take a wooded walk if you showed a bold interest. She was saucy, outwardly happy, and made a stern life more bearable. But, she was desperate to love and be loved. It did not matter with whom. She loved all the boys. Even the master would find an excuse to rearrange the straw and work on chores in the barn if the opportunity arose. I often think that, thanks to Mary Jewel, that farmer must have had the tidiest barn in the whole of Cornwall.

Mary Jewel did not hold my father's interest for long but, on reflection, I think that was mutual from what my father had related to me one sultry summer's evening many years later. The only things that moved as he spoke were the last of the day's flies as they tore back and forth across the rays of the sinking orange sunset in front of us. After several hurried gropes and fondles his interest drained, he had said, and she was soon fluttering her eyelids at another young love struck boy who had been lucky enough to see her in full flow over the milking.

One Sunday, much later, when my father was over twenty years of age, he told me he had plucked up the courage to walk to Porthalloe with Margery, my mother. It was the first time they had any sort of talk, beyond the formality of the farm. They had spoken of the other farm servants and he had asked about her family. At the journey's end, near her mother's cot, she said goodbye and he gave her a posy of wild pink campions he had picked from the hedgerows and verges along the way. They had both smiled and their friendship had begun at that moment. Before that, no one had ever shown my mother such attention.

Their world was to become an island, where all schooners sailed by, unnoticed. There was no need for either to be rescued from this spot. To them both it was a blessing. With all promise before him, his past unhappy life was forgotten. He opened and showed her his world as a young independent man. He showed her the verdant woods, cool streams and bountiful orchards. He took her to the hills edge, above the bay, at the Beacon, where you could sit amongst the wild thyme, look across to Falmouth and Saint Mawes, and imagine life amongst the dark cots and wet cobbles. There, on the brow, the sea breeze cooled their gazes and their new found freedoms flourished and became entwined, as one.

Thomas, my father, said he had always intended to marry Margery, my mother. He said that it was not an obligation brought upon him by any sense of duty, or the fear of Bridewell ordered on the disobedient by those stiff white wigged masters of our laws. Once he was told by her that their passions in the wheat fields and fern glades had led to a conception, he was clear and resolved. It was what mattered to him. It was time to drop anchor and find a sheltered bay to settle. He had resolved to be a better father than his own father had been to him.

Thomas found work nearer to Porthalloe, for Margery wanted to be near her mother, and also close to her mother's help. In any case, she was unable to stay at the farm where they had both worked. To be with child was to be a hefty burden. They would find a way to manage, despite the tight fists of the landowners, who were forever driving down the daily wage. As soon as the summer harvest was completed they would marry. The date was set. It was to be a feast to celebrate and bless the produce of the land, the passing of Margery beyond twenty one years, and their union.

Drinking, dancing and singing around a crackling bonfire all made it a night to remember for the village, and also a morning to forget.

In those first few months they were happy together. Like two bees weaving invisible thread in a dappled and forgotten flower meadow. The cot was small but it was warm, cosy and theirs for a season. They had grown up with hardship and had made light of it. Now it did not matter. They were in a place of their own with nobody else to turn to but each other. They were in love and somewhere they loved. There was a kindness in their neighbours and, at last for them both, a joint purpose to their lives.

What, possibly, could break this blissful spell?

Then Thomas junior, their first born, arrived in March 1822. It was a difficult, agonising birth. He became twisted and stuck, rousing old superstitions from behind the cobwebs strung in the rafters. It took an age to release him as my mother pushed, strained and laboured through the night. Both were nearly lost.

When the baby did arrive there was no sign of breathing. Grandma Margery Saunders was there. She took the baby by the ankles, held him up and gave him a rough slap across the haunches which persuaded the mite's soul to stir into life with a cry. As the candle burnt in the soft early morning light, tiny blue Tom began to bawl and turn a healthy pink.

It was not a peaceful start for my older brother and fate had been truly unkind.

Everything was to be different after that first birth. Thomas, my father, had been reminded of all his past troubles. Shaken, from that time on, instead of joy, he only saw the problems and the mistakes.

3. The Early Years

George the fourth was the king of England when I was born in Porthalloe in 1823.

My mother had an easier day giving birth to me than the night she had endured when my elder brother was born the year before. She had carried me the full term without too much complaint and so I suppose she hoped I would be an easier child and that their home would finally settle into a peaceful monotony.

I obliged by taking to the breast with no need for any persuasion. My dark eyes reminded her of her father. My grand mother, also called Margery, helped with the birth and was so overcome at the sight of me that she had to sit a while. If ever there was a likeness of her dear dead and long departed husband, here it was, she said. Silently I expect she also hoped I would be much less trouble.

One Sunday in late September of the same year, I was dipped in the font at church in St. Keverne and, as the Reverend Pascoe's fingers dripped holy water across my temple, a name echoed out through those ancient arches like a ghost. I was baptised Zebulon Saunders Pearce, a reminder to all that my Grandfather would, after all, live on.

By then I am not sure that my father, Thomas, cared too much. There was plenty of work to do in the fields, barns and mills around Porthalloe. The wages for his sweat and toil was not much for a living. As it became less each year so he would work longer to maintain the balance. My elder brother, named after him, had failed to prosper and was slow to walk and speak. My father had wanted to hide him away. The clear difficulties weighed upon my father's mood like unleavened bread. His young carefree ways were lost under the yolk of responsibility and the daily reality of his new unfolding life. He had realised that this struggle was to be the sum total of his existence. There was to be no rescue or golden moment when all he wished for would appear before him and wait in line for him. I expect he felt like a Jerusalem pony, tethered to a millstone, tramping round a vicious circle. He sought solace in the pleasures of the flesh and we, his growing family, were a tithe on him even for that.

My father was known by all and farmers would engage him for his ever dependable services. He would tend the livestock and produce cattle that were better nourished than we were. The salty breeze of the sea was never far away from his work but he always preferred the spring of lea under his boot to the choppy black of water beneath the flimsy timbers of a boat. He became a shadow we saw only in the light of a weak candle as it flickered at the end of another long day. In the morning he would always be gone early, before even Jude, the cockerel, had blinked a bleary eye, stretched a weary wing feather and cleared his sleepy throat.

He left the bustle of the cot and yard to my mother. What she did not have she did not miss or care for. In all my memories of her she was never without a swollen belly, never without a small, dirty child tugging at her apron strings and never without the fear of God around her shoulders. She had the benefit of great help from my Grandmother, also called Margery, and together they set about preserving and keeping what little they had been given or had fallen their way. We all lived as though the hard won security we enjoyed could easily be snatched away, as family stories had suggested it had been many times before.

I know she loved us all dearly, like a mother hen would her brood of confused and innocent chicks as they learn to peck in ever bolder circles away from the roost. She was not as ceremoniously religious as some other folk but she liked to climb the hill to St. Keverne for church when she could and, when the sun shone, she always found time to lift her face towards it, close her eyes and give silent thanks for its reliable warm glow.

After little Thomas and I, along came Samuel, another son. He was named after my father's brother, someone neither we nor my father ever saw. He lived several miles away over towards Manaccan and, apart from a story or two from the past, that was all we knew. Samuel was a family name and so that was the reason my father gave for handing it on to a son of his. 'I may not know my brother or want to know him but he is still family' my father had explained to my mother at the time. Then, along came Nicholas, named after my father's father, whom he never cared to see again. What a strange reminder these two new young sons became of a past my father had chosen to have no mixing with and to forget.

I can remember the day that Nicholas was born. I was four. It was during the pilchard season and my mother screamed louder than any huer I would ever later hear on the grassy banks above Porthalloe. It was as though she were being ripped apart like another helpless Packet on those mean Manacles rocks. Nicholas was indeed a sturdy baby and it must have been a relief for my mother when it was done.

Soon we were four excited boys, all under the age of six and full of energy and mischief. Where my grandmother only had girls, my mother, it seemed, could only produce boys. My mother must have been sapped, like a tree separated from its root, its leaves and fruits withered at the expectation of having to feed so many hungry eager faces. What a sight she must have had of us all jumping around, our noses running and our earthy hands stretched out in hope of a morsel more to eat than any of the others.

Of us all, only Thomas, my elder brother, failed to prosper. He was slow to learn and unable to carry out the household and other tasks demanded of us. One of us would always have to go with him and assist to make sure that he was safe and that he carried through what was required of him. If he were sent alone for water, he might come back from the stream but it was not always with the water, and, sometimes, not even with the pail. His return would never be straight away, either. He liked to stop people as they went about their business, and talk to them. They would listen, even if they did not understand what he was trying to tell them. Afterwards, looking bemused, they would be on their way shaking their heads as they went.

Nevertheless, we three brothers would stick up for him and shield him from the worst of my father's growling temper. 'Was life not a hardship large enough without this extra load to bear?' my father would scream at my mother in frustration. It was sad to see my father, who was so self reliant and industrious realise, as time strode through the seasons, and years, that his eldest boy and namesake would never be able to discover his wit and to follow in his footsteps.

When 1829 arrived, so did another baby. We all crowded round the bed, where my mother lay, exhausted, in her night gown. Her hair was brown, damp and long. It curled down across her left shoulder. Her eyes were moist with tears, grateful for another precious moment and a safe arrival. We jostled to catch a glimpse. Samuel was always the most persistent. 'Is it a girl at last? ' we all enquired as we stretched over each other to see. 'No', my father replied, 'tis another lad for the plough'. Unsuspecting of such destiny, the baby lay peacefully, crinkled and pink, with his eyes shut tight. Margery, our Grandmother, was on hand to lay out for supper, as she had been to help with the birth and everything else. She rounded us up like a wise old shepherd would a flock of unruly lambs. As we sat, elbowing each other in the ribs between gulps of scalded milk, Gran said 'I think we have another Peter'.

Peter Saunders Pearce was named after my two Uncles, called Peter Saunders, who both lived within a mile of our cot and who were always on hand with help and support. One Peter was my mother's brother, the other her Uncle and they must both have neglected their own families to help tend to ours. They were kind and I'm not sure anyone told them so back then. My father just left them all to it. We were growing like crops exposed to a strong sun after a full week of lashing rain. At that time, if a litter of piglets were born I think some folk may have mused upon that and viewed our family as a comparison.

They were unsettled times to be raising a family. There was anger at the scarcity of corn and the ever higher price of food. Landowners and farmers were lowering the pay for a day of labour. Muttering and concern reached even this remote, sheltered corner of the kingdom where nothing was ever wasted. What was the answer? Even the question was forgotten once the winter candle was blown out. My father's gropes and my mother's giggles were to lead to only one conclusion. My mother would again be with child. In the mornings he would smile, belt his britches, eat his breakfast and be off for another day with the cows, cap in hand. She would sing to us amongst the bedlam they and God had created before her good mood wore off and she tried to rescue the day by bringing in some sort of order. She did try to steer us towards piety and obedience. That was a thankless daily task, along with the provision of enough daily bread.

There was no complaint of pain from my mother when William was born in 1830. He was the sixth boy in eight years. I know the vicar was counting for he remarked upon it. I think his bushy eyebrows were raised to the rafters at the time. 'Heaven help us' I think I heard him mumble as he rolled his eyes. Thank heaven William's arrival was smooth. Gran said he would be an easy, undemanding boy and she was not going to worry about him.

While the babies kept arriving, Sam, Tom and I explored Porthalloe, watching the fishermen, checking the drying nets for a forgotten fish and sitting in the boats drawn up on the bay front. We threw pebbles into the lapping surf and squabbled over who was the strongest thrower. There was no schooling other than what we found at the shoreline, in the countryside and from each other. Sam and I preferred to be out and we took Thomas, our brother, with us. He was beginning to learn. Sometimes Frank or another friend would come along. Nicholas was too young at that time. Baby Peter was always ill and crying. Our new arrival William just slept, quiet as a mouse.

These were innocent, happy times for us, as young boys. We had no desire or ability to understand the weight a society of landowners had placed on our father, mother and neighbours. It had continued for generations. If my father could work he was of use to any farmer or landowner of the Parish who cared to employ him. If he could not, the same farmers and landowners felt he should not be a yoke upon their shoulders.

What did this mean?

It meant my father's work was of less value each year even though what he produced for others increased each year with his experience. It meant that he was breaking his back sowing and growing the corn only to have to pay more to buy back some of it to feed his family. It meant no one was ever satisfied. They always wanted more from him.

He doffed his cap and my mother curtsied when they were in the presence of these tinkering men of power and their decorated ladies. They would bend over backwards all their lives.

But, we never heard them complain out loud or saw them buckle or give in. Thomas Pearce was in work and he remained grateful for it. Yes, the undeserving fortunes were made elsewhere. Yes, it meant each penny we saw was squeezed until it bled, like a chicken stripped to its white, over boiled bones. Yes, it meant there was never any likelihood of money being squandered in our house on the latest fancy feathered hat, 'yet another' fashionable jacket or whatever it was that pleased her deserving ladyship.

It suited the few to keep the majority in ignorance and serfdom and, little did we know it as we tore up those steep banked fields that we, the sons of Thomas and Margery Pearce, were to provide the next generation of poor labourers, ready and prepared to toil without complaint. Our births into that humble little cot meant we were bound like prisoners to the ship of destiny's mast. The captain, sipping port in his wide, warm cabin, had cast his compass, consulted the sextant, and already determined our passage, without the need for further enquiry.

Well, for the majority of us.

In November 1830, whilst we were helping salt and barrel thousands of pilchards, Peter, our young brother, died. He was not even two years old. We stood, bowed, while his little lifeless body was placed in the ground, now silent and limp after eighteen months of sickness and misery. He was going to a brighter place the Vicar said. If the Reverend knew this to be true, why, I wondered, did he continue to live there, amongst us?

We had to grow used to death early. Even the King, George IV, had died so no one was beyond the fateful finger if it chose to point your way. People could be there one day and gone by the time the sun rose on the next. In

Porthalloe, that November, four lives were lost to death and three of them were young, having hardly started on their journey or uttered their first words. We did not ever know our brother Peter. We only knew his cry. He would never play in the streams and leas with us or look up the hill at the thin grey church tower on the St. Keverne horizon. We shed more than a tear, for here the deep sorrow of death had been experienced close to hand, in our own family, and for the first time.

When Thomas, the eldest of us all, was ten, another baby arrived and we were six brothers once again. In defiance or in memory, this new small wriggling package was also baptised Peter. He was a determined fighter, with his fists clenched and arms thrashing as if already pushing demons off. In spirit alone he seemed equipped to stand up to those tough times.

As baby Peter settled in, Thomas, my elder brother, moved out. He went to lodge a few doors down the lane with grandmother Margery where all hoped he would be of some help to her and that she would be of some guidance and help to him. We would still see him every day.

I had in any case grown used to taking the mantle of the oldest, in charge of a regiment of two small, disorderly footmen in Sam and Nicholas. Mother was the General, sending us on missions to raid the hedgerows for nature's current bounty or to the Mill up at Tregarn to fetch any scraping's from the day's grindings of barley. We were always hungry and must have eaten half of all we picked. Blackberries were a favourite of mine but I liked them sour and on the turn from red. That way there was no need to wait and find that another scavenger had spied the ripened fruit first and filled their belly. I grew used to my food cold and unripe, for it was more plentiful that way.

At the age of nine I was beginning to have an awareness of my surroundings and where Nature's goods could be found. I had many a cut through of my own amongst the paths and lanes that crossed amongst the cart ways, streams and folds. Coming across the quickest path meant more time to forage or climb trees. I understood that Nature was a great provider so long as you did not try to control or destroy it. Why break a branch to reach an apple? If you did, there would be no apple in the same place next year. It was better to be a husband to it and hope that she would repay your attention to kindness with a rich variety of flavours and tastes.

We became miniature husbands of a quiet, fertile landscape. We were far from cares, as long as there was food. For a time we felt like kings of all we saw. On a baptising Sunday, as we shuffled, pinched and fidgeted, the Vicar would talk about the beauty and bounty of Eden, some far away place he said we could only dream about and wish for. But was it not here, spilling out across our green rolling hills, our wooded valleys and our calm blue sea? What could be better that lying on our backs in the sun on a grassy bluff, hands behind our heads, watching the clouds and ships go wandering by?

We were the Pearce boys, known to everybody and everybody was known to us. No door was shut and we were in and out of all the houses, like summer flies, noses into everything. We made sure we did not miss out on anything. Francis Noye, known as Frank, became a great friend. We lived a few doors from each other and we all quickly became entwined, like ivy on a weary tree trunk.

In spring, summer and autumn we were often called to work in the fields, orchards and at the waters edge. Picking apples, cutting the hay pastures, planting corn or potatoes were mixed with helping land a pilchard sean when Porthalloe was blessed with one. Any pennies we earned would be turned over to Father and Mother for we quickly learnt the order of things. We were each but a minor bell in a full peal and, should you refuse to ring, it would put out the tune of the whole canticle.

I was used now to this way of life and the freedom to explore. I knew all the granite gate posts, mud creeks and tree lines. I knew where the rooks would gather, when the weather was changing and the demands of my mother according to the length of the shadows along the valley's edge. I felt truly alive and wrapped in a silent world broken only by the song of a thrush, squawk of a jackdaw or mother, calling me home.

It was not to last because, for me, there was then some bad news.

I remember it was a frost bitten Sunday in 1833, a year after the birth of the second baby Peter and a day when my father was home. My father came up to me as we were preparing to walk to Church up the hill at St. Keverne. The first bells were beginning to call us up. 'Zeb, my boy, it will soon be time for you to tie yourself to a farm' he said as he strapped his boots. He did not look at me. I was ten. I suppose I had known this moment would come. It meant I would soon be leaving home to work, and to live, on one of the local estates. 'I've had words with Mr. Roskruge and he has kindly said he would keep by a place for you at Pengarrack'.

Mr Roskruge's wife had died in June of that same year, he had given up a little, and he needed help on the farm. I knew there was already work to be done and I knew not to argue. Now I was ten I had to be a man and to be strong. There was nothing else to be discussed, but I was going to miss my mother.

Before the week was out I was on my way. I had nothing to take apart from the clothes I stood in and my wits. Frankie Noye had said that it was not too sorry a life. He had been sent away six months earlier, in time for a full summer of work. I had walked many times to see him, along the cliff path, to the farm at Gillan where he was working as a farm hand. 'Mrs Williams, the farmer's housekeeper, is kind and feeds us all enough' he would say. Nothing bothered Frankie. He was a comfort and he always brought a smile. He made any hardship a small one and with him by my side the great unknown I had in front of me was always easier to face.

Pengarrack Farm was up the hill from Porthalloe, on a cart path that hugged the bank and, after some Cornish miles, eventually led to St. Keverne. It stood on its own, with a good view across the bay to the castle at Pendennis. There they grew corns and barleys and ran a herd of cows. The corns and barleys went to the mill below. It served the people who lived locally and was a living for the tenant farmer and the landowner he paid his annual rents to. It was a short brisk walk up the lane from home so not as bad as Frankie's fate. My father had said 'when you be taller Zeb you'll see the rooftops of Porthalloe from the farm. Don't forget to wave'. I could tell he was going to miss me.

My work at Pengarrack was hard and unforgiving. Each day was full and long, tending to the crops of winter and summer barleys, the wheat, the cows and the pigs. If it was not tilling, it was removing the rocks from the ground through the changing of the seasons, and re-building hedges with them. Mr Roskruge's sons always wanted more, wringing a damp cloth bone dry. Some boys did not last. What became of them, I do not know. Maybe they joined the militia and had their heads shot off. When the choice was laid before me, I was not afraid of the work. I was afraid that if I did not work I would have no home or food. I imagined my father in a rage, refusing to take me back, slamming the door in my face as I begged for a roof over my head. It drove me on to carve a place at Pengarrack that was only mine to loose. At the end of a day, exhausted, I would settle for anything there was to eat. It might have been a piece of hardened cheese or stale bread. Surely no one else would want it? Yes, I ate what no one else wanted. I ate what had been forgotten. It was food and it was welcome and you had to be clever to get enough of it.

So, for the next two years my bed was in the main barn, where all the young farm boys slept. As soon as my head touched the straw I would be asleep. If I washed, it would be in the bottom stream and only if there was time. The master, Mr Roskruge, was kind but distant. He was a man of few words and I did not see him about that often. If I did see him he was usually in his dark funeral weeds. As his wife, the mother of his nine children, had just died, I was not surprised that he was withdrawn. The death of your wife was not a speck of flour dust to be brushed from your shoulder. It is a sore tragedy that will forever be carried with you.

Most of the direction in the farm came from three of his sons, Richard, Henry and John. Whatever you did, you had to be careful of Richard for he could quickly turn and his mood would change day to day. Henry was more gentle and even, happy if not too much were expected of him.

John, the youngest son, was eager for work and I learnt much from him.

I did also learn my first written words at the farm. I had no schooling so, before then, pens, paper and ink had been a mystery to me. Eliza, one of Mr Roskruge's daughter's, taught me a few words and how to write my name. She was kind. I also learnt the counting of money so that I could be relied upon for the accounts and deliveries if I was required for carting duty.

Eliza was a year or two older than me. She was the youngest of the master's family. When left with time to herself she was not afraid to seek the company of those who were her own age, like me. Her kindness made me dare to think on her as a sister and friend. She was a guide and helped me to see more than my own view of my own world.

Where I felt safe in a world I could see, Eliza was sure that the unseen world would favour the brave. She was always clear in her belief that her life would be on a farm but she would say 'there are farms and mills in many places and people will always need to eat'. She doubted that this sheltered corner of St. Keverne could be the only beautiful place in the world. 'I have been reading words of far off places' she said, adding 'They promise riches for all who venture beyond the horizon'.

Across the bay to Falmouth would never be enough for her, I thought.

Two years after I left home I did have a sister, when darling Elizabeth was born. She was a daughter for my mother, at long last, and at the eighth attempt. My mother was overjoyed, relieved, so totally complete. Elizabeth, or Bessie as she was quickly called, was truly, truly cherished. Little did she know it for she slept soundly as the brothers who were still at home crowded curiously round another birth, trying to catch a glance.

We were all there round the font when Bessie was baptised in the middle of September 1835, later that same year. She cried and upset Edith Mitchell, the other baby there for baptism. The whole church was filled with the echo of lungs at full blast from the two of them as they strove to out bawl each other. Only Edith's mother was there with her so perhaps she had more to cry about. She was already seeking attention from an absent father who should but would not or could not care less. Our tears that day were for the happiness Bessie had brought my mother, who could not let go or stop smiling. She constantly gazed into her daughter's little dark brown eyes, holding her close in case she was going to be snatched away. My mother had her triumph and was soon walking around Porthalloe showing Bessie off with bright eyes and a renewed purpose.

I never lived with Bessie at home but when I was there to visit I could see that she was a binding, happy influence on the family. It settled every one during those thin days, even if, by comparison to up country, it was a peaceful and bountiful part of the world. She was a blissful escape.

Troubles elsewhere were speculated upon and worried about. Now and again a nameless body from the unknown world beyond us would wash up on the beach. They were poor, pale, bloated and lifeless souls sent to remind us that death was never far away. We could only guess about their lives and what fate had befallen them. We knew, however, that we were all but one step away from our maker and one step from being washed up ourselves on some bleak forgotten shoreline. I tried not to think of that person I had seen lifelessly riding over each incoming wave, who had finally come to rest amongst the scattered seaweed, stranded far away from home like a storm swept shell.

But, that person would be there, nameless, floating in the worst of my dreams.

Somewhere there would be a mother waiting at home for the return of her beloved. She would fade in her twilight years, forever wondering about what had become of her loved one, the one with whom such a tight bond had been joyfully shared. Had he cared so little that he didn't send her word of his wellbeing? Her life would remain on hold, consumed by daily sorrow, waiting for those words of comfort that would never come. I expect there have been many mothers like that who never knew what fate has bestowed upon their child. I expect there will be many more. If you had seen the bulging eyes, the torn grey and purple skin and the loneliness of those who had drowned unknown, perhaps it is better that those mothers never know the true outcome.

So, I did not resent the way my mother held Bessie tightly to her bosom. 'Cradle her and savour every sweet moment' I had said, more than once, to myself.

I also resolved to work hard, always do my best and, most of all, to keep close by my mother for her love, I realised, was a pure one.

In 1836 I was joined by Samuel at Pengarrack. The haws and cow parsley's were white with flower and the lush leas were almost as tall as he was when he came pushing through the grasses. His sandy brown hair was flecked with seeds and petals. He was undaunted by the new life now facing him. He had been engaged by Mr Roskruge to help me with the growing herd, the calves, and other chores. As an old hand, well, one with two years experience, I cannot say that I was able to take him under my wing for Sam was confident and purposeful from that very first day.

'Come on, Zeb' he had said as though it was I who had just arrived.

He had been arguing with father and he wasn't going home, he added. He was here to make the best of what lay before him and not what lay behind him.

Over the next few years Sam developed a solid frame to go with his independent spirit. If he did not believe something was right or just, he would be defiant. Some would say headstrong. On many occasions he might have lost his position at the farm had I not decided to sit on him, holding him down, until his anger had dwindled, like a brook in high summer. He was too quick to react if his view was overlooked, dismissed or ridiculed. It was right that he should be there with me for I was able to steer him towards a calmer berth and not take such a stormy view of the world and those who lived in it beside us.

Sam and I did work closely together in those years. We grew to know each other well and we learnt how to labour for the benefit of the farm and for each other. I felt I could settle for a life like this, knowing my position and the seasons. I was born to follow my father and his father before that. Sam, however, was always restless. He did not want to live his life in the ruts left by our ancestors. Even the clouds were moving, he said. Where were they going? What did they know that we did not? Why should he remain here? 'The money we earn cannot even buy a sip of the roughest cider, overlooked and rotting at the bottom of the last barrel. What future is there in that?' he had said.

We were still young and learning the farm trade. Sam did realise that time was on our side. We were growing stronger with each passing season and we could work well, without the need for direction. However, whilst I had

Sam with me in all my dreams of a prosperous future, I think he only had himself in his own thoughts. He was already making plans to follow those clouds.

In June 1837, we heard that after a short reign, William IV was dead. Victoria, young and not much older than us, became the Queen of England.

A year later, I was stacking the barley at Pengarrack one hot summer's morning when my younger brother William rushed up, flushed from a charge up the hill. His eyes were wild, as if he had been chased up from Porthalloe by an angry stampeding bull.

'Zeb, come now, tis Mother' he cried.

I could not leave my duties but Willie was tearful, pulling at my sleeve.

'She's going. You must come now' he continued, clearly agitated.

I found Mr Roskruge, the oldest son and master, and explained that there was a pressing need at home for Sam and I. Where my mother was going I did not explain.

'If you stop work now, forget today's pay' he said, shaking his head. 'Be back by sun rise' he continued 'otherwise others can be found to do your work and you need not return at all'.

It was a quick tumble down the hill from the farm to Porthalloe. I may have ripped some skin on a bramble, but I forget and it mattered not. We arrived breathless.

Inside the cool cot, my mother lay on her bed, peaceful, sleepy, but hot with a fever. She was weak but managed to open her eyes as I reached for her hand. I could not contain the tears at seeing her there, exhausted and drained. She seemed resigned, unable to recognise Sam and I properly. It was a shock to see her so rudderless and limp. She had been our reason, our direction, and our one true support. I was fifteen and it had never crossed my mind that one day she might not be there, in her cot, up to her elbows in flour and washing. Up until now she had been there every day, treating us all equally, showing us all love, and asking for nothing in return.

Nicholas said she had cut her hand badly six days earlier, whilst gutting a catch of pilchards at the water's edge. She had bound the sliced wound with some cloth and carried on working. My mother needed the money and could not stop work. Other tasks could not be held back either. Dirty chores and children demanded that she struggle on even as her hand began to swell uncomfortably. She had gone down with a fever that then raged across her, eating into every sore corner of her body like a fire, blown by a strong wind, consuming a dry hay rick.

Bessie, only three, and the youngest, had cried loudly with an anxious fear. With arms outstretched, she begged to be picked up and comforted. William obliged. The rest of us held our breath and prayed. We prayed hard and like never before, searching the empty skies for angels.

It counted for nothing.

The sparkle left the sea, the wind dropped, honeysuckle hung listless in the eaves and, as the sun slipped from the sky, my mother died.

It was a Saturday, the 16th June 1838, days before the Coronation of Queen Victoria.

Margery Pearce was buried by Monday, the 18th June. She was on the cusp of being thirty eight. May God rest her gentle soul. She will be forever in my heart.

4. Hannah (altrewan)

After my mother died, Margery Saunders, my grandmother, picked up the pieces and threads of our lives and became the female head of the family. We were crushed, like kernels under a heavy grindstone, and she was a vital and steady pilot, able to steer a sound and safe passage away from trouble. She was well suited for the task of sweeping up broken pieces. After all, she had already had to do that many times before in her own life.

Thomas, my father, could not stop work so life, for him, had to go on much as it had done before. The family's livelihood depended upon it. Nothing changed for him in his role of looking after the family. He had to carry on rising each day, as he had every other day of his life. If anything, he now worked harder, throwing himself into caring for cows and heifers, hoping they would help him to forget the leaden cloak of tragedy.

William, who was eight in 1838, and the oldest son still at home, had to grow up quickly. He became close to father, helping father where he could and picking him up where he could not.

Peter, who was six, and little Elizabeth, who was three, were both too young to know the full force of this family loss. Gran took control and set them to a routine. Thomas, my eldest brother, who was now eighteen, moved back in. He could help my Grandmother. They were companions. However, he was still unable to work in the leas or to be on his own like the rest of us had been since we were ten years old. The one time when he was left alone to mind the cows for father, William had to be called to herd then up before they had trampled and eaten all of Mrs Sowell's prized vegetables.

My brother Nicholas was eleven and had been sent away to work for Mr Retallack at Trewothack, just inland from Gillan. He was not far away, let's say a couple of miles walk, and he had his Porthalloe friend Thomas Martin for company. They were both occupied with the dairy there. It is a beautiful place where the cows enjoy God's view and produce the reward of thick rich cream. Gillan has many hidden coves to explore. Father was pleased that he had secured the place there for Nicholas. Perhaps there was some sympathy in it from Mr Retallack for there were many requests from men in the district with ten year old boys who needed work. Nicholas was not so fond of it. He undoubtedly missed being cared for at home.

Sam, of course, was with me at Pengarrack so we were a comfort to each other at a bleak time. Not having mother to see at home on a Sunday was like a fisherman setting off to catch fish without a net. Something vital was missing. But, we knew we had to get on with it. We had never heard of any one coming back once they had left for heaven apart from in those passages read from the bible on a Sunday. Sam said he had seen mother there in the mowhay, singing soft melodies, and watching over us when it was dark and we were supposed to be asleep.

My grandmother did her best. She had to be a mother all over again at the age of sixty three. I suppose if you were a fisherman then left your boat idle for ten years or more, you could again go back to sea. 'Once you have learnt, you never forget the ropes' I had said to her one day, repeating what some one with a head on his shoulders had once said to me. I had called by during an errand to see how she was. Gran agreed but said to me that mothering at her age was not as nature had intended and, if she were a fisherman, the bottom of the boat would be in need of a few pressing repairs.

And what was my father to do? He was in his forty first year so he was still young but there were the children too, hanging like noisy cowbells round his neck. Who would be prepared to take them all on? If they did, why would they not be married already? It was marriage that he would require, "plus all the trimmings and comforts" he would add with a knowing chuckle and elbow when with his labouring friends. In a few years Elizabeth could look after him but in the meantime, his mother in law ran his house. It was not an easy arrangement. I expect he felt like a lodger but it suited for a while and it was born out of necessity.

St. Keverne got to chittering.

The women fussed and clucked together over their chores and the men mused in small groups as they clutched their pipes on the corners of its lanes. Who could help the poor unfortunate Mr Pearce who had lost his wife at such a young age? A tragedy it certainly was they had all nodded in agreement. The message was sent out to Helston, and further on to Falmouth. Mr Pearce was a man of little means and limited prospects, with three young children at home who were almost orphans. Who would take pity on them all? Who would take him in hand? Did they know what they were letting themselves in for?

Perhaps some one with similar prospects would suit? Surely in these circumstances, Mr Pearce, aged forty one, would be a good catch?

Then Willie Tripcony over at Treleaver Downs made a suggestion whilst three sheets in the local kiddlywink. His family had lived at Tregarn with Peter Saunders. Everybody knew each other. They had all worked together from time to time. So, when you happened across them after church you could get to talking about all sorts of dreams once you'd had a drink or two. The chime of the church bells would soon be drowned out by all the chaff and chatter. God's message would be long forgotten by the time the sun slipped down as quickly as the cider already had. Willie's suggestion was speculated upon long after the uncritical moon had risen to usher folks home across the fields.

Willie Tripcony had worked in Devon, quite a few miles away. He had never let on why he had gone there or why his new wife came back from there six months later with a baby daughter. As he held court he said he was experienced in how the world worked beyond the corn scapes and hedges of St. Keverne. He had seen a thing or two, make no mistake. He would tell you, too, given half a chance. He drank more cider at other people's expense in those days than anyone I know and the stories he told grew longer and less believable every year that passed. He liked to see us laugh. I suppose, on reflection, we also liked to encourage him.

He had also been to Camborne, he said. It was a mining town full of people. Where there were people there was drink, he had continued. Where there was drink there was cavorting. Where there was cavorting there was bound to be a wife, lurking. Camborne was 'only twenty mile away, walkable in a day', he said. 'Not much sacrifice for such pleasure' he had concluded, looking at my father. He, in turn, dipped into his pocket. It was a thought that had merited another cider each.

Willie had heard of women left at the altar by men they loved. The men had loved them back but had left them pregnant, still single and in disgrace. In many cases it turned out that such men were already married, or seeing someone else on alternate Sundays who, in time, had drawn a keener fancy. Willie said these men had often moved on, or disappeared, leaving the women, the children and yet another set of troubles behind. This all sounded familiar.

'If the men stayed in town', Willie had continued, tapping his clay, 'they often denied all knowledge of what lay behind a woman's apron strings'. Willie told one story of how an accused man had said to defend himself 'I saw her with a different Tom each night that month. She were up that alley at the back of Tyack's. Some fella were squeezing the life out of her and she were holding on as though her life depended on it. I never touched her so that babby can't be mine. It don't even have my likeness what with two eyes an' that hair an' everything.'

Who could believe that such things would carry on? In some cases it might only be that the husband, usually a miner, had died young, leaving a widow in want of company or in need of food for her baby. Maybe God's local servant would help, Willie suggested. 'That is if his hands were not full enough already' he chuckled.

Over the next few months my father caught hold of this thought, cupping it like a baby bird. It grew in confidence. Then, one Sunday, he went to the Church and after service the Reverend Pascoe listened quietly before saying that he felt it was a good pursuit. He agreed to help. A letter was written on my father's behalf by the reverend Pascoe and sent to the vicar at St Martin in Camborne. Did they know of a young woman who was in need of saving by way of a husband? He would be a husband of sound character, with love to give and only available because his wife had unfortunately died young.

Then they waited. At first the weekly postal pony had to trot its way up country to Helston. There the message of hope was eventually sorted into the right pile for the Camborne cart. After that nothing else was heard and so, like turnips in a frost, the idea went cold.

But, news did eventually come, by letter, addressed to the Vicar at St. Keverne. He spoke of it to my father at the church door one Sunday, at the back end of May. 'Shall I read it to you?' Reverend Pascoe asked. 'Yes, if you have a care to' my father Thomas politely replied, expecting the letter to at best contain a mild refusal.

"Dear Reverend Pascoe,

Thank you for your letter of the 20th April. Your proposal has been given due consideration and I am of the opinion that there is some value to it. I believe that there is a young woman who may prove to be a suitable match for your parishioner, Mr. Pearce. Her name is Hannah Barratt and she is a God fearing woman with a young daughter who is now six years of age. Hannah has been of great assistance to me so if she were to accept Mr Pearce's proposal then she will be sorely missed. I have discussed the matter with her and she is disposed to a meeting as soon as it can be satisfactorily arranged.

I remain, yours,

The Reverend Hugh Roberts

St Martins".

A broad smile broke out across my father's face. 'Bless you, Reverend' he said, holding his cap whilst stooping gently forward. His hopes were revived.

Hannah was born in Camborne in 1809, the last of ten children of William and Anne Barratt. Her father was a tinner who had died, exhausted, of phthisis, at the age of fifty three. Hannah was seven. Between 1814 and 1816 she had seen three sisters and her father die. Only one brother and three sisters survived into full age, in miserable, hopeless conditions where even rainbows had feared to cast an arc.

In the early 1830's she met a man called William Collins and fell in love. He had pronounced his love for her and expressed it in short torrential shudders and bursts between quarts down darkened back lanes and out in the bracken, brambles and brush around the town.

When Hannah's daughter was born in August 1832, Mr William Collins was long gone, perhaps to sea, and with him went his promise to 'do the right thing and marry, making an honest woman of her'. Who would want her now? She was disgraced, deflowered and destitute. How could she have been so foolish?

Hannah made up for all the weakness in William's heart by resolving to keep her daughter. There would be no sweet poison. She named her daughter Hannah, like her, to show union. She would be cared for, sometimes with help from the Church.

At other times help came from her sister, Kitty, who at forty was seventeen years older than Hannah and so almost a mother or even a grandmother. Kitty's husband, Henry Bartle, was a quiet, kind and mild man who spent his days down a mineshaft and his nights caring for his family by stretching the little money he had earned until it groaned. It would now have to stretch to two more mouths whether he minded or not.

Hannah also took in laundry and the vicarage was amongst her customers. This helped her to get on her feet and to show that she was independent. She resolved that she did not need a man with cruelty in his heart and no backbone to his soul. She fought for all she had and then she fought again to hold it. When she was approached by the Vicarage offering her a solution, she did not, at first, believe it to be true. Then she dared not think of this as her salvation. Surely this man would be the devil's goat, untethered, unwanted and uncaring. He would beat her, be vicious to her daughter, and treat them both like slaves and nothing more than common whores.

Beggars could not be choosers. She quickly agreed to meet my father Thomas.

With one thing and another, time's pages were turned and it was July of 1839 before they were able to meet. It must have been a queer sight. She, small and slight, was as pale and thin as spilt milk. He was bronzed from the sun, sturdy, with a mop of brown hair, flecked at the edges with grey. She was dressed in plain pallid colours, he in rough country browns. It was awkward but there was no point in beating about the bush. She could come and live with him, take care of his children, be a wife, have a new life. It was far from Camborne, a different way of carrying on. She would be safe and would not have to do laundry for others for a scattering of worn pennies. He would treat her daughter like his own and she could carry his name.

The age difference was over ten years for he was into his forties and she barely thirty, still of child rearing age. She liked him but knew that she would need to barricade her position there with him. A child with him would provide her with security. Then she would be able to run their lives her way.

He liked her and felt a young woman would do him good. In any case, what did he have to loose apart from his old mother-in-law?

They were married in Camborne, after the harvests were safely in, on the 11th November 1839. The main holiday Feast at St. Keverne was on the 20th November. They got to know each other with dancing, music and song. He had wanted to touch her long before, to sample the fruit, but she was set against it until those words 'you are now man and wife' had been pronounced.

Willie Tripcony was rewarded for his idea by being a witness. He had himself so liked Camborne that he moved shortly after to a small farm there, sheltered between Penponds and Hayle.

We, my father's eldest sons, had not even met our new mother before we saw Hannah standing there by the hearth of the cot. With her arms crossed she let us know where we stood. We were not to interfere. We were not wanted. There was to be a different tune to the one that had played before.

Elizabeth did find an older friend in Hannah's daughter. Peter had a new mother. William calmly accepted all the change. One tune was very much like any other, he reasoned. My grand mother moved out again, her purpose once more served and her presence no longer needed, or required. My brother Thomas followed her, like a lost lamb.

For my father it was as though he had Margery, my mother, back. He went about his business the same way, whistling up the lane, carrying on as though nothing had changed. Even if it had, it mattered not to him now. He had a woman back in his bed and what a bewitching wonder she was.

Sam, Nicholas and I looked in on a world where the scene was the same and most of the people were familiar. But it was no longer our life.

A new broom had swept the past and its lingering ghosts firmly off the threshold. The dusty corn doll that had hung forlornly above the door since 1821 was burnt. It was the clearest sign that from that time on it was to be Hannah's way.

In late 1840, a year after Hannah married my father, my half brother Henry Bartle Pearce was born. Another boy, yes, but a new son, and the new heir.

5. Penare (Pennare)

Mary Ball was my friend at Pengarrack. We grew up together in Porthalloe and we were the same age. She was the only child of William and Mary Ball and I expect she had always been lonely. Aged six or seven she'd come and look round our door to see what we boys were up to and she would watch, leaning against the frame and keeping a safe distance. I suppose she thought we would chase her off if she showed too much interest in our noisy house.

William, her father, worked on the land with my father and they would often both drink too much strong cider together and console each other over how their lives had turned out. We would keep our heads down at such times because that sorrowful mood could quickly change into something more threatening. If you were then caught in such a thunderous red fog you would be lucky to navigate safe passage out of it without being the subject of a bruise or two. I pictured her trying to stay out of her father's way so as not to catch his eye and therefore give reason and direction for his rages.

Her father was forty when she was born and her mother was older still. Although her parents had clearly gone step by step through the conception process on many occasions, Mary seemed to be a surprise to them both. When she arrived, neither really knew what to do with her or what to make of her. Mary was an unwelcome intrusion into their steady, quiet lives. 'What wrong have we done to deserve her?' they had asked of each other. They were too weary to change their way. Over the many childless years that selfish nature had become an easy habit for them. Even the clustered cobwebs had been ignored in that cot.

When Mary was twelve, she came to Pengarrack to milk the cows, make cream and butter and help in the running of the house and farm. She went wherever her help was needed. She said she would not be missed at home so we all knew she was already suited to us, her new family. She was slight and as quiet as a church mouse but as reliable as the vicar when Sunday's bells rang their calling to us in the Parish each week.

For four years on that farm we had spent our lives together, working, eating, sleeping and talking. We had experienced the same background and we shared our thoughts. I know she saw me as her only real friend. 'You have treated me better than any brother could' she had said to me one dark winter's evening. I brushed this off by saying 'but you don't have a brother.' I did not mean to hurt her.

In time, there we were, both sixteen, and our bodies had changed. I had grown muscle and sprouted hair in unlikely places. What devil had driven such change in me? I was forever searching for a new sack cloth which would fit my widening frame. She had herself changed from a wisp of straw. That is what happens when you are in charge of the butter and cream. Her breasts brought new curves to her slender shape and I was amongst those who noticed.

I grew fond of Mary and I found myself staring at her as she walked across the yard. I could care for her in other ways, I thought. She became a different attraction. She was my first love.

As we turned towards spring and the air warmed, we began wandering together through the leas and lying amongst the lush ferns and bluebells in the nooks of the hill sides. For me, it was a delicious exploration as we lay hidden from the world between the gentle green fronds that bordered those shaded gullies. We had our favourite places. They remain secrets, perhaps even from the wood nymphs. She let me touch her soft skin in places usually covered by her farm smock. 'If it means something to you Zeb', she had said, 'I suppose it'll be alright'. It did mean something to me. I discovered the soft feel of a woman for the first time.

Days grew longer and I found I could not wait for those brief moments when sunlight and leisure combined to produce that heady mix. For a season a trip to the calm cool of the woods was all we could think of.

But, in time, as the trees shed their blood and ochre shades and winter drew in again, our love became a troubled matter. She wanted more than this. She did not want ruin which was where she felt this path led if our passion was left unchecked. She wanted a home to call her own and a husband to provide for her. She wanted an unknown number of children and she had a whole multitude of eager demands that no merchant in anticipation of a feast day could hope to ever stock.

At least not there, in Porthalloe.

She changed. Instead of a friend, she began to see me as her provider. I became the answer to her prayers, a Dorcas ticket, which would give her the first taste of meat for a year. She clung to me as her means of escape. 'After all', she said, 'I have given you the greatest gift of all, my virtue.'

All I wanted was more of the same. I wanted those sweet moments to last and for us to stay as we were. I could not be her key in the lock to a big family. I saw how it changed my father and remembered what had happened to my mother. I did not know what I wanted, beyond simple pleasure and distraction, for I was young and on no wage at all. I could not provide a certain future for I was uncertain about everything except those snatched moments of physical bliss that we had secretly been sharing.

I was not my own master, I reasoned, and, if I was not, how could I be the master of my own destiny and take her with me? Marriage meant a chosen path and a weight of expectation. I wanted us to work together on the farm, to share our earthy pleasures and to remain friends. The only harm I meant was to the broken blue bells on top of which our bodies had rollicked. So, for me, the trade I was offered was not one I was ready, or able, to make.

As we could not agree, a difference grew between us which kept us apart and made us unhappy. We did not speak, for words were not enough to untangle a knot that had become tight, and eternally twisted.

That's how it was. Yes, I know now that I let her down when I ran.

In October 1841 I left Pengarrack.

I was sad to leave. It had felt like home, perhaps more than my own home ever had been. I had been there almost as long.

Mary left, too, but not with me. We were both eighteen. I think Eliza Roskruge had a hand in helping Mary, who was upset. Perhaps she fixed it for her to work on another farm up country, or as a maid in Helston, Falmouth or Penzance. Perhaps Eliza even weighed up a perfect husband for Mary, a match made only in the most blissful of dreams. I do not know. I often wondered what happened to her but, having run, I kept low.

After Pengarrack I found work with Mr Tripcony at Penare. It was a new start and he was a new master, keen to overlook all past history. He was a young man, only about ten years older than me. He was brave to try his luck by taking on an Estate tenancy so early in his life and to make a go of it. He had also taken on the widow of Penare, who was older and more fertile than even my father. She was the mother of eight children from her previous marriage and three from her current one to Mr Tripcony. A formidable woman she most certainly was and we were all in no doubt about who was in charge and what was required of us.

Like my father's friend, this Mr Tripcony's name was also William. However, this William was no story teller and he moved about the farm in the shadow of his wife's previous husband, Edward. I admired William for trying but nothing he did was ever good enough by comparison. In everything that was measured he came up short and Mrs Tripcony was not slow to tell and remind him. She did not care who heard about her dissatisfaction.

When I lay in the barn at night I could sometimes still hear Mrs Tripcony shouting over at the main house. I was sure then that her previous husband must have reached heaven when he died, for if his ears had suffered such buffeting and punishment when he had been alive then he must surely have been a saint.

Everyone in those parts seemed to carry the same name as someone else, apart from me. It could get mighty confusing or amusing when you were talking about people. Official gents from up country trying to track down a smuggler or a tax payment were often given the run around. Some people even had the same first name as their surname, like Mr William Williams in Churchtown. Any stranger making enquiries about some one in the area swiftly attracted suspicion. They would find themselves with a drink in their hand, then another and then another. Meaningless stories and generous hospitality would flow, diverting attention and stirring the confusion. The stranger, often from somewhere like Redruth or London, would soon be so twisted and befuddled with this tale or that tale that they forgot what they had gone there looking for. Later, they'd wake up in the back of the post cart, with stalks of straw in their ears, short of a belt and shoe or two, and trotting gently back towards Helston. They'd have nothing to show for their visit south but a pounding head ache and the resolve to never set foot there again.

Not for me, though. If it came to smuggling, and with a most singular name like mine I would be caught, now wouldn't I? 'I'm looking for a ruffian by the name of Zeb Pearce. Do you know him?' 'Yes, there is but one. You don't forget a name like that. It must have been him. You are quite correct, he is a notorious vagabond round these parts. You will find him loitering over there…..'

Well, I was hiding at Penare where there was plenty to occupy me. These were hard, changing times and the farm was a mite run down and would need a strong measure of courage and brawn to pull it round. With so many children there were also many mouths to feed.

Thomas Downing had moved across the way to help his family at Lestowder and I was his replacement at Penare.

It was a beautiful spot, set back from the cliff's edge, overlooking the sea.

When the sun shone you could see across the bay to St Mawes, Falmouth and in to the pleasing wide mouth of the Helford. At certain times of the day, the sea would shimmer in front, glistening like silver below the blue sky. The farmhouse perched above on the knap, like a grey eagle, cast in weathered stone and keeping a watchful eye over the bay. Across to the left and over the Helford was Mawnan, with its white shoreline cutting into the sea like a blade. The gulls circled here, looking for offerings from the speckled tides. Ah, there should be nothing to trouble me here, I thought.

Penare was but a mile from Porthalloe and so it was close to my old home and to where my father was living with his new family. Not that I saw much of him. Hannah was keeping him busy. The shortest path to walk was along the face of a steep cliff, where the cows clung. To the left of the path there you could hear the water lapping hungrily against the black rocks down below. You treated it all with respect and kept watch for the slipsey stones, those dark ones with a bit of an evil shine. The second you did not tread with care, especially in a hard frost, you could loose your footing. A trip on a slipsey and you could be gone, tumbling into angry foams. On top of you, I expect, would come a cascade of earth that had bound so hopefully to the land until you, the fool, had come along and disturbed nature's temper. Missing your step at night over stone stiles laid by ancestors was always a sobering jolt on evenings when even cider had not intervened. But, if my forefathers had managed to survive these perilous paths, then so could I. It was best to get a face full of mud or dung than to go sliding when the ice was up. Rounding up the cows on those abundant slopes always ended in breathless relief, a pat on the last hairy backside as it passed the gate post, and a smile or two for having survived another day with a stiff measure of good fortune.

And I saw, for all the hazards at the cliff's edge, that it was also good fortune which gave me work at a place like Penare.

In daylight, when the fog had burnt away, I sometimes stood and watched the frigates, and other ships, as they sailed by. On their decks, sailors ran like ants, whilst others hung in the rigging preparing the sails for their long journeys in search of some undiscovered beauty. Little did they know but there was one beauty, a jewel, right here, under my feet and under their noses.

What sea monsters awaited them as they set course on their quest? Would those sailors be flung into the raging froth as they sought to escape the creature's leaping jaws? From Penare you could see the different moods of the sea all in one day and experience all the seasons of the year in one week but, there were no monsters. Well, perhaps only Mrs Tripcony when she was in a swirling temper. There were only ferns, lurking in damp corners, with green fronds like dragon tongues which unfurled gently during May.

It was no hardship, really, to be out in all weathers there. I hated being soaked to the bone but shelter could be found behind the hedges and beneath the twisted branches of the wind blown sycamores. I would soon dry out once the sun cut through the clouds and cast slivers of white light across the sea again.

I got to know the paths between Penare and Roskerwell well, as my father and brothers did. Between us we had worked those sloping lush grass pastures with its red mud and cheerful blue skies for more seasons than I care to mention. My brother William, who was twelve, was close by in the dip at Treglosack and Nicholas, who was thirteen, was at Flushing. Peter was at home, Thomas was in Porthalloe with Gran, whilst Samuel, who was now sixteen, was still labouring up at Pengarrack.

I came to Penare for my labour, as I had done at Pengarrack before that. I had no apprenticeship so I could not claim to have a craft. There was no value attached to any skill or craft that I brought with me. In my first year, in exchange for my sweat, I received a place to lay my head at night, and some food. My father said a youth should expect no more unless he were to be born to a gent like Mr Vyvyan up there at Trelowarren Manor.

So I had to get on with it and learn to turn my hand to most things. I'd look after the cows, seeing to it that they had water and fodder to fatten and cream them up. We had to introduce the bull to the herd and be mindful of his horns. When he'd taken care of things I'd have to move him again so as to let the girls settle down to their grazing. Even when you are as endowed as Hercules was, there is only so much nonsense a lady will put up with before she tires of it.

I minded the pigs, making sure they did not take to robbing the crops when out of their pens. They loved the green acorns that I gathered from the crouching oaks down in the gilly's. Sometimes I'd come across my brother William and we would share the load. He was a shy and lonely boy. I thought he would be alright but your time did not belong to you if you wanted to keep your position and I could not do more for him. There was plenty of fetching, carrying, ploughing and repairing. I regret now to say not much time for resting, sleeping or dwelling on family.

The farm was up against it. A rent demand or some one who needed paying was never far away. There was always something to occupy your energy as the master strove to earn his living.

When the salty wind blew in from the sea it could spoil the crops and livestock if the hedges were not set right to protect them. If this happened the master would surely be ruined. Coppicing the trees on the hedge walls was a chore I liked. It was a skill to find the balance between cutting too much, or, indeed, not cutting enough. Shovelling the hollows gave you a ditch to protect the new tree shoots from nibbling animals and you could build up the height of the walls, packing squares of granite to hold it firm. What kind of tree would resist the wind and not fall, ruining the whole lot? My father Thomas liked blackthorn for this task. If it bent in the wind it would be stronger, he said, and grow into a thicket. Mind you, he also said 'You can make a coloured gin with its small purple berries, the slones, and that will shelter your insides'. I suppose there does have to be some pleasure.

Yes, Penare was a pleasing time. Mr Tripcony and the far from merry widow may have been wrestling with demons of their own but I was happy there, like a drowsy tick on a fat cow's backside.

6. Mary Ann (keresik)

By the end of 1841 I had started seeing Mary Ann. Frankie Noye teased me and said it was courting. Well, I suppose it was. Mary Ann had become my shiner. We kept company mostly on a Sunday and I often walked her back the three miles from St. Keverne church to where she lodged at Trevathen, on the downs above the sea at Coverack.

Mary Ann Heyden was the daughter of Jane Bastian and Lewis Heyden.

She said her father raised a musket at Waterloo. He would recount his stories of the battle to any listening ear this side of the hedgerow. Drawing on his old long necked Belgian clay, the tobacco billowed like gun smoke as he described standing firm against the slashing blades and hot grape of Napoleon. Were it not for him we would have surely been defeated.

Lewis Heyden, his name, will not be on any record or etched on a memorial wall for standing between French balls of lead and Wellington as the army skirmished all over Europe fighting for foreign causes. He was, however, remembered by his long suffering wife Jane for never being there when she, or his children, needed him.

He was born in Penzance. That much we know, for sure, of his past. All his stories may have had a grain of truth in them but, although I was too young to recollect him directly, I preferred to believe that he must have had a wild imagination and was able to tell a good tale. His stories were often repeated by others over the years and, like Willie Tripcony's, each time they became a little more fanciful. How could all that have happened in other parts when it was so peaceful there in Porthalloe? How could all that have happened to one man alone? At times he must have been the luckiest of all men to still be alive. At other times surely he was the most unlucky of all men to find himself in such a number of close scrapes?

Jane Bastian was the daughter of a fisherman and was born and raised in Porthalloe. She had lived there all her life. She had fallen in love with Lewis, who at the time said he was a soldier for the Cornish Militia. He had been passing through St. Keverne, just as he seemed to pass through most places. What brought him here would surely move him on in the time it took to burn a candle down. What thoughts made her reason that he would now surrender to this secluded bay and drop anchor there with her?

Jane was spellbound by his stories. I am told he could certainly talk. All it needed was for someone to show an interest. She clearly did and he brought the unknown outside world in to brighten hers. All she had known was life around the pilchards landed from her father's boat. She thought there must be more than that and now Lewis praised her for her belief. He told her that there was indeed more and that he could show it to her if she would only let him in to hers.

He rolled up a sleeve and showed her an arm wound, which he said was caused by the nip of some flying grape shot. It had been fired at him by an agitated enemy. Such fortune in avoiding death meant his heart was not heavy with lead and had been preserved, for her, he said. Her heart was won over, too, by this stranger from another world. She was a ripe fruit, ready for picking, and she dropped willingly into his waiting lap like an October apple after a gentle nudge of the tree. Never had any one so beguiling ever come her way like this before, she thought. She married her brave soldier in July 1804 and Lewis was allowed to stay in the Parish by the Church. A year later their son, Samuel, was born.

Then, almost as soon as everybody had settled back into their lives of daily routine, Lewis the brave was gone.

He did not set foot again in the Parish until after the battle of Waterloo, over ten years later.

For all those years no firm word had come of his whereabouts, from any quarter. Each day Jane had woken, looked out across the grey horizon beyond the waves, and wondered. Each day brought a new question or doubt. They were pitifully heaped in her mind, like the bodies of netted fish. Why had he not come home? Was he dead? Was he with another woman? How dare he leave her.

There had been stories, and possible sightings, but nothing was backed by money. Some said he had been carried off by force to a destiny not of his making. Others had heard that when he was returning from Falmouth, in a newly purchased boat with provisions for his family, he had been blown off course by a sudden storm and stranded in France. There, some hostile villagers had stolen his boat and mistaken him for someone who was worth a ransom.

When they decided he was not even worth a beggar's groat, they must have taken pity, and had released him back on to the open road.

I believe he escaped from Jane and Porthalloe, all those years before, to the safety of a single life across the bay in Falmouth where he had enjoyed weeks of beer, gin and freedom. Whilst there I expect he heard of the need for men to fight for Wellington in Spain against France. His passage from Porthalloe, and fatherhood, was assured. To be certain, I'm sure he kept below deck on the troop transport as it passed by the Lizard, in case the fishermen on the waters there should have recognised him and hauled him back to captivity like a flapping pilchard caught in one of their seine nets.

When he did re-appear in 1816 he was tired and bedraggled. There were no alternatives left, it seemed, but to beg forgiveness. He had worked his way home, he said, after being released from soldiering, making and selling goods of doubtful virtue along the way. Most of the time he had been away had been spent walking or marching and so he had covered many, many miles. Thankfully for his feet, he was very good with his hands and he had learnt to work with leathers in Spain. He earned extra pennies helping some of the other soldiers with their foot ware repairs and belt adjustments but had not otherwise worked his way beyond the rank of a private.

What a sight he was, I'm told, when he returned, having hung up what he called his fighting boots. He was thin, dirty and he looked like a vagabond who would normally have been moved on from the Parish with a penny or two for food or subjected to the grind of the Treadmill as a punishment for his vagrancy. He looked older than his forty scattered years.

Jane had taken pity, put an arm round him and taken him back in, accepting that he had not had any other means of getting back sooner. Of course there had been no one else. He had been a victim of circumstance. Besides, she had reasoned, his battles had been for a worthy cause. She had chosen to forget that her own battles lay fully unresolved.

Whilst Lewis had been away, Jane had had another son, John Henry Heyden. She had gone to Manaccan to have the baby and avoid the disgrace, for the father could not have been Lewis. How could Lewis have been? He was away shooting blue coats and repairing boots all over Europe. Who the father was remains unspoken to this day.

Despite the constant reminder that Jane had taken, briefly, to another man, Lewis seemed content for a while. He settled with Jane in a run down cot in Ladenvean, on the stream, just outside and below St. Keverne. There he made a living of sorts with his new skills, as a cordwainer and maker of shoes. In 1818, Mary Ann was born, a product of this loving reunification with Jane.

But it was not to last. Like the boots he made, everything came apart at the seams. Lewis took to wandering again, happy to be selling his wares and telling his stories as he went. Mary Ann's mother scowled and said he must be more afraid of a baby girl than a French musket and, if that were the case then he was a turncoat and should change his name to Louis. By her mood when she recalled those days I fear she was none too pleased to be left alone once again.

So, you can see that Mary Ann led an unsettled and uncertain childhood. When her father was gone she did not know if he was alive or dead. If he were alive, when would he show? He could come whistling down the lane at any time, greeting folk like he had only been out working for the day. When he did come home, he would turn out a few coins from a pocket, the gin would flow freely and he would light up their lives for a week or two. Then, unannounced, he would be gone again. She loved her father but hated his long absences. She also hated her mother's emotions which swung like un-tethered brig barrels caught on deck in a swell.

Her brother Samuel had instead been the helpful influence in her life. He was thirteen when she was born. He was already used to looking after his mother. He was as strong as a bull. His son was later a Cornish wrestler, full of muscles and the undisputed champion of Helston. We all looked up to Samuel Heyden in Porthalloe. If only we could be like him. We let him have his way and so he had a good run of the place, for certain. We were all sure to be firmly on his side in any dispute, however wrong he might have been about the cause. He stood for no nonsense. Pilchards had little chance with him at the net. He was more of a father to Mary Ann than the several men who passed through the abandoned and lonely Jane Heyden's life whilst her husband was away, who knows where, doing who knows what.

After 1826, Lewis Heyden stopped coming back. Mary Ann was eight. Then, a while later, rumour had it that he had died in Penzance, where his journey had begun. He must have been no more than fifty years old when he disappeared for good.

In 1830 Mary Ann left Porthalloe to go into service. She was twelve.

She held a number of positions over the next few years with people who needed scullery help. In return they gave her food, and what passed for lodgings. Unlike her father, who had trouble staying in Porthalloe, Mary Ann could not stay away and kept coming back. She became firm friends with Margery, my grand mother, and would also help her son, my uncle Peter. She taught Peter the skills of a cordwainer and shoemaker, which she had learnt herself from Lewis, her father. When Lewis took to the lanes Mary Ann always had to finish the work on any outstanding boot orders.

Mary Ann also took an interest in caring for my brother, Thomas. She felt useful there, and wanted, and so she wrapped the life of Porthalloe round her shoulders, like a comforting shawl.

Mary Ann's mother Jane married for a second time in 1831, over five years after the last sighting of Lewis, her wayward first husband. She had suffered a long time and she was now in need of happiness. It was the least she deserved and, at forty six years of age, she felt she was still young enough to find it.

She had grown friendly over many years with Nicholas Johns and had sometimes acted as his housekeeper during the months and years when Lewis went missing. He, at fifty four, whilst beginning to show signs of wear, like his boat, was also still young enough to be a prospect for the lonely. His first wife, Alice, had died in childbirth at the age of thirty eight back in 1815 and since then he had steadfastly worked and brought up his own children. His sister was also the mother of Jane's son Samuel's new wife. It was an easy fit. To Jane he was all that Lewis was not and certainly all that she needed right then.

Where Lewis had walked the byways, Nicholas sailed the seas. He was a sea pilot from Coverack, and so a crafty, experienced waterman. He made his living from rowing out to ships with his crew and offering himself as a guide for safe passage round the fearful and treacherous Manacles rocks. A steady flow of stories about unguided brigs which had broken their backs on the reef kept his prices high. There were other pilots but Nicholas was the most experienced, the best, and had the fastest crew. That helped him reach any approaching vessels first. He knew the rocks, the tides, the ebbs and flows and kept an unwritten chart in his head so others could not profit. He also made a living from plain old fishing and, maybe, the odd touch of smuggling or contraband. I can't say. Anyways, sometimes we called it salvaging. All I can say is that the main beam of his cot was from the wreck of a vessel which had probably refused his and any other offers of guidance into open waters many years before.

So, back to Mary Ann. When Jane, her mother, moved for good to Coverack to be with her new husband, Mary Ann was no more than thirteen years old. She wanted to be close by to her mother. Although it was only a mile or two along the shoreline, the cliff walk to get there was more suited to a goat. So, she moved again into service at farms on the downs nearby. Her mother, now Mrs Johns, was fixed on Nicholas and their cot was all aglow with smiles. It sounds like it was a proper young lover's nest and, Mary Ann had said, with so much carrying on, she could not have stayed there.

In truth, I had never paid too much attention to all this for in 1833 I was but young myself and about to be occupied up at Pengarrack. What was happening to me occupied all of my days. I lived hand to mouth. You heard word when people died but otherwise you took little notice of a persons coming or going. You either saw them or you did not. If you caught word that some one had not been seen for a while you knew they were not gone for long for how far could you venture on foot, unless you were like Lewis? Where would you go? What reason would you have to leave? We were here, existing in a safe, beautiful spot. Just do the master's bidding and God would provide your loaf and fish, as the vicar would often remind us on a Sunday. Indeed, what more was there and what more could you need?

So, the next time I remember seeing Mary Ann I was sixteen and she must have been on the cusp of twenty one. It was on the wedding day in October 1839 (what a wet morning that was) of her other brother, John Henry Heyden.

John Henry had stayed in Porthalloe. He was a labourer, regularly falling in and out of work, and in and out of all the local kiddlywinks. You could depend on John if there was nothing you wanted. He was well suited when he married Jane Richards, the unreliable daughter of Oliver Richards, a reliable local fisherman. She had an uneven temper and was quick to give up on anything worth fighting for. Such a shame it turned out to be. It was an ill fated match.

Mary Ann had struck me back then as quite plain. She was dressed for the wedding in a maid's simple thread. Her brown hair was pinned into a tidy bun. It was not down and flowing as was the hair of the other girls. She held a posy of seasonal flowers, freshly picked that morning from the stream's edge. Later, she sat on a bench watching the dancing and jigging through silent dark brown eyes. Her brother Sam danced his way up and down the mowhay with his wife Mary. Mary Ann kept a watchful eye on Sam and Mary's four younger children as they tried to imitate their parents and join in. No one apart from those children had danced that evening with Mary Ann. I expect not many recalled her being there. I felt sorry for her and wanted to take an interest but I also had my eyes firmly set on the cider. No one cared if I helped myself and it was the end of a barrel that had been made from a good season of apples.

The wedding of John Henry Heyden and Jane Richards had brought Mary Ann back to Porthalloe but, before the garlands had even faded, disharmony fell over their thatch like a heavy sea mist. Mary Ann tried to keep the peace for both of them, anxious to prevent the ghosts of the past from gathering around her again.

Trouble still seeped, like water, through the cracks of most days.

In passing I would see Mary Ann and we were friendly if fate landed us in the same place at the same time. I began to notice her on a Keverne market day or other village occasions. Although sometimes with her mother, a brother or a child, she always seemed to somehow be alone. I must say that continued to interest me. I liked the thought of being protective. I tried to befriend her and would ask about her day. I could see that she was always trying to help others and that she could be troubled by their problems.

She was kind, like my mother had been.

Then her brother John Henry Heyden disappeared, and her sister in law could not explain this turn of events. It set every neighbourhood tongue alight with mischief.

I took Mary Ann under my wing, shielding her from the speculation and association. There was no one else who would protect her, I thought. I began escorting her back to her lodgings at Trevathen farm.

One day walking her back we held hands. She had allowed me to be her friend. In time there was no flinch when we brushed against each other. The walk back became longer and we started to leave the path, in search of fresh green pastures where we could sit in the warm sunshine against a hedge wall and amongst the daisies. It started with a kiss, or two, before slipping to quick fumbles. Ah, the warmth of her. She wasn't sure. She thought of her mother's treatment by her father Lewis. She thought of Sunday, and God. He must have been full of disapproval, she said, as he shone through the gathered clouds above us. 'What of your brother Thomas'? Mary Ann would also ask. She was fond of him and I knew he was very fond of her. They were of a similar age and she had taken care of him. She had been ready to settle for a different life until I had taken an interest.

Then, with her mind troubled by the choices before her, my brother Thomas was caught stealing.

It was the 27th March 1842. My brother Peter came to tell me. He was almost ten then. It was his turn to bring me the family's terrible news.

Thomas had done the unthinkable and punishment was certain. He had made a bad choice and stolen from someone who had been good to all of us. Together with John Rashleigh, who was seventeen and so two years younger, they had broken into Mr Roskruge's barn, entered it and then stolen nine gallons of cider. They were caught red handed drawing the cider from a large storage barrel. Thomas and John had run off into the night, leaving their candle and flagons.

We lived in a part of the world where everybody knew everybody else. Apart from Lewis, where could you hide when all were looking for you? John Rashleigh and my brother Thomas were soon apprehended and they were not long in confessing their guilt.

On Friday the 15th April they attended the Easter sessions at court and were both sent down for two months of hard labour in Bodmin. They could have been transported, never to be heard of again, but Mr Roskruge's son was kind enough to ask for mercy, for Thomas was a simple soul. I was grateful once again to Mr Roskruge for turning as blind an eye as he was able to do in such matters.

With Thomas sent for hard labour, it hit the family to the core. Thieving was not common and the Parish could punish you with a cold shoulder and the withdrawal of charity if you were caught. For John Rashleigh it meant the loss of a valued apprenticeship with Mr. Martin, the village blacksmith.

For Mary Ann this incident resolved her mind of its choices. One day, when we again talked of these troubles on a walk back from Church, a passion arose in her and we fell to the ground in the nearest lea. We did not notice the nettles and we laughed after about the cows. They had been witnesses to a flurry of excitement as they stood, unconcerned, silently chewing the cud. What enlightening stories cows would tell, if only they could speak.

And so we continued to keep company as the summer sun of 1842 warmed the estuary, the blossoms grew into fruit and the tall grasses were cut and dried in the pastures. We were like bright clouds, alight with the sun.

In the heat of August, when Mary Ann said to me that she was with child I know she wondered if I would decide that my fortune lay elsewhere and that the day she told me would be the last day she would see me. I was minded not to be like Lewis, her father, and run for the cobbles of Falmouth and the shelter of an infantryman's uniform. 'I'm happy about it. It is a good development' I said. Besides, if her father Lewis had spoken truthfully, why would I want to sail to the Continent and then be chased all over it by angry souls firing musket balls at my retreating backside?

Yes, I was happy there at Penare. Now I had Mary Ann and a babby was on the way. I felt at peace with my surroundings and the animals, like my father and grand fathers before me. There was certainty to my day and a harmony in my soul. The promise of a child did not feel out of place with that. I felt this was my world and everything I knew and wanted was there.

Was it much to ask for? No, for I had not asked for much beyond some simple pleasure. I had found that pleasure in the companionship of a woman with similar desires and no demands. I now had the promise of a child to protect and care for. I felt no obligation to marry. I was happy to do so, and so was Mary Ann.

My brother Thomas returned, much altered by jail and hard labour.

The red welts of heavy chains were still upon him when, again, he was taken in by my grand mother in Porthalloe. He had been fond of Mary Ann for she had shown him consideration and understanding, helping him with all his difficulties. When he was told about Mary Ann and I he felt I was taking her away from him and he struggled to contain his anger. The memory of his days of punishment may also have welled up in him. The matter was distressing for him despite the calm hand of our Grand mother Margery. She explained to us all that he had seen such terrible things and that his soul had been agitated. It was now so agitated it did not know where to look for peace, she had said, drawing on the memory of her own dead husband.

Maybe my brother Thomas had thought that Mary Ann would be his answer but now, because of me, it was not to be. I vowed that prison, and all its chains, lashes and hate was a place I did not want to experience. Not even for all the silver up there at Trelowarren Manor and certainly not for a barrel of cider.

Mary Ann and I were married at St. Keverne Church on Sunday the 16th Oct 1842, just before the full moon, surrounded by some of the family, who wished us well.

Mary Ann was twenty four and I was a close shave off twenty. I remember that I could not borrow my father's Sunday best for he had agreed to be my witness. I feel I was still presentable before God in the best togs I could muster but, in truth, my mind was on my bride, Mary Ann. I expect she felt any clothes I wore that day were an improvement on my normal rags. She was dressed in her Sunday best and carried a garland of her favourite autumn daisies. What a pretty picture she was, my sweet Mary Ann.

Mr. Peel was Prime Minister at this time and there was a mood of unrest, swirling like a gusty wind ahead of a storm. But, we were like two dancing leaves, happily in a whirl and looking forward to our whole lives together. A baby was growing inside Mary Ann and her belly was beginning to show.

I spoke to Mr Tripcony at Penare. As a married man was I not now entitled to a higher wage? I wanted to stay there, amongst the lush green grass, never to leave. I was sure of it. I knew the work and it was no trouble to me now and my happiness was secure. He replied 'I am obliged to you, Zeb, for your good labour over the past fifteen months but I regret I am unable to keep you on'.

Indeed, he said he was thinking he might give up the farm himself. Yield was low. Cost was up. Those wages paid would have to be cut. Everyone would have to work more. He only felt the obligation of a single man's wage. It was easy for God to recognise my union but God did not have to find the extra shillings that came bound up with it. 'I will have to make do with a younger farm boy, at a much lower cost' he said in a firm but resigned tone. As he spoke, I am certain my face must have looked like a whitewashed wall.

What would I do? All I knew and wanted was there. I sought the counsel of my father but his words were not what I had hoped to hear. 'Your brother Peter is now ten, and ready to leave home', my father said. 'I have an arrangement with Mrs Tripcony that Peter will take your place over at Penare'.

7. Leaving Porthalloe

Mary Ann and I took a little Estate cot in Porthalloe next to Willie Perrow. It was not much but big enough for a place to lie and for us to gaze into each others eyes, whispering sweet nothings. Besides, there were no nettles.

Or cows.

We were like two mice who had found half a pound of prime cheese. What more could we want?

The cot had been abandoned shortly after James Rogers had died there in May of 1842, a full half year before. All his family had left before he died apart from Peggy, his youngest daughter, and her obedient husband. They had cared for the poor suffering and failing Mr Rogers until his death of decline at the age of seventy nine. He had lived there quietly for many, many years. It was far longer than anyone still living could recall, whenever the question had been posed. No one had known much about him. He had been quiet, as though keeping some unspoken tragedy from others. No one had lived there since his death. Why? Perhaps old Mr Rogers would still be there in spirit, damp in the dark blistered walls and ready to start mischief when the babby arrived.

To me, it was fine with or without the ghost of James Rogers. He might merely have wanted the release from solitude that only other folk have the gift to bring. From the window there was a sight of the shore, beautiful even in the mizzle, and it was close to Mrs Pentecost's grocery shop where there was always a tale to be had. What a clacker she was and better than any messenger at passing on the latest line. I'm surprised she ever sold anything as you could easily forget what you went in there for, what with all that laughter and triddling as a distraction.

After the loss of my work at Penare, living in Porthalloe meant I could still be close to any labouring that might be found. Besides, we knew all the folk nearby. Why, most of them were family in some way or other. A cousin there, an aunt here and even my step mother Hannah over yonder.

Hannah, my step mother, had given birth in the middle of 1840 to the first child of her union with my father. The baby was a fine boy with a thick crop of hair. They called him Henry Bartle Pearce, as I have said. He was my half brother and my father was proud of his healthy new heir, smiling and laughing in a way which we, his other sons and daughter, could not recall ever seeing before. Their happiness was like a door slamming shut between them and his old family. 'You keep your noses out of it' he would say if in no mood for enquiry. Even Elizabeth, my five year old sister, became a stranger to me.

Hannah's daughter from her Camborne days, who took on our Pearce name for a while, was more independent and certainly knew her own mind. 'I have always been ignored and overlooked' she said 'but here by the shoreline air is a better place for it'.

She also said to Mary Ann that from then on she was to be known as Anna, as indeed her mother had also decided to be. There was no more need for all the 'H's. No one used them anyway. They only served as a reminder of a past they had now buried and forgotten. My father Thomas had offered a new start and a better life. He took to calling her 'Anna', leaving her H's silent. Camborne and all that happened there was now just an unseen cloud over the horizon of a clear blue day.

Another child, a girl, quickly followed for my step mother. My father, in a good attempt at making peace, named her Mary Ann. She was a mite and not expected to live long until she took firmly to her feed and began to thrive.

However, my father and Hannah, or Anna without the 'H's, were not the only frolicking lambs in Porthalloe. I had news of my own. My son was born in early spring, 1843. Mary Ann, my wife, wanted to call him John Henry Heyden Pearce in memory of her own brother, who, you may remember, had disappeared almost two years before. Her brother's wife had then been found dead in her bed shortly after Mary Ann and I had been married. What a mysterious tragedy it all was. I hoped my son John Henry would fare better in life than Mary Ann's second brother had.

Amongst these early family days I did happen upon some fortune with work in and around Porthalloe. It was not regular. I might get a day or two working for one master, then a day or two working for another. Sometimes at busy periods you might get work by the fortnight.

I never took anything as my right. I could turn up ready to start and the farmer would say 'I don't need you, come back in a week or two and we'll see what needs doing then'. I had to believe that I was not now fit only for the mullock heap. I could hear my mother say 'Be like the birds, Zeb. They sing their hearts out every new morning'.

There was some steady labour with the boats in July, and for dunging, ploughing and harvesting the leas. Even work at some of the Mills nearby could come my way if illness of another made a vacancy for me. I could turn my hand to most things on the land, like building, stone work, hedges, and anything to do with animals and crops. I did not take to most things on the water although I was happy enough to take an oar on Nicholas John's boat or haul a tuck net into the shoreline when a pilchard shoal was caught. It may not have paid well but, somehow, there was always something to pass the days so that there was something later to pass our lips.

I loved preparing the fields in autumn and spring for new seed. When Frankie Noye's mother suddenly dropped dead in 1843 due to 'Visitation of God' I found an opening for a time in the fields, in her place. Why God should visit

Annie Noye and take her away so suddenly and early in her life was not easy to fathom for she was an easy person to please and a difficult one to upset. Were she a sea, no ship would have sunk.

There were many of us, all starving mouths, looking for proper paid occupation. So, with such demand the rates again lowered and what I earned was no good, really, if it was meant to be a living wage. The Church Overseers arranged some employment when the idle seasons were upon us and I gratefully dug stones out for roads, maintained hedging and broke the ground for the laying of pasture parks. The rich tapestry around St Keverne owed much to the hungry unemployed.

To say money was scarce would be an exaggeration. It was a perfect stranger to me. But, I had grown up a master of these green rolling folds and lews so we scraped by with the help of a touch of scramming and scrumping. I did not feel that I was depriving another, especially a gent, for I was taking silently from forgotten places where nothing was noticed before I passed through and no changes were remarked upon after I had gone.

Not even the trees grumbled.

The money the Overseers paid over to me was to be used on food and so we fell behind on our rent at Roger's cot. Crumbs of work, potato blights and bad harvests meant an ill temper was brewing in our little valley.

Whilst I was well known by all in Porthalloe, we resolved to move up into the Churchtown of St Keverne where we hoped there would be more work. It was a walk of a couple of miles or so. Whilst we would be under the full eye of scrutiny at the Church we would also be one step closer to shelter. For that, as we said on more than just a Sunday, may the Lord make us truly thankful.

Mary Ann was pregnant again and baby John Henry was full of angry, disappointed tears. I could almost hear him cry 'What life is this that I have been born in to?' I wished I could dissolve the anguish with a wave of my hand but, in truth, only a better prospect could do that.

Around this time, Samuel, my brother, turned eighteen and decided to leave Pengarrack, and Porthalloe. He was no longer a lad and Mr Roskruge could not now afford to keep him on for a man's wages. 'No one is making a living worthwhile', Sam had complained, 'so why should I stay where I am not wanted'. I did not say anything. 'Money will never travel to these parts to find me' he continued, looking down at the worn soles of his boots.

I still said nothing but he went on as though my silence meant I had agreed with him. 'Indeed, what reason is there to stay?' he said, adding 'there are no women here that I care for enough to keep me here and I see your baby John Henry and desire a future with a little more peace in it'.

He would be away from his family, I reasoned, at last.

Sam replied 'Father is fully occupied in the bowgie and with the distracting ample bosom of his new family' before adding miserably 'Besides, he does not have the answer and I need to provide my melancholy stomach with one'.

Mr Bryant, the keeper of the little Inn at Porthalloe, said he had discovered the answer. Relations up Camborne way had talked of mining work. He had said to Sam and others like me in the same fix that he had heard there was much work available there for those that wanted it. 'The farthing should outweigh the fear' he said. If he meant that, though, then why was he trifling with a sleepy beer house in these parts?

Where I had travelled a few miles up to reside in St. Keverne, Samuel had decided that he would go further up country. He was not alone and travelled with Henry Noye and other friends, none with any money and all with not much more than the clothes they stood in.

Old and young alike were leaving due to the shortage of work. They were even encouraged by the Overseers, who for centuries until now had earned a reputation for wanting to hold on to people of the Parish for its own means.

Apart from men like Lewis Heyden, until now no person around here had ever before moved far from the sight of their family. If they had been forced to move by argument, they were still within throwing distance, as many cut heads could testify.

Yes, moving away from this sweet corner of Cornwall had become a well trodden track along which grass no longer grew. The earthy prints of hopeful boots all pointed one way. When the day came for Sam's departure I said my farewells and looked on from the edge of St. Keverne as he walked the hill. He was like a rigger on the ocean's horizon, disappearing a little with each gust of wind, until finally he was gone with not much more than a glance back. Gone to somewhere unknown, ripped from our hearts, and already changed.

I missed my brother and his happy nature, even before that day he left had expired. I hoped he would one day return home and that I would be fortunate enough to be there to greet him.

But, around me it all got worse.

Pilchards may have been bountiful but the harvests coming off the land were not. With less grain to sell, the prices rose, and Mary Ann and I began to worry deeply. It was enough to curdle her milk. I could not carry on working aimlessly, with odd jobs here and there. Neither could I keep relying on charity, as the kind souls at the Vicarage would regularly remind me each week as they handed their spare pennies over.

News came back of Samuel. He had found work at a mine called Wheal Treasury, at Horsedowns, south of Camborne. There was a demand for more men, who were rugged and not afraid of hard work. I was sure that he had so far survived a worse ordeal than my own but I considered that the mine's name had a deal of promise in it.

At the beginning of 1845, Mary Ann gave birth to our second child, Margery Ann, named after my Grandmother, my mother and Mary Ann. With a name as good as that she should have a certain following, if only with the family.

She was healthy and brought a heavy appetite for mother's milk with her. Trying to settle a baby was not the time for us all to move but moving was much on my mind by this time. Skilled work like the smith or carpenter was still always in demand but there was a new usurper for those men like me who merely offered brute force and the daily strain of every sinew and muscle. It was something Mr Kinsman, a farmer at Kerris, called 'the machine'.

It was nothing you could ever imagine, or I be able to describe fully to you. This machine was all iron and wood with links, belts, wheels and levers. All parts seemed to move at once and of their own accord. It would throw out dust as it roughly separated the drowsy ears of corn from their stalks. It stood in the field and rattled like a temperamental washerwoman at the board. It was called a threshing machine. To us it was a black reaper, looming over our futures. Yes, a reaper of innocent souls that cared not for the value of a man's sweat or his daily toil.

We had all been in favour of a tool that saved our back or helped our cause but this was a devil. This machine intended to do away with us and did not even demand a meal in exchange for it. If this beast had been given eyes, they would be shut to the misery it would create. I reasoned that these new thoughts on farming must also be to blame for the blight on the potato that had cut our already meagre rations.

My father Thomas complained that manual skills learnt and mastered over generations were being put out to grass overnight by machinery much faster and more powerful than any horse or man. So much would be forgotten. The craft of the agricultural artisan would be trampled beneath the harsh wheels of the machine. Having come face to face with a machine in the barn he did not fancy his chance of outliving it let alone keeping all of his fingers. 'I 'opes it don't run on my cider' he had also said angrily to anyone who cared to listen.

Or was Frankie Noye right? He had left Porthalloe in 1843, just before his mother had died.

He felt that machines could not be harnessed like a plough horse or have a settling ring put through its nose like the impatient bull up at Mr Tripcony's tenement. No, this was a beast that needed to be better understood and would have to be admired. As long as you did not try to overcome it, its power could be directed. Surely this was a new opportunity? There must be work for those who were willing to stand astride these huffing monstrosities and care for them. 'All you need to do is grease them instead of stroke them' he had said. He had set out to find out if this was true.

I still did not want to leave and nor did Mary Ann. We were uncertain about the path to take. Here was everything we knew and all the folk that come with it, good and bad. Away from here there was the dark unknown and in our imaginings it would rip us all asunder, casting us like storm tossed sailors into the foams of despair. We had two very young children to care and provide for.

However, if we did not leave, we would surely find ourselves the slaves of Helston workhouse. A few months back the workhouse had claimed my elder brother Thomas. He had disappeared through its cold detached doors as quickly as an innocent passing fly swallowed up by a hungry leaping trout.

I did not like the idea of mine work. Samuel and others were saying it was hot dark work deep under the ground where air was a stranger. Not that he minded. Indeed, he felt he had slipped the noose.

On a visit home he said 'There is work for you and you will soon get used to it. It is no different cutting rocks than digging the fields here, only you do it as though at night'.

With a big smile on his face, he showed me his reward for regular work. In the outstretched palm of his hand lay a small collection of brown coins. I noticed he had lost a tooth since the last time I had seen him.

Willie Tripcony, my father's friend, who had helped my father with the search for his second wife, Hannah, also moved away in 1845. He took on work as a husbandman about twenty miles away, at Mellanoweth, which lay between Copperhouse and Camborne. On a visit back to say how well he had settled there he offered me a few days of lodging and work. 'It will mean that you can see what plentiful labouring work there is to be had without being quickly swallowed by the change, as others have been'.

Some folk never came back, so there was no way of telling their fate, but it was true that those who did come back to visit or collect their families were soon gone again, leaving tales of better places and better times. Few ever came back to stay.

Nicholas, my brother after Sam, was now eighteen and agitating to go. With a heavy heart I made arrangements for us both to travel together. When there is no going back and no standing still and only one path in front, what other choice was there open to us?

Whilst I was gone, Mary Ann was to stay with her mother Jane, in Coverack. She would have help there, and food from the plentiful sea for her and the two little uns.

Nicholas Johns would keep a watchful eye and I trusted him.

On my last night, after everything was done and everything had been prepared, I went down the hill, following the cut of the shaded streams, and sat alone in the calm of a dying day, high above Porthalloe.

I looked out across the twinkling sea and felt it was to be for the last time. I sucked in the cooling air and, under a young moon which spread like butter over the darkening ocean, I said goodbye to the spirit of my mother and to the last echoes of a happy childhood.

I left the following day with the post cart, and a pebble from the beach in my pocket.

Harry and Willie Borlase, from Trenoweth, came as well, and so did my brother Nicholas. Harry was short of work after Mr James the butcher had released him in favour of work for his own family. We could all understand that. Willie and he were going to travel on to Camborne and see what benefit there was to be had there. Nicholas and I would stay together.

Many had said it would be an adventure and that there was more to life than Porthalloe but I know I was contented where I had been, even if where I had been did not wish for me to be contented there.

I was going to miss the green dappled hillsides where the shadows and lines of light change as the sun nudges its way up and into a new day. I was going to miss the stacked sheaves, the autumn blush of crimson and tan leaves and the constant tumble and rumble of waves along the shore.

It was goodbye to the damp dew drying as the wild pea and vetch unfurled. It was goodbye to fern banked holloways, the fertile red earth and the mists on the slopes of the Helford. It was goodbye to the sea, with all its colours and moods. I would no longer see the mossy stones of a local wall or hear the wind whistling through it.

I expected it would also be goodbye to most of the people even if, like my father, they had not wished to say goodbye to me, and, if I was going to disappear down a cold black shaft, it was also going to be goodbye to the glory of sunshine.

8. The Rail Way is Coming

I missed Mary Ann and the babbies.

I would take my grey Porthalloe pebble out of my pocket. It had thin white lines which cut through the middle. I'd run my fingers over its smooth surface, remembering my family with a smile before clasping that rock tight to my beating heart.

It was 1846, and I suppose I found Willie Tripcony's position at Mellanoweth very pleasing, given all my earlier fears. I had escalated these fears with years of speculation and now, at last, having seen everything with my own eyes, I felt more at ease.

Willie had settled with his wife, Ann, daughter Elizabeth Ann, and son Francis, in a narrow sheltered valley where there was still a demand for grazing cows, the froth of fresh milk and his considerable eye for a good animal.

Down the middle trickled the Angarrack stream from which several mills borrowed and harnessed power to drive the wheels and turn the grist. Amongst the bustle of the trees a breeze gently meandered deep in thought and the low chatter of the birds went largely uninterrupted, until the whistle blew.

The whistle came from the mouth of the valley and what was there was yet another new discovery for me. It was what Willie called a snorting iron horse by the name of 'Cornubia'. It gave out a shrieking call, not like a man but forged by him. The sound could startle you upright in seconds, giving you a sore head and bleeding ears. Horses would scatter at the noise the engine made when it approached.

This iron contraption gushed hot steam and fiery smoke but it did not rear up on its haunches. It was controlled by two men, dressed in black jackets and caps, leaning out, pulling leavers and shovelling coals as fast as they could into its hot hungry mouth. They waved for people to move from their way. Quite how much control the two men had of the reins should this beast decide to bolt it was hard to tell.

This humdinger moved on iron wheels, guided by two iron rails and it pulled open carriages laden with minerals. Three times a day this monster would also tow people in coaches along the rails to Copperhouse and Penpol. In the opposite direction would go coal, timbers and what seemed like the same people, holding on to their bonnets and hats, travelling back from whence they had come earlier that very same day.

I had never before seen the like. I was not accustomed to such an idea and this was a rude jolt. All I had known was in reach of a walk and could be lifted by hand. This iron horse carried people at speed and would disappear from view before I had even set my stride. The occupants would travel a mile all in the time it would take me to scratch an ear. Their errands would be done and they would be returned to their homes again before I had even climbed a stile. It was a wonderful and busy new principle. Until now the fastest thing I had seen was the hasty trot of a tardy post cart after James, the postman, had overslept.

This new system was in great evidence on the gentle slopes at the approach to Angarrack from Copperhouse. There, a double rail incline led to the top of the hill above and to another connecting set of rails. The first engine would usually be relieved at the foot of the incline, for it could not climb. Should you need to escape from one, climb a slope, I thought.

At the top, around 185 feet up and 2000 feet on, a second engine named 'Pendarves' waited for a coupling before a journey along the ridge and on to Camborne. A third engine, fixed with no wheels, strained as it winched the carriages up and down the incline. What my father would make of it I have no idea. Willie said this work used to be done by horses but the engine was more powerful and did not tire. He said there was still work for men.

This interested me more than the tin mines and forges, whose chimneys were rising like dismal grey fingers all over the hillsides around us.

The valley was a refuge from the smog shrouding Copperhouse, Phillack and Hayle in the bay below. Fires in the furnaces of foundries there lit the night sky and, should you venture to these towns the smoke of industry choked the air and left black grime on your collar, like a noose around your neck.

I escaped from this into the seclusion of Mellanoweth, which lay behind Angarrack. In exchange for a straw bed and a daily bowl of whatever was cooking, I helped Willie in the fields for a month. In turn, this helped me to get my bearings and saved me from some of the sorrow of not being with Mary Ann and the two babbies.

Willie explained that when he moved it brought much change and every one struggled. He had even dropped 'cony' from his name and he was now known as Willie Tripp. The 'cony' was a sign that he was a rustic and easy to fool by those in town that willed it. He was too clever to be shigged, he said. He did not think I needed to change my name for Pearce was as common as a smoke stack around these parts.

One Monday morning, shortly after I had started to help Willie, and whilst working in the exposed fields above Mellanoweth, we heard sounds I had certainly never heard before. It was the pitched scream of a hundred voices combined with what I now know to have been the crashing and moaning of iron against iron. The high screech was coming from the rail way incline. Willie and I looked at each other's faces, searching for the answer to the question we must both have had in our minds. What is that? What has happened? As the screams faded a little, we began running towards the incline, with a mixture of fear and curiosity.

As we drew near, along the crest, it was clear from the commotion of a large number of people who had congregated that there had been an accident on the rail way. An engine and three carriages were calm and stationary there at the top of the incline. On the brow were another two enclosed carriages with the distressed faces of people at the carriage openings. They were screaming in panic, their cheeks streaming with tears. Down on the slope were several folk lying scattered about on the ground, their clothing in disarray, their faces a turmoil of pain and bewilderment.

Beyond the incline, on the plain, Willie and I could see a chain of four open wagons disappearing at a gathering speed along the rail back down through Ventonleague, Copperhouse and towards the docks at Hayle. Passengers inside were waving their arms as their noise faded.

One young lady lay on the incline, her leg fractured. Another lay motionless with her head all bloodied, with a man leaning over her who also appeared to be in pain. In all, I would imagine there must have been a dozen or more who had leapt or been pitched from the descending wagons as they had gathered speed. An employee of the rail way was muttering that he was applying a brake to a wagon to slow it when a gentleman had dropped on to him from above, causing him to lose control of the brake.

It was clear from the carriage that remained at the edge of the incline that a coupling chain had broken and later several people said the engine towing the carriages had struggled and strained under the expectation of so many folk. It had groaned, unable to pull the weight. It had lurched and shuddered, before some vital cog or link had snapped, throwing those on board back down the cavernous incline.

The open wagons that had broken away finally came to a halt two miles down the line. They were still on the rails. On the outside of one they found a man who had clung on for dear life and, apart from the fright of such a ride with death staring you in the face, he seemed quite unmarked in a bodily way.

I secretly expect his hair stood up with fright and that it did so for the rest of his life. He will have been easily recognised wherever he went. 'Are you not the man from the runaway train?' I could hear them ask as they stared at his hair standing on end when he ventured into a public bar. 'Look', I am sure I could hear him always reply with a sigh 'I only came in here for a quiet smoke and a considered gin. The story has already been told a hundred times too many. Now, if you were to buy me a drink......'

The run away wagons were gathered up like stray hens, towed back up the incline and attached back up to the patiently waiting engine. The train then set off for Gwennap, where a service and prayers awaited. All those who had been on board the train seemed content to remain aboard. It was as though nothing had happened or nothing was to be allowed to interrupt a prized excursion for over two hundred people. No doubt when they all arrived at the end of the line the survivors would give their grateful earnest thanks to God, if they had not already done so over and over during their onward journey.

We had watched on in the sunshine whilst the injured were tended to and removed. Willie said to me 'I ain't seen 'im before but runaway wagons often happens here. They all smash themselves to atoms once out of sight o' the hill'.

Before that day none of those smashed wagons had ever contained passengers. That day all the wagons survived, along with the people in them. It truly was a miraculous escape. Perhaps the vicar at Church all those years ago had told the truth. If you look after God, he will look after you.

The runaway train would stay long in my mind. Alas, my brother Nicholas had not been there to see it. He had been restless for a new beginning and quickly joined my brother Samuel at work in a mine. They were at the Strays Park, sunk on land at Camborne owned by Mr Basset.

This progress into the unknown suited him more than work as a farm hand, which he could have carried out blindfolded. He lodged with Samuel and his new wife, in exchange for which he seemed happy to part with half his weekly wage. The other half gave him a giddy introduction to the ladies of Camborne and the blurred delights of beer.

Samuel had taken up with a feisty young woman called Avis Rodda, from Horsedowns. She was one for a firm opinion and took issue with much of what she saw, including me. She also had the reins on Sam, who was easily led. It had been a quick romance and one that in the beginning Avis's father Edward had not much cared for. I do not know why, for his own life was more restful once Samuel became a distraction for his daughter.

Either with Edward's encouragement or displeasure, Samuel decided to move closer to Camborne to an address which was away from all the irritable gazes. As Sam and Edward Rodda had worked together at Wheal Treasury I am sure that this was a good idea. You never know when, for no reason, a pitch pine timber, a ladder or a rope might give way.

However, once secured in employment in Camborne, Samuel began to call on Avis again.

He would meet her at church, where he was keen to catch her eye. He had brushed his hair over especially and acquired a new second hand suit. It must have worked a treat because Avis and Samuel were soon married. She had just turned seventeen.

From what Samuel had said to me I thought he had wanted some peace, but this must have changed. What discovery had he made? There was certainly a sudden rush and, within the year, Avis was with child. I suppose that when you spend your days working so far under ground, where danger is all about and pleasure as thin as the foul air, you have to have your life as you would like it once you make your escape back to grass on the surface. It may only be a short while before a rock fall or blast claims you, so Samuel was living each day fully, as though it was surely his last.

There can be no doubt that Samuel was a good worker, and keen to earn money. He was not one for mutting. Deep in the ground around Camborne there were untold riches of copper, tin and lead.

To Samuel, they were opportunities waiting to be discovered, and the daily hardships endured below ground were just obstacles to be overcome. He had always been a fast learner and never let himself be troubled by what he did not know or what he had no care for. If mineral sprites were lurking in the tunnels he kept them charmed with his cheery way and in turn, he said, they helped him to seek out a lode from the gloom of the dark rock around him. Nicholas was just happy to follow along.

After I had found my feet, I took labouring work in Camborne, where there was plenty of building taking place. Tin and copper mines were hungry for men and they were matched by labourers coming from all parts of Cornwall and beyond, looking for any work they could find.

This usually meant down the mines.

I did not wish to be swallowed into the wet black gloom underground. It was not for me and I was happy on the surface where I could be sure of my footing. So, I fetched and carried, helping the masons build cottages for those who intended to stay in Camborne. After all, the miners needed to have roofs over the heads of their families.

I was still without Mary Ann. Until I was able to afford larger lodgings, I stayed with Frankie Noye and his new wife Ann.

Frankie had found work on the Hayle rail way at the mineral yards of Camborne. He moved wagons, unloaded coal from them for the mines, and filled the very same wagons with ore dug from the mines. This was fast work if the reloaded wagons were to be ready in time for the train carrying the ore on to Hayle or Portreath where it was to be smelted or carried for use somewhere in the World. This kept him occupied and fully employed but he often spoke of improving his pay by joining the platelayers out on the rail. 'For that I will need new skills. I will need some learning' he had said, smiling at me.

When we spoke of an evening, Frankie said that from what he could see, it was a busy time for the rail ways.

Cows were the past. No one would now ever be needed to look after a cow. It could chew grass all by itself. Here, on the rail way, there was a future full of promise. Demand was high for willing labour. These machines could not run themselves and nor could you pick an engine off a branch as you would an apple. They were being made by the sweat and clever endeavour of man. Each bolt and nut was devised for a purpose and, with a feed of hot coal, each piston hissed with the force of a thousand men.

Engines would open up new work, for some engines were employed to pump water deep from the ground to keep the mines dry enough for men to dig deeper. Other engines were for pumping air down to the depths so that those very men who dug could continue to breathe, and dig even deeper. Then there was a stamp, which crushed the rock and splintered the pieces into digestible sizes. Yet more engines were taking the heavy loads to and from this place and that, he had said excitedly. There was much talk of expansion and fortunes to be made. Tongues were wagging everywhere with the sound of golden dreams being delivered to the ordinary man. Many people would be required for there would be engines everywhere. 'Iron rails will sweep up the quiet hamlets with its mania, stretching to all the corners of Cornwall' he said, waving his arm around the room.

'Why' Frankie had continued, 'all manner of goods and people can now travel the nine miles from Redruth to Hayle in well under an hour'. The station master of the rail way at Camborne had talked to him of rails being laid by a Mr Brunel which would soon take a train all the way to the metropolis of London. It truly was incredible and it would bring great opportunities for all involved. 'People will soon be able to travel by train to Penzance where they will be able to sit and take the air by the sea' he said, stretching his left hand in the direction of the coast. I thought it unlikely that people would want to do that, for I had lived by the sea and I had seen no demand there for idleness.

After a few months I found lodgings in Union Street and arranged the little spare time I had towards settling my family there with me. It was a small space and no more than two rooms but it had a fireplace which gave us a place to cook and a backlet to rest up with a smoke. John Henry, my son, who was now three and Margery Ann, my daughter, who was now passed her first birthday, also had space to run around. For me it was mighty fine and a reward for my effort. However, Mary Ann was troubled. She had not settled.

Mary Ann did not like the dirt, which fell everywhere outside like a fine black dust. The air smelt of coal and sometimes of human waste. There was no running stream here, like Porthalloe, or shady pasture in which to rest a while. There was no help from a caring mother. The peaceful leas had been shut out by high stone walls. Whilst there were goods to buy, you had to have money to do it. Getting enough of anything for the four of us was difficult. She was like a lapwing trying to pull worms from the belly of a rock.

Where before she had been free, now she felt like a captive. Man had built a fortress against the greens and blues she loved. She choked on the coal dust that had been captured within Camborne's ramparts. In Coverack Cove she had been surrounded by nature's colours. She missed the salty gust of a sea breeze, sucked deep into grateful lungs. She was ill at ease with the hustle and bustle of life in the new town and said she was struggling to settle amongst such grey dark streets. The tiny rows of terraced houses crowded in on each other, huddling together against the cold, their windows like eyes, dark with sorrow. They conspired against her, sensing that she was an outsider and that she did not belong there.

 'What am I to do each day and all day whilst you are at work, Zeb?' she asked in a distressed tone. A strand of hair had escaped from its bun and hung across her eyes. I was at work for six days in every seven and I only saw the light in the eyes of the children on the Lord's Day. 'I have two small children to tend to and I am not feeling well' she complained, brushing the hair away.

The air was stale, the food rotten and no one was eating well, especially Mary Ann. But, was this not a better life? Was this not what we had been striving for? Mary Ann and I never went to school. I was labouring on ground where a school was to be built and our children may one day learn to read and write there. Then our children would be able to read the newspapers brought from London on the train, and adopt new opinions that were not independent or of their own making.

News came of another son for my father Thomas and my step mother Hannah. The babby's name was Francis.

What had he intended to do with all these children, I wondered? Perhaps leave it to providence as he had thus far? He was now the father of nine sons, two daughters and a step daughter. He now had a herd of children to compete with his prized cows. Apart from the first Peter, who died very young, the rest of us were aged between twenty six and nothing.

Had we flourished? The land could not keep us all. The sea could not oblige either. We were now scattered like seed would be if thrown up into a howling gale. I was twenty four and I could not recall that he had ever given a moment to enquire about me. I was a child of his. He should know us all. We had grown forth from his nocturnal escapades. His pleasure should never have finished there.

But, enough of self pity. Mary Ann and I had news of our own. She was again with child and in late 1847, our son Nicholas John was born. He was named after my brother, my grandfather (whom, I confess, I never knew) and Nicholas Johns, my wife's step father. Shortly after, Avis gave birth to a little girl. My dear brother Samuel, too, was now a father.

Although not for Mary Ann, Porthalloe was slipping from my mind, like a gently retiring tide. I was enjoying steady labouring work, and, at last, the jangle of pennies in my pockets at the end of week after week, month after month, season after season. I had feared such a change but it was not so bad. Wasn't anything better than the disgrace of the work house? I thought so.

Camborne was beginning to feel like a home. It was growing with every mine shaft that was sunk and there was a fierce demand for men who were eager to try their luck below ground. Where they went women and children followed, employed to break the extracted spoils once the rocks had been brought to the surface. Everyone in Union Street owed their living to the mines, apart from the widows whose men had died because of it. There was a growing tally of those, too.

Aware that Mary Ann was troubled, Frankie came to me one day and invited us all on an outing for the day with his family to the 'Riviere'. We would travel with him as passengers on the Hayle rail way for a nominal sum. How grand! It was set for a day in August when we could expect a warmer day.

None of us slept the night before. We were all excited about what this brave adventure might bring, apart from Mary Ann. Her eyes were wide with anxiety. When the large black engine loomed on the approach, then rolled unhurriedly in alongside the platform at Camborne, Mary

Ann raised her hands to her ears, shielding them from the whistle and hiss of the steam coming from the engine's wheels as they slowed to a halt. Frankie said it would be all right. 'I have been in a carriage before' he said, opening a door to one. We climbed in amid the clunk of doors slamming shut, up and down the platform. A man ran by, already holding his hat, eagerly looking for a seat.

Our fate was sealed with a whistle and a lurch as the train began to move forward. It was too late to climb off. We would now have to ride. My daughter Margery Ann distracted her mother, I took Nicholas on my lap and John Henry sat excitedly pointing out the passing streets, then livestock, all of which grazed on, ignoring the noisy commotion as we rattled by.

It is true, you could be in fear of such power but I was in awe, for I had never before travelled at such a speed. Nor had I enjoyed such a passing view. A glow burned across our cheeks from the rural air. As the soot of the town slipped away behind us our nostrils filled with the fired scent of the iron beast that pulled us forward.

Mary Ann gripped the carriage as it swayed from side to side. The train jolted as it ran over the rails and whistled as it passed by waving farm servants. At the Penponds and Angarrack inclines we held our breath as the carriages were tugged, raised and lowered and then, shortly after, we were there, at Hayle Riviere, where the gulls circled, crying out their hungry greetings.

Ah, yes, it was a good day out. We climbed until we were above the rail way station and all around was water, sand and bright light shimmering in the estuary. Birds flocked behind luggers returning to the bay on the tide, hopeful for a catch of their own. Sails dropped as they entered the narrow channel to the port and craftsmen of the tides steered their fish hauls safely to the quayside. Larger ships lay slumbering at anchor and up there on the sand hills the sun now warmed our faces as much as the view before us.

The children ran around tumbling and exploring, returning now and then with a whitened shell or other wild curiosity. It reminded Frankie and I of days gone by. We lay on a flat bed of tight scrub, stretching out amongst the surrounding sea holly and marram grasses. We put our hands behind our heads, looked to the heavens and remembered all the good moments. I picked a long chain of little white daisies for Mary Ann.

Up there, in the warm breeze we all forgot the aches of our labour, the craving for food in our bellies and the greasy black cobbles of the streets we now called home. Mary Ann found and picked some pink heather from amongst the furze and placed it in my button hole. When she arrived back at Union Street she rescued the sprig and it then lay for a while by her bedside, until the small flowers faded and crumbled. For a time that hot day had made her happier.

My son John Henry said, as he later fought sleep, that he would like to ride again on the rail way. Next time, could he stoke the engine and make the smoke? 'Someday I would like to work on the rail way, too', I replied. Frankie had told me that there was fevered talk of expansion. 'It is a secure prospect for men like us' he said. 'The wages for a platelayer are good' he added, 'and I mean to enquire of it. So should you'.

Mary Ann was pregnant again. I was going to need to find more money from somewhere, somehow.

9. Prosperity and Hardship

I heard we were on the brink of a fine new world and that the constant sweat of grimy men like me would provide it. This message was repeated to me on many occasions, and not just by Frankie Noye. I truly wanted to believe it. But, for what had been a long time, I had not been able to see any signposts which pointed me towards any money in exchange for an honest day of labour. I didn't know about any one else but I certainly needed a shilling or three to help grease my part in the delivery of an Empire.

I could see those, like me, who were prepared to work hard to forge that powerful new world but I also saw those who possessed the money not wishing to part with it in exchange. Their behaviour reminded me of the fisherman who wished to catch his supper with a rod but he had expected and attempted to land his prey without the aid of a worm.

Wealthy men used seductive words to draw labour in but they harboured a stronger desire for an ever higher profit. Indeed, once those with money had drawn the smell of it up their nostrils, like blood, they only seemed to want it more. The law makers allowed them to do this at my expense and at the expense of others like me.

The streets of Camborne filled with souls, thrown together from all the corners of Cornwall. We were searching for better lives than the ones we had come from. We had heard Camborne was a prosperous place. What we found was not quite what we had been told. Hope was short lived, like a new born spring lamb stolen by an experienced fox before the lamb had been able to dismiss the wobble and find its legs.

More men and their families were arriving daily, all seeking the same cure: Money for a better life, in exchange, if you please, for work.

But, enough money and enough work were not being supplied. We knew that only money from working could cure the hunger. It would bring bread to the table and the dusting of flour from the crusts would soak up the tears. The warm dough gouged from the centre of a freshly baked loaf would swell bellies and shut off the stomach pangs. It would bring crumbs of comfort. Yes, work would bring bread but the words that had enticed us here were as empty as our stomachs and now we would do any work, and we would do it at any price.

'Work at any price' meant another downward squeeze on my daily labourer's rate and I was forced to work longer for less. I was reminded that, should I fail, there was always someone else who was willing and who was bound to succeed were he fortunate enough to be in my shoes. Mr Hocking there on the corner, a threadbare cap like mine in his hand, would seize the opportunity in the flicker of a candle flame and do anything for a farthing less than I.

Whilst I was proud of the work I did, I was minded to keep working on without complaint.

I decided to watch my step and close my mouth.

Where people gathered in such large numbers there was an increase in the spread of disease. It festered as invisible clouds and was invited with open arms into the damp clammy rooms of Camborne. It sat in overflowing buckets below the open mouths of the latrines.

Lungs of miners already thick with the dust from the daily burrow for tin below, clogged, and gave up their fight for clean air. Inflammation of the lungs, typhus fever, scarlet fever and consumption were alive and thriving. They were greedy killers, spoilt for choice with rich pickings down every street.

Some folk were too weak to fight it off and the young, the old and the not so old could all equally cave in should pestilence arrive and call out for them. With the death or decline of the bread winner came the certain ruin of the whole family.

Avis, Samuel's wife, had now delivered two children and both had died shortly after they had been born.

It carved at your heart and pumped it full of sorrow.

Camborne had started to make me bitter. It continued to make Mary Ann unhappy. She had decided from the very first fresh shoots of our new lives that this was no place to spin our fates on a gamble, nor those of our young children. She was set on a move from the growing turmoil and slime of the blackened town. She talked longingly of a return to the breezy cove at Coverack where the sea raced its crystal foams up on to the shore. She remained anxious about our growing brood and aloof from me. She saw me as the one to blame for all the mire. I raised my arms in protest for I felt I was but an innocent pilchard caught in a fisherman's net along with the rest of a flapping, dying shoal.

I did not believe our beloved Porthalloe, or Coverack, now held an answer. They, too, were in the clutches of despair.

I had looked to the rail way for my salvation, as Frankie Noye had said I should. It would keep me the right side of the grass, I thought.

I sought work at the offices of the Hayle, but it had fallen foul of speculators and gamblers in the guise of a new company, the West Cornwall. After clearing the debts it was discovered that there was no money to improve the rail way as the West Cornwall had promised before their take over. Their fevered talk of expansion had not even led to one fresh sod being cut.

I still went to their agent's office to enquire about work and stood in line, awaiting my turn. When it came, the clerk looked over his glasses and scratched my details across the page of a large leather bound ledger which lay open on his desk. 'Your name will be passed to Mr Ritson, the contractor' he had said through a tidy but ample moustache. He pulled a silver fob watch from his waistcoat pocket to check how soon it would be time for lunch. There was another large clock behind him. This rail way seemed to count on the tick of time as its master. 'I expect you will hear soon but in the meantime please be sure to call again' he said, motioning for the next fellow in line to take my place before him.

The investors had brought plans, backed by men with lengthy titles and a passionate knowledge of expensive French brandy. Those plans and promises were for the expansion of the rail way down to Penzance and up over moorland to Truro. In Truro the rail way would link with other rails owned by other great speculators. These men of words had all waved pieces of paper they said were as good as solid coin itself.

In this I had some hope, but promises would not put bread on the table. Where was the money itself? Was the intention of these honourable men just to make money for themselves from the rail way by influencing where it would run? I heard that if the rails were to run across their land then that would be most acceptable to the Gentlemen concerned. However, these generous concessions would require a hefty compensation and that this would be paid by the Rail Company. Money would be an adequate measure, they thought. It would console them for the loss of land which could not possibly be of further use to them or the poor tenants who for many years had scraped a living upon it.

These much maligned gentlemen would, of course, also require their compensation to be paid to them before a rail could be laid or a rock blasted from the spot God had always intended for it.

For three years the arguments had blazed, draining the coffers of gold that had been promised for the building and improvement of the rail way for the good of all in Cornwall. Then, like the sun breaking through the clouds on a rain swept day, all speculation and delay quickly dried away. Turpin's ransoms had finally been agreed upon! Men were at last to be hired. Work was to commence.

Harry Borlase and I went back to the clerk at Camborne station and stood again in front of him and his imposing time piece. I have no idea what it said but I didn't care. The clerk took a look at both my hands to feel the roughness and my boots for signs of recent work. He did the same with Harry. Satisfied that we would not shirk, he wrote us both a ticket and told us to seek out Mr Ritson at Polstrong. We were to hand our papers over to him.

We had at last found ourselves engaged for work on the magnificent West Cornwall Rail Way.

We got as drunk as lords on quarts that very evening and sung our way home in high spirits. Mary Ann was not pleased to see the state of me. I could not win favour with her in those days. I had found good work at 2 shillings and 8 pence a day, where before there was precious little in the way of luck, and she was still not happy.

We soon found that the West Cornwall would want a good return from us, too. A few men were engaged from around Camborne. We joined men who had dug and excavated earth in many parts of England, reshaping it entirely from God's original vision. Others from a far away place called Ireland said they had been invited by Mr. Pike, the superintendent, to work on the line, for it needed finishing urgently. Everyone was in a hurry to get to Penzance and those already there, I expect, would be in a hurry to finally get away.

We made up a motley gang of men, detailed to dig new sections of line. It was an exciting project with a promise of work for many years. An engineer Frankie had talked about, called Mr Brunel, had overseen the plan and had put forward an idea for rails to span across the valleys on a set of viaducts. They were to replace the incline workings where the trains were hauled up and down the levels by a series of engines, pulleys, large ropes and counter balances. These alterations would cut the delays and would smooth the passage of the train through the terrain. The viaducts were to be at Penponds, Angarrack, Guildford and Hayle. People wanted to travel faster. I was not so sure they wanted to do that up in the air.

There would also be new rails down to Penzance and up to Truro and it would be cut through the sleepy folds of hills lying in virgin countryside. My work was to be on the section from Camborne to Hayle.

We blasted rock, dug out the track bed, laid ballast, built up embankments and levelled the gradients. Harry and I had never worked so hard breaking rock and shovelling it into wagons. We had no machine for help. We had our muscles, our spades, our pick-axes and our wheelbarrows. We dressed in moles and lived in turf huts. It was not work for the faint of heart and, despite differences between the men working, we all had to team together for the greater good. I was to quickly learn that this was not a skill some of the men possessed.

About this time, Mary Ann and I moved to Penponds, a mile or so south of Camborne and near to Polstrong. It was close by the work which had commenced on the first viaduct there and the changes to the rail line. It reminded us of home. I had to have Mary Ann near and where the air was sweeter, for she was with child once more and tired quickly when on her own. Soon after, on Tuesday 8th January 1850, William Thomas Pearce, my third son and fourth child, was born.

Then, I admit to it now, I lost my way.

Whilst every chain of that rail was planned and was certain of its destination, I was not. The fan tail viaduct built at Penponds was a magnificent man made creation.

It was seven hundred feet long and forty five feet high, towering above the village on outstretched timber limbs, with embankments of earth on either side. I had more than a hand invested in it. Each day I had been exposed to extreme danger and challenge. By surviving each day I filled my head with too high an opinion of my worth and drank to celebrate it, as did all the other men.

Drinking in celebration of outwitting the day's dangers became a habit. At the end of a day I put it first. You have to understand that the work then moved along. It was all new rail south of Trenowin, where the old Hayle line peeled off towards the Angarrack incline. As the work moved away towards the site of the next new viaduct, I spent less time at home. Mary Ann became stranded, on her own, with four young children.

I had no sympathy for her. I was hard pressed. Work was every day with only a few days off at the end of each month when, with luck, we would be paid. When the money and spare time came we all drank and argued. Was I not entitled? Why go home to be scolded? There was more pleasure for me on the rail and it was a new life for me. It was a discovery. I lived in the shanty's set up along the rail way and was amongst men who fought, sometimes over women who had shown us an interest amongst the muddy workings, and sometimes over nothing more than an ugly look.

I admit life had become a daily walk through an overgrown bed of nettles before entering the mouth of hell's cave. Most men stole when the money ran out. There were no rules apart from those that suited the fiercest of these men. Power lay with the wickedest amongst us. My meek acceptance of the devil's kingdom was pitiful. I did not steal but I was swept along by this torrent, like a dark serpent sliding brutally through a thick putrid mud in a slippery dance with vile Medusa. As we curled through the green leas, pick axes and shovels swinging against all in our way, I forgot my duty to those who were innocent and helpless and who had relied on me. My suffering family's anger, when I saw it, was directed not at the corrupters, but firmly at my failure to be strong.

Payment for our labour was irregular. When we were paid, it was quicker if we accepted cheques, which could then be presented back to the contractor's Tommy shop in exchange for what we all knew was over priced flour, butter, salt and other necessities. What choice did we have if we wanted to work? And eat. Those were the rules set by educated men and it was a condition of our engagement when we were taken on. There were many issues we would have liked to have been better but we had no say in it. We sought escape from our privations by spooning out our own justice against one another and in yet more drink. Brewery barrels that travelled with us took a steep levy and I found myself short, unable to provide money for my family as I should have done.

So, I gave up our lodgings in Penponds and Mary Ann left with the children and went back to far away St Keverne, where she stayed with her mother at Coverack. Nicholas Johns, her step father, was now over seventy years old and my eldest, John Henry, who was eight, was engaged to help him with his fishing and to 'learn the ropes' from him. How else would wise ways be passed down through the generations unless those who were older and experienced took time to show you? It was the best place for him for he was not going to learn anything from me, apart from how to sin.

Instead of correcting my ways and seeing what was important to me, I took a fancy to Caroline Heathorn, a neighbour from Penponds. She was twenty five, with freckled skin, long brown hair and rose petals for lips.

She worked at West Stray Park copper mine with all five of her sisters, the youngest of whom was seven year old Jane. They all lived with their widowed mother in what amounted to little more than one room and they encouraged me to take sincere pity on them. I obliged. There was no other man there to help them and Caroline was ready for the trappings of marriage. She was like a hot oven, ready to receive freshly kneaded dough. I was ready to viciously burn and I was truly distracted, like a fox in an open henhouse.

Caroline and I took to sitting by the brook at Penponds. There, in the dell, we could bathe in the clear shallow waters as they languished peacefully before surging down towards the new viaduct. We also lay on the warm sweet grass to dry, sometimes between the passing rain showers.

'If you stay with me, I will care for all your needs' she had whispered to me as she ran her finger deliciously across my chest and down towards my belt line. I can still see those vibrant drips from her wet hair running silver trails down her goose pimpled skin and in to the moist of a steaming meadow. But I awoke, as though from a dream. It was a taste of what might have been, not what was to be.

My brothers Samuel, Nicholas and Peter, who were all now mining a huer's cry away, smiled knowingly to each other and said I was a fool, an iggit, for, in their eyes, it was nothing more than the last resisting embers of youthful lust.

Delays in the construction of the new sections on the West Cornwall occurred at the beginning of 1851.

Money was scarce as capital demands were made against the share holders, who then ignored the wails. The weather was unfriendly and hindered the work, skeat's making the ground heavy underfoot and our man made embankments unstable. A lack of daylight in those winter months was another reason progress was slow.

We had reached the hills behind Hayle when the contractor laid many of us off.

We then sat huddled in the camps, our spirits soured, waiting for the call of re-engagement. I remember watching the rain tumble and splash on the thin canvas of our tents, day after empty day. Once, whatever the weather, I felt free but now the rain did not cleanse or release me. It just washed my hopes away.

It was the warm welcoming soul of Mrs Millett that saved us. She was a tall thin lady, of stern expression, all elbows, always dressed in black and with her dark hair tucked beneath a tidy bonnet. She was a widow but still young enough to possess all her own teeth. I believe her husband, before his death three years before, had been a man of God and a soother of souls. Her son had taken up a darker science, using bandages and balms. He was a soother of physical ills through the practice of medicine.

Mrs Millett forgot her standing and set up a soup kitchen near her home at Penpol. There she provided a free hot meal once a day to all the excavators. It was close enough for us to walk and all she demanded was that we conduct ourselves well. If she feared this band of dirty men in rags and moleskins she did not show it or she chose to look beyond it.

We were starving and her benevolence eased this pain in us and brought back our strength in both body and soul. She had reached down to us and pulled us from oblivion with her compassion. Walking to Penpol, and back afterwards, to the camp, became a time when I reflected hard on my position. I was full of praise for Mrs Millett and the charity in her soul. Perhaps there was a God, after all.

As the weather improved, and the clouds parted, work started again. We cut a new track along from Hayle to Angarrack and, at both ends and in the middle at Guildford, work commenced on the new wooden viaducts. At Angarrack and Guildford the viaducts were set on stone footings which then supported wooden beams. These beams reached up 120 feet at Angarrack, each cluster like a hand with its fingers outstretched to the heavens, ready to support the passage of the rail across the gaping wide mouths of the valleys.

It was dangerous work, hammering nails and bolts the size of my arm in to stubborn wooden beams whilst suspended that high above the valley floor. The land below echoed a warning to the noise of the hammers on wood. 'If you fall from here you will be dead' it drummed. I have never felt more alive. I could wave to Willie Tripp and his daughter Elizabeth Ann as they ran to frighten the crows from their crops down below at Mellanoweth. It could be that their wave back was one of goodbye. From where I hung, without the wings of a bird, I must have looked nothing but a damned sorry fool.

I cared not. What a magnificent monster I was helping to create, I thought. This truly was the future and it was full of hope and achievement. Up there I had a view only birds had enjoyed and had never before shared. It had been their beautiful secret. As summer stretched before me, like the shining iron lines of the new rails across the viaduct, I resolved to make my peace with Mary Ann. Over the past year I had been dead to emotion and had not missed my family. Now, full of joy, with the glorious warm rays of the sun shining off the water in the distance at the sand hills of Riviere and Gwithian, I realised that I missed them dearly and knew that they were indeed what I truly wanted.

Our family needed to be reunified for my son Nicholas, now three, and my daughter Margery Ann, now six, were at this time in lodgings with Willie and his family. His daughter, Elizabeth Ann, who was thirteen, kindly looked after them in exchange for a few pennies.

Mary Ann was still in Coverack. She came to visit, bringing little W. T. with her. I asked her to come back and she agreed. We fell into each other's arms and we let relief in. It poured through us both with a passion.

She quietly forgave me. I had not been used to that in my life.

Money remained scarce and we had to work on trust. In this regard, our faith was constantly being tested.

At the end of April 1851, Mr Elkington, a sub-contractor at Hayle for Mr Ritson, had run away with the wages of over eighty men, including what was rightfully mine.

Although the money was entrusted to him by authority, he had lived the life of a glutton with it and squandered what was owed to us for our many days of back breaking work. The amount rightfully owing to me alone was nearly seven pounds and the sum total must have been over three hundred pounds when all the aggrieved men were added together. I could have exploded like an overworked boiler as I thought of all the children going hungry because of this one man.

Mr Elkington was then sighted swilling gin twenty miles away in Truro. He and drink were regular bedfellows and in his pursuit of this weakness, cheating his fellow men was merely a shameful necessity. I am sure that our deprivation and the deprivation of others, due to his dark deeds, was hardly worthy of any passing thought from him.

Four labourers from the camp were given the task on the first free Sunday of tracking him down and extracting, from him, the money that was owed to us all. In this they had some fortune, for Mr Elkington was about to elude them with an escape to Exeter with the mail. By the time they caught up with him their tempers must have been high for they ransacked him there in the street. I am sure pennies were rolling everywhere but only a small sum of money was ever recovered.

So, we were paid back some of what was owed. But, this event made me angry because, besides this, Elkington was not held accountable for the remaining debt.

I remembered in my anger that the punishment for my brother, Thomas, for stealing cider, was two months of hard labour. This man, Elkington, pleaded his innocence and pointed to everyone but himself as the guilty party. He accused others at his lodgings of stealing all the money from him and they were arrested by the Police instead. It was too late for our money, for most of it was gone, but Elkington tangled the judge up in polite, clever words, protesting that he was the victim of sharpers. The judge, as a fellow gent, showed him sympathy, believing that Elkington must indeed have been an innocent dupe of unfortunate circumstance, set upon by those of a lower standing. I know the truth but it counts for nothing. Elkington was set free, no doubt to repeat his stealing elsewhere from other easy prey and those less fortunate than he.

The debt he left was so large that he could not possibly bear the burden. All, apart from him, would have to share the cost of these upsetting events. I pitied his family, if he had one, and any wife, for they must have suffered their entire lives from his cheating, lying, stealing and drinking.

I grew to hate Mr. Elkington, contractor to the West Cornwall rail way. He was a truly selfish and unreliable man whose only beneficiaries were the purveyors of drink.

Mary Ann understood the reason this time for a shortage of money and that it was an event over which I had no influence. I think she worried more about the accidents that could occur. She was with child once more and when this babby was born it would mean we had five children, all under the age of ten. If anything were to happen to me, what would she do? I doubted my father or brothers would look after them all any more than I could look after their families, should anything happen to them. One false step from me and it would mean the workhouse for them all.

Terrible accidents occurred underground in the mines and there were several every week. It was a rock fall here or a broken rope there. Some men were never found or recovered. Others hobbled around Camborne saying they had left a leg or an arm somewhere below ground. The best of them would say 'I don't worry. I shall be back down there for it tomorrow morning'. Yes, some of those men could be rescued from beneath a scale of rock that had fallen on top of them on a Tuesday and be back at work by Wednesday.

Above ground, the construction of the new rail way was safer but there were still incidents. Why, in one week in early June of 1851 Bob Harvey fell off some scaffolding, which had not been tied securely enough. One of the poles then fell heavily across his thigh, fracturing it badly. Dr Millett worked up some science to save his leg from being sawn off.

The other railway accident that week resulted in the death of a man by the name of Roskilley, up near Redruth. He was a brakesman and was helping to run a nine wagon train filled with copper ore from the mine at Dolcoath to the quayside at Portreath. After applying the brake to the first wagon on a sloping section of track, Roskilley slipped and fell in between the wagons. The heavily laden iron wheels passed over his head, killing him instantly. No one was to blame.

He left three young children and a widow in trouble, for the money he earned will have stopped. It would be easy for his family to be swallowed whole by despair. I hoped that they would all be able to rise, despite this tragedy, and make good lives again for themselves.

On the 20th October 1851, our fifth child, a son we called Richard James, was born at a cot we had taken to again in Penponds. As we gathered round, before I had to hurry back to work, I hoped my children would all know me, their father. For that I would need a better fate than the poor unfortunate Mr Roskilley.

At the end of November of that year I had a few days of leave and went home to Porthalloe for the feast day and the baptising of my son, William. Mary Ann was already there where she could rely on the help from her mother.

The holy ceremony had been delayed due to our differences and troubles. William was the last child to be christened in 1851 in the font at St. Keverne. No babies took the iced water blessing once December was breached.

It was a quiet baptism. I suppose because it was a Friday most of the family were unable to be there. Elizabeth, my sister, had left home and was working as a house servant for Mr John Roskruge and his family at their new farm down Landewednack way. Samuel, Nicholas and Peter were all occupied in Camborne. My grand mother, Margery Saunders, who was now seventy seven, had come up on a walking stick from Tregaminion to be there. Mary Ann's mother was at the service, as was my eldest, John Henry, who had grown tall since I had last caught a sight of him. His arms and legs stretched out of his clothing.

My father, Thomas, was working in the fields up at Roskerwell as usual, as was my brother William. They were like two peas in a pod. They came to share a cider after wards but, in truth, we talked emptily about a new world they neither knew, understood or cared for. I felt I already knew all there was to know about Roskerwell. It was a life I had been forced to give up so it grieved me to dwell on it. I was much altered and, whilst Porthalloe had not altered, everybody was busy surviving their own cruel lives. When I left on Sunday afternoon to resume work on the rail way, I did not know when I would next return. I was sad but I felt Camborne was now where I should belong.

On the 16th February 1852 the West Cornwall Railway was closed for the final work to complete the new line. This meant the joining of new track with the old at Trenowin and the abandonment of the incline workings and stations at Angarrack and Penponds.

The old Foundry station at Hayle was also abandoned. A station was built to replace it on the new line which ran above the town. This line now crossed on a 1,200 foot fireproof stone viaduct that spanned the mud flats of the creek and the smoking furnaces and chimneys of industry below. Off these new workings ran a spur which twisted round and down to the harbour, where it connected to the old Hayle rails at the quayside. The old section there still ran past Riviere, where I had spent that day with my family and the Noyes, past Phillack, and then along to those who still demanded rail at Copperhouse Pool. Track from here back up to the old Angarrack incline was abandoned. No more carriages would escape into the valley to the sound of terrified screams. It proclaimed great change.

It was all single track that used the old T section Hayle rails on their stone beddings where possible, to keep the cost down.

The new workings used an invention called Barlow rail which was also very mindful of cost. Frankie said these wrought iron rails are laid without wooden sleepers, straight on to the ballast. They rest on iron saddles and each length of rail is secured by a bar of iron riveted to the opposite rail. Their adoption was on the advice of Mr Brunel, as he considered them to be more durable than the old ordinary rail.

And so, the line from Penzance to Redruth was complete.

There was both a great excitement and a great fear amongst the people. They could see the new structures, towering above their cots, dripping water on to their roof tops. The viaducts creaked as engines drew on to them for the first time, testing the track. The black beasts rattled and roared, spitting out sparks and startling the livestock.

Those trains promised the delivery of good and bad, bringing the remote southern inlets of Cornwall within reach of the chimney pots of London. They would bypass the wild and the dangerous trails but put hard working men out of work. They would allow outside influence to invade our centuries old customs and traditions. They would bring us civilisation, but with all its evil admirers and they would bring us tricksters like Mr Elkington, but also men of stature like Mr. Brunel.

The first whistles of commerce blew as the line opened to traffic on the 11th March 1852. What a heart filling sight it was to see that first puffer pass with passengers over the viaduct at Penponds.

Mrs Bennetts down the lane muttered and mumbled, as she gathered eggs, that it would bring nothing but ruin and nothing would ever be the same again. Was she wishing for a return to the days when your cart's wheels stuck every time in rutted mud lanes on the way to market? She was determined not to let the rail way change her or her ways. Her husband, John, stood silently by her side, his yellowed whiskers heavy with the burden of it all. He had just turned eighty five and still worked down a mine nearby. I expect he descended there every day searching not for tin but for a bit of peace and solitude.

Please forgive me for all the detail here. You must understand that I had come from ditch digging in Porthalloe to building what had until then been just a vision of the future that was impossible to describe to my own father. My arms had hurt with each shovel of ballast I had lifted and my shoulders had been soaked with the drops of a full year of rain. Who would have thought that I, Zebulon Pearce, just a quiet lad from a place no one had heard of, would have a hand in the building of this magnificent towering rail way and that, in the undertaking of the task, I would brush against the coat tails of great men.

All the men involved in the construction were invited on an excursion to Penzance. There we were given a hearty meal of beef, bread and beer to celebrate. To have beef was indeed a treat. I took great pride in what had been achieved and my part in it. We raised our glasses to celebrate the vision of Mr Brunel. We raised our glasses to celebrate that without us, this grand magnificent rail way would not have been built and we raised our glasses with optimism for the future of that new rail way.

Unfortunately, the end of the dinner signalled that, down the line, I would again be looking for work.

How could I raise a glass to that?

10. Mr Smith

People complained about the new rail way and said it was the 'devil's work'.

They were worried about what it would lead to and where it would end.

Many said the iron horse and its followers would erode morality, turn all hearts to stone and plunge us head first into the fires of the inferno below. 'The human spirit will be a chained slave to the rail way' they wailed.

They believed that even the price of oats would plummet and the much loved horse would become a dying breed, fit only for a pie.

I reasoned that you would still need a horse to get to places along the rail way where the train paused to take on water and passengers. Sections of the West Cornwall at Hayle Wharves, mine sidings, and spurs, all still used horses to tow the wagons. Ploughing teams had been employed on the emerald and golden slopes of Cornwall as far back as I could remember and, when the hissing pistons in the engine sheds fell silent again, and the heavy wheels no longer lurched, we would all need the gentle horse to be our friend once more.

So, I had no time for their worry. The world could not stay the way it always had been. We were all going to need to change what we had accepted in the past.

I needed to find work again and I felt the rail way remained my answer, for it was now busier than ever. The rise in industry brought to our door by the rail way had created money, expansion and jobs.

Money continued to be scarce for me. I suppose I could have left Camborne to work on the new sections of line and viaducts being built up near Truro. Most of the other men I had worked with had left, travelling up country to be re-engaged in new gangs. But they lived a different life to the one I wanted. I had to settle my young family. I had five hungry children all under ten and I did not want to leave them to the Parish. Moving every week was no life for a married man and Mary Ann and my children had suffered enough because of my long absences.

Camborne again it had to be.

It may indeed have been the hand of the devil that saw me find that work again on the rails, for there was an accident near Hayle less than a week after the new line had opened in March 1852.

An engine with carriages in tow had passed over the Guildford viaduct and was slowing before the new station at Hayle when it ran off the modern Barlow rails and over an embankment.

I had helped dig and prepare that bank less than a year before. The engine had slid on to its side and dragged an open carriage with it, throwing passengers out. Thankfully, the remainder of the train had stayed on the track and so a terrible accident was averted. All was well, apart from a few bumps, bruises, muddied leggings and ripped coats.

This accident brought refreshment for the doom mongers. They also complained about engine sparks, blaming the rail way for fires in the thatched roof tops of cots that crowded along the tracks and below the raised banks. However, men of influence, used to having their way, were making too much money from the increase in commerce that came from using the rail line. They had too much of everything invested in it to be put off and they scoffed that they could not just let 'all this magnificence' be reclaimed by nature's creeping fronds. They argued that they were a long way from giving up formidable mechanical progress on the basis of what they saw as the babbling unfounded prophecies of local grief merchants.

However, none of these new dreams would survive if accidents continued to happen.

Men were to be sought who would check the ballast, maintain the fences and cut back the furze along the rails. Through Mr Brunton, the West Cornwall therefore engaged me, as well as others, to work up and down the line along side the platelayers. 'The engines and wagons are to run smoothly on the rails at all times' Mr Brunton had announced to us. I was thus able to gratefully agree with my new benefactors that the rail way was, indeed, a good thing and that in my estimation it was important that it should continue.

Mary Ann and I had moved back in to Camborne's cramped rows and we began to feel settled like never before. Up until that time half way through 1852 it had seemed as if we had always been on the move, seeking a day of work here and another there. We became part of a community, even if that community was constantly changing around us.

The usually quiet Mary Ann now began to open up and speak to many people. She met some folk through the children. The tots made friends just by running up and down the street with not a care in the world. With so many open doors every mother had to mix.

Besides my family, and my brothers, we knew the Noye's, Sowell's and the Borlase's from back home. These familiar faces gave Mary Ann a great confidence. She was not alone now. Others we knew from St. Keverne were coming to settle and there was a familiar face arriving from home almost every month. They came with the despair of a torrid few years marked across their pallid faces but with hopes of a better future warming in their hearts. They came without questioning their welfare and they accepted any offer of work that they could find. It was almost always down a deep mine shaft. But, they felt fortunate. Work was work.

I escaped along the sulphur trails, walking the tracks up to Redruth, down to Portreath, and across to Roskear. I became the eyes of the rail way, clearing the land either side of any scrub and branches that might catch fire or endanger the safe passage of the daily trains. Preventing the theft of railway property such as hinges and rivets and keeping livestock off the lines also fell my way.

I saw industry rising up along side the iron rails, eager to take advantage of this faster and easier method of transport. I met some of the people as they scurried in and around these soot covered new places. They said they were forging a brighter future, fusing coal and water together to produce metal objects with names I had never heard of.

It was the edge of a new world where your soul could be swallowed if the forces around you allowed it. Why, even the raw grain of the fresh timber fencing that stretched for miles each side of the track was heavily pickled in creosote.

Camborne opened its arms wide to embrace these big changes, hoping to profit from its mineral bounty whilst the swarming hoards it attracted clung to the dream that their human spirit would survive and thrive.

Because of the work I had above ground I did not need much else to sustain my spirit. A bowl of food each day, provision for my family, a good pair of boots and enough brass left over each week for a John Barleycorn or two.

Was that too much to ask?

Mary Ann and I also found a common cause we could understand where people were brought together for social events, music and services. It gave us the belief that we were not outcasts here on earth. We believed, for the first time, that we had a value and a purpose. On Sunday's we began attending the Centenary Wesleyan Church where God was the central figure but all people were included as equals beneath him. You did not need to read to be able to pray there and loud singing was warmly embraced.

At other churches we had found that the front pews were only for the gentry. It would also be difficult at other churches to follow the service. Usually a tired old vicar would read a dusty well leafed passage with no passion in his chords. At such services we had assembled to mumble along. We had looked at each other silently, thinking the same doubting thoughts. Sometimes in those churches you were forced to sit apart from your family and I did not care for that either. God, if no one else, had surely meant for us to be together with our loved ones, as one, under his magnificent canopy.

At the Wesleyan Church, apart from God, George Smith became our inspiration.

Mr Smith was a Wesleyan Methodist preacher but, in truth, he was much more than that. He was a leader of our community and a man who merited respect and admiration for his actions and his mindfulness. If you were ever drowning, and in need of rescue, he was the person you would want by your side for he would know what to do and how to do it.

He lived up the lane at the big house known as Trevu. Yes, it was on the prosperous side of the rail way but no one begrudged him that for he did have humble beginnings. The large house was a long stride from those early days but his right to enjoy Trevu's high ceilings and airy panelled rooms was fully earned. He had not inherited a title. Nor had he ridden on the weary aching backs of others. All his wealth had been earned through his own honest and clever endeavour. He then sought to improve life for everybody. In all he did I believe he had stayed true to his soul.

His father had been a small local farmer, struggling to make ends meet. As a boy, like me, George had worked on the land and with cattle. His father had then given him the gift of education which George had seized with both hands and ears. He had strived each waking day to improve himself and to put his education to good use. Then, as a young man he had worked as a builder and learnt the skills of a carpenter.

With all the knowledge he gained from his books and his hands he set about life with a purpose. He lived his life to the brim. He was thirsty for such learned topics as the history of our land and its language. He wrote books on these, his favoured subjects. He would see a subject, learn about it, confront it and improve upon it. Then it would be ready to help others.

He believed God had given each and every one of us such a power. It was human spirit. 'It cannot be placed in a bottle. It lies unmeasured in every one of us. Wake it, shake it, nurture it, and never loose faith in it' he would say, looking at us all from the pulpit.

We would be roused by chapel. When we left after service we believed we could be a force for good. We went home fortified and determined to be more like him.

When I look back now, I realise that Mr Smith could not have ever found time for sleep.

At the age of twenty six, whilst still working as a carpenter, George married Elizabeth Bickford, the daughter of William Bickford. Shortly after, Mr Bickford announced an invention. It was an explosive fuse for use by miners in the mine tunnels where they dug.

All miners had begun to use explosive powder under ground to help them in their work. They used the force of explosion to blast steadfast rock into unwilling little pieces for this was quicker than hammering away at stubborn black walls with nothing more than a blunt tool and a yard of space.

You do not need me to tell you that explosions are dangerous. We had used them to great effect near Camborne on the new path for the rail way and in moments it had shattered the peaceful earth, scattered the birds and opened up whole hillsides to daylight.

Mr Bickford had observed that miners below ground were lighting trails of gunpowder, running for cover and sometimes killing or maiming themselves and others when the explosion they planned for had ignited earlier or with more force than they had reckoned with. It was more of a butcher's yard than a place of work.

Mr Bickford perfected an alternative and much safer method. It gave miners a controlled fuse and a measured explosion. They could now run for cover without the fear of chance wanting to play and trifle with their lives. It was a triumph. Nature was overcome.

He protected his idea, and decided to produce his invention at Tuckingmill, next to the new church between Camborne and Pool. George Smith had been eager to help him for he had immediately seen the value of this new creation.

Alas, Mr Bickford was personally unable to defeat nature and succumbed to death before the factory was open. George Smith was left to continue with the work. He ran the factory, produced the safety fuses, saved many lives and made himself a large golden fortune.

Mr Smith's money from the factory has been put to good use. Worthy causes have benefitted greatly, like the building of the Centenary Chapel. His children have all been educated and encouraged to make good connections in society and enter businesses which promised growth and posterity for years to come. I had never been to school but, having seen at first hand the value of it on another who had started life like me, I resolved that my children would have some learning and, with God's encouragement, a trade and skill.

In 1853, my brother Peter left Camborne. It was sudden. Like Samuel, he was curious of what lay undiscovered and was not afraid to poke a stick at it. Talk around town had been of great riches to be found far away over the sea at the end of a leading wind. Agents from mines in other lands were seeking young single men. The agents then promised better terms and working conditions to the men they found. Peter and a group of friends had talked excitedly over beer and were going to try their luck. Beer can certainly swell your expectations. They were hoping for riches at a place called Calumet. Stories came daily of a rush there for copper.

'Large rewards for those who venture' was a beguiling mistress that had whispered daily in his open ear. After all his work in Camborne had amounted to so little, he had felt strongly that there was nothing in Cornwall for him except more of the same. 'That miserable reward was not worth the penance' he had said, shaking a head which had clearly been turned.

Peter and I had followed the same path in Porthalloe, but at different times. He was no more than two when I left home and six years old when mother had died. He had endured the sour treatment of our step mother but the sweet pleasures of Penare. Above all, he was my brother. Our features were from the same fountain.

There had been a measure of improvement for him in Camborne but, was this to be the sum total of his mark? Maybe leaving Cornwall now would provide another step towards a better life. 'I have no wife or children to worry for' he said, smiling at me through the candle light on our last free evening together. 'I am as free as a bird and I aim to soar' he had added.

It was done. He told me he had a free ticket on a sailing rig called the Western World and a contract with a mine captain's signature to recognise that, even before a shovel's worth of ore had been lifted, he was already important. 'I will be able to have a proper Sunday waistcoat with a row of metal buttons and a set of pockets at the sides to rest my thumbs' he joked. He had skill and knowledge, in pumping and hoisting, and would earn a percentage of what was mined. 'Don't worry, Zeb. Others I know are going too. The Americas will seem like Camborne because of it but I will be of better use to others and myself.'

I wished him well but I was sad, for I believed from his excited stories that, whilst he was travelling to a beautiful unspoilt place full of snow covered mountains, it was wild, lawless, and near the ends of the earth. Mr Rosewarne said there would be one hundred miles or more between each man. It was not going to be just another place to perch.

Peter said he would be back. I would have liked to have believed him but I was sure none of us would ever see him again.

My work changed once more.

The old Hayle rails, adopted by the West Cornwall, were wearing out with the heavy toll of daily wagon and passenger trains now running between Truro and Penzance. The flat stones on which the rails sat were groaning under the expectation. Had they not been laid with pride and thoroughness by earlier gangs they would have given out long before then.

I found myself as part of a team sent out to replace the fatigued rails between Penponds, Carn Brae and Redruth. I learnt new skills and it was heavy, fast work. I felt a part of this life and my spirit was fulfilled. There was also the extra pay. I had traded up from the furze clearing.

It began a time where work like that was available on the railway in short intensive bursts. The company did not seem to ever have much money or perhaps it did not wish to spend it on the rails, where it was needed. So, only in times of extreme necessity was there a call for men to work the line.

The newer Barlow rails were troublesome and not wearing as well as the Hayle rails had done before. There were some accidents. Blame was placed on those that smelted the iron, saying it was too weak, then those that laid the ballast, saying it was not in the correct place. All I can say is I did what I was told and I was paid for that. I was not rewarded for my view. This was not why I withheld it. In truth, I believe I would have been swiftly dismissed by the contractor had I dared to question any part of my task, even if I sought, by my own experiences, to help improve the track for the benefit of all. I can say now that Barlow's rail was an experiment that did not work as well as Mr Brunel had planned. I did hope he was not laying it elsewhere.

My little daughter Mary Jane was born in February 1854. I remember her skin was white, and soft, like a dollop of freshly clotted cream. I look back and think that she must have been small enough then to fit in my pocket, alongside my faithful pebble. She was so peaceful, and quiet, that I would have forgotten that she was there. Bless her, for her life was to be a constant struggle.

I now had six young children. I was thirty one and the oldest child was John Henry, who was ten. Margery Ann was eight. She was able to help mother with the daily chores for our lives were busy and full. The other three boys were all in to mischief around the cot. I cannot think who that reminded me of but certainly you could not forget about them. They were always there, tugging at my britches seeking answers I was always too tired to give.

As a country, we were in the midst of another draining war, in a place that sounded far worse than any before it and known as the Crimea.

When work on the rail way stopped again, our family moved once more, back to Angarrack.

I took to labouring where I could find it, so long as it was in places I knew. I cared not what task it was so long as it was above ground, and not at sea. I knew that if something needed doing, I would do it and I could do it. A penny tossed in my direction would ensure employment fell my way.

Far off adventures in the Americas were a fancy for men prepared to leave their family behind or for men in search of a family. How could I leave for the unknown when everything of value to me was what I saw before me with my own eyes? My wife was still happy, surrounded by her children, their faces gleaming in the spring sunbeams that cut through the shelter of quiet leaves in the trees above us.

Money did not need to be a king here.

We lived in the shadows of the rail viaduct, just beyond the drips, and I worked with horses down at Phillack. It was a short easy walk, no more than a couple of miles.

My son, John Henry, would come with me and we would walk the old abandoned line from Angarrack incline down across to Copperhouse Pool.

Nature's barbs and twines had crept back across part of the rusted path, throwing out belled flowers that attracted bees and the song of small birds. John Henry was a town boy but it was there, in the peace, solitude and heat of the sun, that he discovered his love for the country and the tie to his other big love, the railway.

11. Mr Burgess

On the 7th April 1856 my third daughter and seventh child, Elizabeth, was born. She was a healthy lively baby right from the beginning. She was named in memory of my own sweet little sister, who, had it not been for cholera, would have just turned twenty one.

By then I was back on the rail way again, grateful for the steady work each week where many had none.

At the time of Elizabeth's birth we were also lodging once more in Penponds. I certainly stuck to what was familiar, didn't I? It seemed to always be but a stone's throw from where the rail way ran.

1858 saw yet more familiar change. We moved back up the line again, towards Camborne, and Mary Ann was once more with child. She had reached the age of forty and her pace was beginning to slow. She said she was feeling her back. She complained about aches and strains caused, she said, from following me about.

We all carry a burden. My back, shoulders and ankle pains brought on by the daily stoop over rail ballast, the lifting of heavy rail and the swinging of a pick found no sympathy either. Looking back we could have been kinder to each other.

Her belly swelled and she struggled through the swelter of that summer until, on August 20th, she gave birth to my fifth son and eighth child. We called him Zebulon, after me. What a poor little mite, born into such uncertain times. He slept, unaware of turmoil, and his thick black hair spilt from one end of the shawl in which he had been wrapped. For Mary Ann's sake, and my pocket's sake, he was surely going to have to be the last.

Baby Zeb had been born at the edge of the spreading sprawl of Camborne. We had taken an old cob cottage in Stray Park. A small sum of money had been put by for it. It was no Trevu but it was in a row near to the station, close to both the town and country. 'There will be no more moving' Mary Ann had said, falling into a chair and not really believing her own words. The new cot also gave us more rooms and a small parcel of land.

Indeed, we had enough space to fill that we were able to take in a lodger now and then. It was usually a railway worker. They often had nowhere else to go or were working away from home, as I had been. Sometimes they were just lonely, and passing through, with no family or ties. It helped us to pay our way, as did the pig, called Bertie. We kept him down in the crow at the bottom of the yard. I felt giving a pig a name was a trifle but Mary Jane, my daughter, had a ceremony one afternoon and gave it a name in memory of Prince Albert. Had she understood that Bertie would one day be carved into breakfast bacon, she might not have become so attached.

If the cottage was to remain our home, then everyone needed to help. Money earned by our children was used to make ends meet. John Henry, who was seventeen, and Nicholas, who was thirteen, were now engaged on the rail way. They laboured alongside me. Their youthfulness and the lower daily pay rates for young men helped convince the rail way of their value over other, older men. In return, my boys gained a trade and helped me keep a roof over all our heads.

Trains were becoming more regular, heavier, longer and faster so the track was in constant need of repairs. We had found ourselves working as platelayers. We were among a team of men replacing the failing Barlow's with heavy cut timbers set into the ballast on to which new rails were screwed down tightly with metal fish joints. That should stop the derailments, the engineer had said.

My other sons William, who was eleven, and Richard, who was nine, both worked on the surface at the Stray Park Mine. The engine house towered within sight of our cot. Its sounds and smells drifted across and in to town. My lads would go off at dawn together, their feet dragging. It was dangerous work for men, let alone boys so young. They hated it and moaned daily but they could have no choice in the matter. It was a new opportunity to work and the family needed money. Despite my good intentions, schooling did not happen. Sitting at a desk would not put food in their mouths every day and if it did so in ten years time then that would have been too late.

Two new powerful steam engines had been installed at Stray Park Mine. Costly but earnest work was under way to drive the search for copper deeper and deeper under ground. William and Richard had to take the work when it was available. It was hoped that by digging deeper for those elusive deposits the new investors could turn the mine around. It had been a regular loss maker so far for all investors. Mind you, all of the land on which we trod or in to which we dug and all of what we could see about us was owned by the Basset family, up Tehidy way. So, even when the mine owners lost money, the continued opulence of the land owner meant they clearly did not.

The Basset's made me remember a day long ago, back in Porthalloe, when John Carlyon was thirteen and I was nine. John had come across me one day up by the Tuck. I had a handful of pocked wild apples. He must have been watching me by the tree from a hidden nook. He had fixed his bulging eyes on my meagre haul and said 'Those look like mine'.

'No, they are not' I had said, making to run past him and on down the path. 'Give 'um to me and I'll check 'em over' he continued, raising his voice and blocking my escape. I did not release the little green nibblers and he cuffed me round the ear, making me drop them. As I moved my hand to protect my head from a following blow he said 'You need to be clear, Zeb, that what's mine is mine an' what you think is yours is mine too. When you one day stand 'ere where I do, as king of the path, you will see it the way I does'.

What he meant, I now realise as I recall having to pick the bruised apples up and hand them over to him, is that I should do all the work up in the tree, and take all the risk. He would watch, picking at his teeth, before brazenly reaping the rewards of my effort.

It was now almost fifteen years since Mary Ann and I had said goodbye to Porthalloe. My left ear still stings.

I had covered many miles since.

I must have walked up and down the rail road between Hayle and Redruth enough times to have been able to walk and see Peter way over there in America. I had chased work in all weathers and I think I must have slept in a hundred places but, at last, I felt I was finally able to keep some of the rewards for myself and enjoy coming home to the same house. Mind you, with eleven people all tumbling around within those walls I did still have some doubts even about that.

A family, a fixed roof and useful work was now mine. We were not in the work house. I had what I wanted. It had been a slow cooking stew but there it now was, hot, rich and ready to be smelt, spooned out, and enjoyed. I remember hoping that my life would indeed remain that way for a while.

I wanted it to be as certain as the sun rising on a new day.

But, what does ever stay the same apart from that sun rising? You need to be on your guard most when you have the bull by the horns, and his eyes glaze and dull with the acceptance of a defeat at your hands. I know, for the bull at Penare would look resigned and calm after a tussle, lulling me into dropping my arms. Then suddenly he would rise again with a twist and kick before throwing me with a giant heave into the nearest fresh pat.

I only had to look at my brothers lives to see that change was there when you measured out the years.

No news came from Peter although he did send some money which he said was to help our eldest brother Thomas to come out of the Helston work house and to go back home. Thanks to this my brother Thomas went back to Roskorwell to lodge with father. Hannah had said she was prepared to look after my brother Tom if she was compensated for her trouble. He had been rescued the same day as the gooseberry fair. Peter had paid for this so I believed he must have been doing well enough in Calumet. He may even have had that waistcoat he had wanted, with the neat vertical row of small shiny buttons.

Samuel had left Camborne in search of silver, following Peter to America. He had left his wife Avis and his two surviving young sons behind. He said he would be back but that had been some time ago. When I last saw Avis she had received no news of him, had declared her self a widow and seemed quite angry that he should have done such a thing to her. I was not surprised at her rage but taking it out on me with some very bad expressions would not help.

'I'm sure he will come back awash with silver nuggets and coins, sweep you up and take you away from all this' I had said to Avis, as a single coal glowed bravely on the bare bones of the grate. She only ever half listened and never valued my opinion. I am sure she had already decided upon the matter and was defiantly telling others that she had no further need for a man. Mind you, she was right to give up on Samuel for, in reality, I expect my brother was spending all he earned on women he had recently met where ever he now was. Yes, easily distracted, our Sam.

Of my other two brothers the news was better. William was settled at Lestowder, a salmon's leap from my beloved Penare. He was happy with farm work and always said he had no plans to move. As others had left, the work fell his way. Why should he change a view of the open sea for a view of a steep cobbled wall like mine? Even his pigs enjoyed a better view and fresher air than I. At the end of 1858 he had married Ann White, the daughter of old family friends. They had worked together and shortly after their marriage their first son, Samuel, was born.

My last brother, Nicholas, who was four years younger than me, had met a steady Camborne girl called Teresa Martin. He had whispered his love amongst the flowering heathers before they were married in 1853, just before

Peter left for America. Nicholas had carried on working as a copper miner up at Dolcoath and helped obtain work, through a connection, for my boys at Stray. He kept an eye on Avis, too. I think he was always very caring towards her but she had married Samuel and everyone had to make the best of it.

Nicholas endured a hard life below ground. It dampened his spark like heavy rain on a camp fire. His wife, Teresa, was very loyal to him. He, in turn, stood by her whilst he dreamt about the lives of others and the courageous lives he believed he might have led, if only fortune had favoured him and belief not deserted him. They lived in the middle of Camborne at that time with two quiet, obedient children.

In the days before I gave up drink, we would meet up with Nicholas and his family at the annual Camborne fair. We would amble past the booths and stalls of the travelling merchants and our children would take turns on the swings that had come to town. He took delight in the sight of dwarfs and bearded ladies. I wondered about him sometimes.

My attention was always drawn to the caged animals. Like Nicholas, their spirits and claws were subdued. How timid and bored they looked. I felt sorry for them although I did not wish for them to discover their roar again and make me their next meal. Thank the Lord they were not found in the wilds of Cornwall and were locked behind sturdy iron bars. As they yawned I could see into their gigantic pink mouths. I imagined their large sharp white teeth sinking with relish into uncertain sailors as they stepped ashore in virgin territories like America.

Those years were steady and safe ones. I was happy. I remember them fondly.

But, there is no comfort for long. There were many different opinions of how the world should be and, as our family grew, we fell under a mix of new influences and people.

I was urged by folk Mary Ann had befriended to turn my back on the evil of alcohol. Some felt our lives should contain no drink, for it caused man to lose his soul. Some felt our lives should contain more drink to help a man to sooth his soul. I had liked a drink and it helped me work but I also saw the holes into which others regularly fell. Usually those holes were large and black, and appeared, causing chaos, on pay day.

Our family continued to be engaged by the Methodist views and the travelling preachers who spoke of the virtues of self improvement and respectability. We felt good standing proud and keeping as clean as we were able to. We tried to eat as well as we could and not waste a morsel of the bread we had been blessed with. God was on our side and would help us look after one another. If we gave up beer and gin we would be able to survive the gambling, starvation and heavy drinking which inevitably led to fighting and misery. So give it up we did and our thrift meant we had coals for warm hearth fires round which we gathered as a family, unified against malevolence and firm in our Godly beliefs. That bond meant more than crust on the table. The meek shall indeed inherit the earth.

Nevertheless, sometimes religion was still a mystery. We could see reason with many of the arguments but it was clear there were many ideas on how to worship God. In Camborne there were people who believed in the Anglican way. Then there were the United Methodist Free Church, the New Connexion Methodists, the Primitive Methodists, the Bible Christians and Roman Catholics. Each group wanted their views to be heard the loudest.

I am sure that the Almighty did not mind how we knelt or how badly we sang as long as we were true in our hearts and kind to our fellow men. For some I think that message was lost only moments after the chapel doors had been re-opened and they had risen from their prayers. For some, I think making others see it their way was what mattered most.

At the end of 1863, on the 28th November, my eldest daughter Margery Ann, who was suddenly eighteen years old, was the first of our children to wed. She married Ed Burgoyne.

Again, our lives changed.

The weather was boisterous on their happy day. I remember us all having to hold on to our caps and bonnets. Like our family togetherness, they were in danger of being blown away on a gale. I had to accept others into our lives, or be blown away too, like last summer's leaves.

Ed was a rail way man like me and our rail gang had a break in work which allowed the wedding to take place. He had lodged with us, and then with my brother Nicholas after he became too amorous for my liking with Margery Ann. But, they had continued to see each other and over that last year I had seen enough to know that Ed was a good worker. I did not doubt that he was a strong character who would provide for his family when it arrived. He was seven years older than Margery Ann but this was what she wanted and so Mary Ann and I were glad for them.

We were back to work shortly after so Margery Ann stayed at home with us. Then John Henry was gone after he announced he would have to marry. His marriage to Elizabeth Anne James was on a crisp clear blue day in January 1864. Hardly a cloud smeared the sky. She was a quiet and loyal girl of twenty one, a couple of years older than John Henry when they married. We had to say he was also twenty one for it was viewed as bad luck to marry an older woman, as I had.

No one spoke openly about Elizabeth Anne clearly already being with child. She did struggle to hide her family way under that neat dress she wore. The girls tried hard to disguise the issue but to no avail. I smiled quietly to myself amid the whispers of 'is she?' and 'what do you think to that?' We had become used to it in our family.

John Henry had stayed on the railway and was plate laying as part of Frankie Noye's reliable team so there was some prospect for the little one of a happy and long life. John Henry was a hard, fearless worker. I was sure the cloistered mutters would soon be forgotten and those with nothing better to do would find another squawking fowl to chase from its restful perch.

As though eager to trump in life's game of cards, my son Nicholas did go one better and delivered an ace. When he started to court Christiana Jewell from Illogan, she just brazenly moved in with us. I wasn't sure. Their noise making kept me awake at night. Those two would never be as deep as Dolcoath. I suppose when Nicholas was away on the track, it did give her a family to be part of and she needed that. I understood when she tearfully explained that she had nowhere else to go.

I just wished that her ardour with my son Nicholas would cool a little so that Mary Ann and I could get our slumber. Mary Ann would just giggle quietly next to me and say we were once like that. 'It weren't the nettles, Zeb'.

Now I don't expect you to keep up with all these comings and goings because I can tell you that it was hard enough for me. I had to work and my hours were long and exhausting. That kept me fully occupied. I then had eight children and their family friends as well as a wife, lodgers, brothers, their families and friends to remember. Oh, we'd best not forget Bertie the third, another pig, who had fattened up nicely and was almost ready for the chop.

The question I asked most in those busy days as soon as they had left the house and departed into the night was 'who was that'? Over the last few years I had grown used to my own rules. Now I had to fit around the lives of others again.

I had trouble with all the names so what chance do you have, dear reader? Using the same names for everyone was one answer and this worked well when my first grand babby was born on the 7th March 1864, to John Henry and Elizabeth Ann. They called the new babby after my wife. I could not help making conversations more interesting and there was always a fair bit of head scratching from those I spoke to.

'How is Mary Ann?' they would ask.

'Oh, she is as full as a tick' I would answer.

'She don't look bad on it, do she?' they would reply.

'Yes, she's good on the breast and suckling well' I would say, before enquiring of them 'and how is your wife?'

Yes, it amused me to confuse these matters with a bit of dumb but wilful intention and to see how long it took folk to work the matter through. There is nothing quite like a bit of a nip with your tea.

Towards the end of 1865 the West Cornwall Railway was bought by another railway company called Great Western. The new company ran on a broad gauge rail system but left the West Cornwall to run as before, on standard, so long as a broad gauge rail was added in with it.

I am pleased to say that the constant change of mind by the Company authorities meant more money had to be spent throughout 1866. That money provided more work on the rail road for my two sons John Henry and Nicholas, for Ed Burgoyne, and for me. William also came to work laying rails. I did not want him to go down the mine when he came of age so I was glad. We were employed in gangs to widen the embankments and strengthen the viaducts. This would allow the heavier rail to sit on a broader track bed and we were then engaged in the teams to lay the extra rail.

Yes, 1866 was a good year for work and for the birth of two more grand children but it was also a sad year because it brought the death of my elder brother, Thomas.

He had not managed back at home. Hannah and my father had no time or understanding for him. His decline was a drain on them and they had said they could not afford to care for him. They had abandoned him yet again. My grand mother Margery had been the only one to always show him compassion but, at the age of ninety one, she was bedridden and in need of some care herself.

So, Thomas went back in to the work house at Helston.

Back there on that sloping hill at Meneage Street he must have slipped into a dark, deep wretched depression. His life had been a sorry and miserable one. It came to a merciful end in April of 1866. He was forty four and alone when he died there of pneumonia. From stories I have heard his remains were nothing more than pale skin and protruding bones.

William had travelled up to Helston with a farm trap to collect Thomas's body, rescuing it from a surgeon's dissection. The family wanted him to be buried properly and privately in St. Keverne. At least then his soul could be saved, as would the souls of those who had failed to care for him in life. That included mine.

It must have been around then that Mary Jane was also struck down by fever. I remember she was about twelve and I remember her lying there, face all flushed and teary, wet through with sweat and heat. She was very poorly and her spirit was within a whisker of being called away but, over time, she did begin to pull through. We remained lucky to have never known the anguish caused by the death of your child.

Her sister Elizabeth and mother Mary Ann kept a vigil and helped to see her over the worst. The fever had left her weak, without appetite and unable to work a full day so we sent her to the new school instead, where her aunt Avis was working. That kept her from being outdoors and exposed to the elements. School also kept her away from the strain of physical work.

Some good families had children at that school.

Edward Burgess and his wife were one. A daughter of his went on to marry one of Mr George Smith's sons so I imagine money was never much of a complaint. Edward was a couple of years older than I was but our children were of the same age and they came across each other frequently. His youngest daughter Mary Elizabeth was the same age as my Mary Jane (we called her Jane, really, using her second name as her first) and his youngest son Henry was the same age as my boy Zeb. Together, they were a couple of tearaways.

Edward was a help to me when my work on the rails began to dry up again. The Great Western sought younger, fresher men, prepared to work for a pauper's rate.

Edward earned his living as an iron and general merchant and lived near the rail way where he kept offices, a store and a yard. I think he lost some money on railway shares but he must still have been prosperous. After all, he did employ three sisters from Phillack, all at once, as house servants, when their father fell ill. Real beauties they were, too. Everything would spill from behind the lace. Edward's benevolent nature rescued them, as did his wife, who decided to turn a blind eye and take to crochet.

Edward knew I had knowledge of farm work and animals. Those skills were becoming scarce. Boys growing up then were softened by town life. They could grow restless if they were not surrounded by blackened bricks. Their hands had often never seen or been marked by soil and their legs had never had to catch and tame a contrary beast.

He introduced me to an older brother of his, called John, who was a land agent, auctioneer, registrar, farmer and gent. Was there nothing the Burgess boys didn't do? John kept a farm up at a sweet spot just off Illogan Highway, still in sight of the Dolcoath mines. It was set in a leafy cranny below the shadow of Carn Brae's towering rocks. It was called Burn Coose.

John was in need of a good man to help him run it.

He also had fifty new acres to grub and convert to farm ability and a dairy herd to build back up. It had not recovered since rindepest had struck in 1866. John Burgess had said that he had previously employed ten men at ten acres per man. Now he had acquired another fifty acres but thanks to progress and new thinking he would only now need two good men and three boys for the whole farm. 'Would you be interested'? he had said to me, sucking on a nose warmer that blew scented smoke all abouts. 'We need to clear the stones and roots, ditch it and make it fertile. Can you do that before the season's start? ' His question reminded me of the grocer on Church Row. You could go in there with tuppence ha'penny for some pasty fillers and come out with nothing but the thought that you'd been on the receiving end of a good turn.

Nevertheless, of course I was interested. I gratefully accepted the chance of work, however hard. I just wanted to work and so, after ten years of stability, we were on the move once more.

I remembered Edward and John's father, William. In his last days he, too, lived near Stray Park. His history goes a long way back and while most people from those days will be long dead I must still be careful with my words. A mean streak can carry for decades, stretching its bony hand from the grave and haunting your grandchildren. Besides, both Edward and John had shown me kindness.

The story I heard was that William Burgess was the product of a lengthy liaison between one of the slim hipped Martyn girls from St. Keverne and the heir to the Tehidy Estate, Francis Basset, who had been on a pleasure trip to the town of Helston with his father in 1777. Francis was a young buck of twenty back then, idling his time sowing wild oats and fine tuning the dark arts of indiscretion. When Francis's son William was born from this liaison he was born just plain William Martyn. It may have ended there but William's mother had died shortly after giving birth to her son. A scandal had threatened to erupt. This was quelled by grand father Basset, with the reputation of his family at stake and the honour of his son to uphold.

Francis was not allowed to turn his back on William, his son. He was made to quietly take responsibility. However, William was illegitimate. Being born out of wedlock meant he could not be an heir. He was also, in part, of common stock. Well, that was no surprise for we are all of common stock down on the Lizard peninsula and the Martyn girl was no exception. To inherit the Tehidy estate both parents of an heir would have to be of aristocratic descent. So, William was adopted by an employee on the Estate by the name of Burgess. A tidy annual stipend and property with in the Estate grounds at Trengove, near Portreath, was quietly arranged to cover this arrangement.

Money is a great comforter and ruffled feathers can soon be smoothed and calmed with enough of it. I am sure it took plenty and that the reminders for further payments were frequent.

It helped William Burgess to become an educated man. His education helped him to see that he was in a position of power and influence but that he held no title to disgrace. He shook the bottle he was given as hard as he could, stirring the contents up just enough without spilling them.

He became a law unto himself, pushing his connection to the Bassets, knowing he would never need to accept the responsibility of a title or set an example to the masses. He was clever and realised that he was easily able to outwit authority and make a great amount of money from unlawful activities whilst doing so. He discovered the nature of advantage over other traders by selling merchandise which had been brought into Cornwall without the usual levies of tax placed upon them. What an enjoyable sport illegal trading was and what riches and power it subsequently bestowed.

I believe, from talking in pubs to those who spoke there with authority, that Camborne turned its face the other way. When William set mine workings on the first accessible cove west of Portreath, every one knew it was for show. No copper or tin would ever come from its shafts unless it was wrapped round a brandy barrel. The mine workings hid liquor smuggling that kept houses like Tyack's and the Plume of Feathers in untaxed drink for many years.

That silent blind cove could berth a vessel at high tide. It was steep, dangerous ground to go snooping. As the tide ebbed and the hull rested on a small stretch of sand, contraband would be unloaded. So the story goes it was then placed in the small hidden inlet until dark, before being rolled across the beach and hoisted up the cliff by rope and pulley. Then it was distributed into many hiding places, scattered amongst the gorse and country wells until delivery could be agreed upon and arranged. The tide would come in, wash the foot prints away and all that was left was the kibble from the cliff top mine shaft.

The fruitless but cheerful search for ore would have started again by the time the excise officer rode by. 'Still nawthun from that mine, Bill?' 'No, Joe, still nawthun. Nawthun so much as a sniff. We'll keep a goin' and see what turns up today'.

In those days did you trust the customs man or William Burgess? You trusted William, for the excise man may have taken a bribe to turn away his gaze. Would you cross William? No. He would make an example of you or sue you if he felt you had cheated him, even if it was over a matter of little real consequence. I was told of a lady called Mary Dawe who was found guilty of stealing liquor from him and was given three months of hard labour for it. The judge, no doubt still suffering from wind as a result of some fulsome Burgess hospitality, sent her down, squashing her like a weevil beneath his very ample boot.

Thinking back on it, William must privately have been a bitter man, harbouring feelings that he had been cheated out of the rich pickings at Tehidy by the low birth of his mother. It must have irked him to see the large prosperous Estate go to a succession of people he considered of less worthy blood than he. None of them were in the direct line for his real father had died without leaving another true male heir. Yes, indeed, that could only have made his temper far worse, leading him to be no respecter of authority and its unreasonable rules.

William was himself a father to at least ten children. All his boys appeared to excel in reputable occupations such as merchants, mine agents and agriculturalists. His girls also married in to the families of merchants. Together they ran Camborne as their business, with a firm invisible grip. Prosperity would not be reserved for those with a title. He would secure his prosperity through trade, by any means. You could only afford to fall out with the Burgess family if you could do so from a distance. Otherwise you ran the chance of ruin over night and banishment from the town.

For me, a man used to being outside in the dark, looking in at men like Mr Burgess as their teeth tore at dripping platefuls of spit roast meat, it was a simple choice. With no more than the most modest of prospects, I accepted what greasy crumbs were left.

So, in 1869, although wary of stirring an irritable beast, I climbed in to the lion's cage and started work for John Burgess, up country, at Burn Coose.

12. A New Life

After the heavy work on the West Cornwall finished in 1866, my eldest son John Henry moved to Calenick creek, near Truro. There he worked as a platelayer at Newham and later on the leafy line that curled down to the shimmering coast at Falmouth. As with my decision to move to the Highway it was an easy one for him and his family for new work was there and in Camborne there was now none.

Not long after our move to Burn Coose, bad news reached us that my grandmother, Margery Saunders, had died at the age of ninety four. She had lived a long life and all in that same Porthalloe valley. She had been the village midwife, a farm labourer, pilchard baulker, mother, grandmother and friend.

She died in March of 1869, as the buds of spring were forming. In her last years she had become blind and bed ridden. She had been cared for by her son, Peter, and his daughter Elizabeth, who was the only good product of Peter's troubled two year marriage to a wayward girl from Coverack.

My grand mother had been buried for several weeks by the time the news of her death had reached us, so I had to mourn alone. In my child hood she had been like a mother to me. Without her steady hand firmly on the tiller, and her gentle guiding love, our family may never have survived. Yes, she scolded me many times, but I know I deserved it. Her temper was never so harsh that it would bruise those in receipt of it. I also knew, deep in my heart, that under that crust her soul was as warm as a freshly baked prime white loaf.

The following day I was working for the Master in the park just behind Burn Coose farm. The heavens opened and an icy rain sliced mercilessly down. I could have run for the barn but I stood there, letting the rain and ice bounce off my cap, shoulders and cheeks. It hid my tears as I looked to the heavens and gave thanks to God. I expect my grand mother was there, by God's side, laughing with him as I stood there drenched, like a shivering sailor clinging to the cordage and spars of an ocean going vessel in the eye of another violent storm.

Life has to march on though, doesn't it? There is no time to dwell on the sharp pain of a cut. Once it has bled out you hope it will heal over tidily enough and that, once the scab has fallen, no one will sense the sad lingering pain, see the scar or notice the limp.

My son Nicholas married Christiana and by the time their second child was born, a daughter called Lillie, they were living on the Illogan highway, just a brisk walk from us. Nicholas still worked for the railway with wagons on the Portreath spur which ran off the main line just north of Pool and Carn Brae. He would go past old man Burgess's property at Trengrove almost daily. It brought back the old smuggling stories and made me smile but my mouth stayed closed for many a nose could be broken by idle words and I did not wish to loose any more teeth, or my employment for that matter.

Through Nicholas I came across a young man who was the same age as him, called George Roskilley. That name sounded familiar to me. Later that same evening, as I prepared for bed, I remembered it was the name of a man who had been crushed and killed on the railway many years before.

Although I had not known that man, his death had affected me greatly. It had made me thankful for each day and I worked the line with more care, always walking on the side of the track instead of between the rails and always looking over my shoulder for sight of the next through train. I was sure that an engine in full steam with its crankshafts pumping hard would not stop if I failed to hear it and move in time from its path.

I had often wondered what had become of Roskilley's family following his tragic death.

I said as much to the younger George when we met again at a meeting of the local brass band. I was taking pleasure in banging a large drum at the back of the room. I am not sure others shared that pleasure but everyone was always very polite, or deaf. George was more musical and his fingers danced with agility up and down on the brass keys of a well prepared trumpet. He produced a much more agreeable sound.

When I enquired he said 'Yes, Mr Pearce, that man who died was indeed my father. I was four years old at the time of his death so, in truth, I can hardly remember him. No one could recognise him from his face after the accident but it was him, the right size and all. He was wearing the same clothes he left home in that very morning and his wedding ring was on his unmarked finger. The clothes he wore that day were kept for my brother and I. We were destitute and nothing could be wasted. The accident left my mother a widow with three children all under eight years of age. She has never remarried or taken another man to her bed and she has kept my father's memory strong and faithfully in her heart ever since. I was the second boy and my elder brother John and I both went to work in the rail way's engine house to keep a coal on the hearth, a crust on the table at meal time and my family from the work house'.

I looked him up and down and congratulated him for his endeavour and for that of his family. He looked prosperous enough, standing there tall and proud, with his black hair combed back over. He wore a neatly tailored suit with a clean and starched white collar. 'Yes, the rail way granted me an apprenticeship as a Smith. I am now an engineer at one of the local mines. My brother and I worked on the boilers of the West Cornwall rail way's steam engines. We worked on the 'Redruth' engines, amongst others. I have been frugal in my desires and I have learnt a proper trade which I hope will one day fare me well'.

George told me that after the accident his mother Mary had quietly gathered the family back up and taken the first honest work she could find. It was work as a charwoman. Her daughter became a tailoress before the age of twelve and Mary then learnt those skills from her daughter, at home at the end of each day by the light of a candle. She had worked hard every day, ensuring all three of her children had food on the table before her. She kept her dead husband's wedding ring, refusing to be so poor that she had to sell it on. That little brass band, with its grazes and scuffs, was the last remaining material memory of her husband and their union together. She hardly ever spoke of the accident or their father but it was clear, George had said, that she quietly remembered him each and every day.

George offered to help me with my search for work for my youngest son, Zebulon. He said he would enquire for us at the Carn Brae Engine works. I was and remain very grateful to him. My son Zeb became an apprentice blacksmith there less than one month afterwards. He now had a trade and a future. I wanted none of my sons to go down a mine where each day you were there would shave a week from your life. I had seen what it had done and was doing to three of my brothers. So, Zeb securing an apprenticeship in a trade on the surface of God's fine earth and out of the grasp of the spriggans and knockers was, indeed, a very proud day for Mary Ann and I.

By 1870 Mary Ann and I had enjoyed the delights of seven grand babby's, born to the unions of our three eldest children. Unfortunately, the four girls and the three boys were all given different names by their parents and so Grandfer, (yes, that was me) giving them each the same name was no longer an accepted excuse, even if the words I used for them was as straightforward as 'my smidgeon'.

I would have to try harder and keep up with these changing times. Three more little pink faces were due in the spring of 1871. I hoped none of them would be a heller like my Richard had been. He'd settled alright by then, I suppose, and was living up at Vean whilst he, too, worked on the wagons marked for Roskear. He had joined the rail way when the mine at Stray Park flooded and had to close.

New life is always followed, inevitably, by the balancing force of death.

My father's end came as the embers of 1870 cooled and turned to ash.

I don't think he had ever missed a day of work in his life. Then, one morning, just after Christmas, before the turn of the year, he was slow to get himself going for the day's labour. My brother William said that father had complained to Hannah about feeling under the weather.

He had thought his complaint might have been no more than a disagreement with a Christmas saffron bun and that he was just being a bit cakey after a day or two's rest from work. 'Turnips need to be grated and cows need to be fed' he had mumbled when told to rest up a while. He had managed to put on his britches and secure his belt. Then he went to leave and collapsed in the doorway, sliding down the frame as he was stepping outside into the first pale light of dawn.

My father was seventy four years old when he finally sunk.

He had been a dependable servant to his masters. However, he had never seen a guinea for all his trouble and he left nothing to those who survived him but his cap, boots and belt.

You took him as you found him and although he lived all his life half way to nowhere, he left children who were now crossing the globe to be somebody somewhere.

When I had looked back I always thought I was mother's favourite and that my brothers had been treated better than I by father. But, now I am older, and certainly wiser, I think he did the best he could and we boys all lived by the same hard rule. What is not in doubt is that I will always believe his short horn cows were above all else. He would often say 'Without our animals we are nothing'.

I never forgot him saying to me as I asked him a question of the greatest importance to me at the time 'Well, Zeb, I cannot stand here idling with you. If I don't go and tend to them cows dreckly they won't be able to recognise me by tomorrow'.

I do not recall what I had wanted to know.

I had not seen much of him over those last few years. I would have liked to have seen how he changed with age and to sit over a cider and a pipe with him whilst we compared the length and thickness of our whiskers. We might have talked about how richly it had all turned out. But, when did I ever get the chance? It matters not now. I shall still miss him and I shall want to shake his hand if our souls do ever meet again.

I remembered him when I climbed the hill at Carn Brae, as I often did when in search of strays from Mr Burgesses' flock of sheep. Up there amongst the silent grey granite, the golden brackens and wild red rose hips you can be alone with the blustery wind and your thoughts.

All around you down below are the mines, including Dolcoath, Tolgus, Wheal Druid, the Crofty's and Cooks Kitchen. They sucked desperate souls down into their hungry hot mouths. You could almost hear them wail as they went. Smoke filled the air as did the sound of distant bells, whistles, and a lamb's weak bleat. You could even see the puffer as it travelled the line and the stone walled fields with the hazy blue sea beyond. Such changes there have been and the landscape below me still changed every day. It could be a new building, a widened path, a freshly felled tree or a shiny ploughed field. Carn Brae, however, apart from the new towering monument, stayed much the same, just like my father always had.

For most people life had become less permanent than either Carn Brae or my father. They could no longer plot their own lives by the angle of the sun, the crow of a cockerel or the ring of a church bell. It seemed everybody who had just arrived in Camborne from the far flung villages of Cornwall now appeared to be leaving again, one way or another.

George Roskilley said he was leaving for a new life in California, wherever that might be. With the discovery of new ore deposits in far off places that take months of travel to reach, the price of tin and copper collapsed in Cornwall. The sun may as well not have continued to rise for it could not have cut through the gloom. The cockerels and the bells may as well have fallen into silence too. The mines had run the rocks, and awaited rescue.

Sam and Peter had already left in search of richer rewards in the Americas. There was still no real word from them. There had recently been a war there which had lasted for several years. May be they had become embroiled in it, I had thought. As mines around Camborne closed, neighbours and friends talked of going and when they went, fragmented stories of their success sometimes returned. Those who remained behind talked once again, firming their intention to do nothing else but follow as soon as a passage allowed.

The sight of flags and banners and the sound of a brass band as another hopeful mining venture opened were now in the past. The expectation of instant riches were now nothing more than chirk burrows next to the silent gaping pits as men were thrown out of work. I tried to keep a positive outlook but I think even John Burgess, my employer, was watching on with some concern.

There were always plenty of advertisements in the papers for men to travel abroad. 'Urgently required' and 'Only reliable men need apply', they read. 'We want a rock tunneller for an Indian railway or a sump man for a mine in Cuba or the Brazils' they bellowed. The way they beckoned, it sounded like an adventure, not an ordeal.

John Henry heard, through an acquaintance, of a Falmouth engineer who had been recruited to build a new rail way in the Cape Colony for a Company called the Cape Copper. John Henry had decided that he was going, for it would be regular work. 'I can take my brother Zeb, for the engine sheds there need apprentices when they open for work' he had said. At the age of twelve Zeb was still young enough and the Carn Brae works had an uncertain future. Yes, they would both be able to have a steady commitment.

Parting from two of my sons was not an easy task for me. Their leaving was a sad day. They were both fine, good looking healthy young men. I was proud of them. I always expected them to for ever be there, watching the same sunrise as I, and the same sunset.

On the morning of the day their train left, I found an aged rock on Carn Brae on which to sit for a brief moment of reflection. Below, in the low clouds and rolling mist, the beasts in the valley were stirring from their slumber for another day of industry and the scuppering of souls. Little did they care for the fragile sentiments of a man's poor spirit. It was but another desperate morsel to be gobbled up without a blink.

When Zeb and John Henry arrived, safely, in the Colony, they wrote home to Mary Ann and I. The letter was many months in the coming but I never minded waiting for news, so long as it was good and brought cheer that we could hang on to.

Mr Burgess agreed to read the contents to me. He seemed to hesitate in his reading when John Henry wrote about the many positions that were available and the beneficial rates of pay that were being offered by the Cape Copper. 'Why don't you come?' the letter had said.

'Oh, dear, Zeb' Mr Burgess said, looking over his glasses and across his study desk at me. 'It seems to me that you are being called away and back to the rail way'. After a short pause he added 'I shall miss you here, you understand, for you do the work of more than one man. However, I could not, in all conscience, stand in your way if you decide that the Cape Copper Company is where your future lies. Why, at those rates even I am tempted and I cannot, in all honesty, match those figures'.

Working for Mr Burgess had been better than I had feared.

I missed my sons more than I had ever imagined I would as those months crept slowly by. I thought especially of little Zeb, the babby of the family, who by 1872 was now a young man of fourteen. Mr Burgess was saying I should go. 'This farm is not earning a living for me any more. I cannot obtain a fair price for the milk' he would say each time a fresh letter from Cape Colony arrived. 'Take your chance and make a better life for you and your family. If you do not and I choose to sell the farm, which I may, what then?'

I could see reason in every word he said to me but I was having difficulty drawing a comfortable breath over such a large matter. I had been in two minds. All I tried had become a tight fit, like I'm sure the whale bone corset on display in the outfitters window down Trelowarren Street would be, if placed round Mrs Trezona.

Crime, low morals, drunkenness, poverty and squalor were beginning to thrive like never before amongst the over crowded streets of Camborne and Redruth. We had been away from the worst of it there on the Highway but, when fighting broke out over a village cricket match and police constables were being hit over the head with bottles whilst doing their duty clearing the public houses of rowdy miners I did decide to talk again about work in Africa with Ed and my sons Richard, William and Nicholas.

What about my wife, Mary Ann, if I went? I also now had three more little grand daughters Mary Ellen, Laura and Annie. Would I miss them growing up? Who would be here to protect them? The boys might have a different view.

They all did and, before the candle in the centre of the table had dripped a drop of hot wax, it was very much agreed upon. In truth they felt there was not much to talk about. Nobody could see a future in Cornwall. I went along with it.

By early 1873 our passage was arranged through the agent. The cost would be drawn from our first wage. The five men of the family would go and join John Henry and young Zeb. There was permanent work there for us all as platelayers and as labourers on a rail way that the Cape Copper were anxious to see completed.

The women and the children would all stay behind in Camborne until money was available to bring them out.

When I look back it was the right course to take.

We would be away from home anyway, laying track and digging the way. We did not know what dangers to expect or even if we would settle or survive. We decided that we would not call for the women to move until life there in

Africa fulfilled the promise given to it by the newspapers. We only needed to take our boots and the clothes we stood up in. That way we could also leave there just as quickly if it all were indeed nothing but a pig in a poke.

Mary Ann and our girls, Mary Jane and Elizabeth, moved into a terraced cot up on Carnarton Street, near to the Camborne rail way station. Margery Ann and Christiana also settled there with their young families. Both now had three children each. Don't fret, dear reader, they were used to a tight squeeze. Like dear Mrs Trezona.

William and Richard did not have wives, or children, that I knew of.

So, that was everybody taken care of.

And I was moving on once again.

I would miss the old pilgrims ways, the thick hedged walls, the roar of the stamps and Mary Ann's plum pudding. I would miss Mary Ann, my dear wife, but was hopeful that I would see her soon. I assured her that it would be like the time I moved from Porthalloe to Angarrack. I did not mention that journey had been but a few miles and the one before me now was to be thousands. We had not been parted much in twenty years. We had shared our lives together, and raised a family. Now, would I be like my brother Sam and not be heard of again? She was fearful of the future. She felt her beauty had faded and she could no longer hide the flecks of grey in her hair or the lines from her face. 'Do you still want me, Zeb?' she would often ask, with hope lying heavy in her question.

'Without you, each day will be dark. I will be living under perpetual moonshine until I see you again', I had replied, truthfully.

She did not know if I was coming back and for days her tears were uncontrolled. I always tried to reassure her.

When the day came for our train I gave her a last big hug and held her in my arms. She buried her face in my chest and collapsed against me so I could not fully see the tears in her eyes. 'My dear, sweet love', I said as I held her tight, kissing the hair on top of her head. I told her again that my brother Nicholas would look out for them. He had made me a promise. I had looked in to his eyes and I believed that he would keep that promise. Nicholas had been forced to give up mining. He had set up a small business in town as a coal proprietor and had five dependent children of his own. If he could make a success of his new venture the Pearce name would not be a thing of the past in Camborne.

The train from Penzance then appeared and slid slowly and mournfully into the station before coming to a halt with a squeak of its brakes and a hissed release of steam plumes from around its wheels. There was crying, shaking and shouting as we hurried about. Someone called out something like 'Don't be late back for tea'. We laughed.

It eased the tension but we dared not miss the train. I think the right people had kisses and the right people were on board the carriage when the train jolted, moved gradually and started to pull away with a gathering speed towards Pool, Redruth and the great unknown beyond.

Soon the family were but dots in the distance, still on the platform, then gone altogether.

I looked down, and around my neck hung a small white daisy chain. I think my grand daughter Emily Burgoyne had placed it there during that final bustle. In my pocket I had the grey Porthalloe pebble, which I had kept. I ran my thumb along its solid edge.

It makes me swell up when I think of that huddle of women on the damp platform, dressed in funereal black, faces flushed with emotion as they waved through the blur of steam and smoke.

I hold on to that memory.

I wonder what would have happened had it all been different.

13. Africa

If the others had said 'This is all a mistake, let's go home' I would probably have agreed and been back in Camborne on the first returning train, rushing to Mary Ann's door, calling up from the unlit street and disturbing her sleep.

Instead, we sat in silence as the engine rattled and puffed up the line.

The gloom was broken when the carriages languidly clunked and clattered on to the new Royal Albert bridge, which spanned the Tamar. Through the metal cages wrapped around the bridge you could see the billowed sails of craft busy on the waters below. Gulls, disturbed by the train, swooped in full cry, searching for a safer perch. My viaduct at Angarrack was a mere thruppenny bit when placed alongside this magnificent golden sovereign.

It was the first journey out of Cornwall for all of us.

Our passage to Africa was on a Union Line mail boat from Plymouth so we left the train shortly after crossing the Albert and made our way to the docks. Ed was joking and trying to keep the mood light and airy. William, my son, said he needed a drink. We had to steer clear of trouble for we had to make the boat at all costs. If he were to find a drink in his hand he might lose all sense of time or take exception to a local opinion of him.

Like sugar for a wasp, he could attract trouble that one.

William once said to a stranger he happened across down by a pond near Brae 'Do you want to see what a proper iggit looks like?' The stranger, suddenly overcome by curiosity, replied 'Alright, young whipper'. William urged him to get up from where he was enjoying a peaceful rest from work, and then to go and take a look in the still waters of a nearby pond. Naturally, the stranger only saw his own reflection looking back and, as soon as he realised the joke was on him, he turned to grab William, who might have ended in the pond himself had he not possessed a set of sprightly legs strong enough to carry him beyond the reach of the surge of anger that rose from the infuriated man.

We didn't want William to take leave of his senses again now and pose another daft question to any person, let alone someone with nothing to loose.

The boat we had to catch, as they say, was the African. A new vessel, freshly fitted and ready to battle with Neptune. She lay in tranquil water, at the quay side, harnessed by large ropes. Men busied about her loading coal, last minute mail, newspapers and the passengers, like us. Her sails remained wrapped and silent. From her stack a thin trail of smoke escaped up into the grey afternoon sky.

For the next thirty five days she was to be our protection and our salvation. As her iron hull was being filled she sank a little lower in the water. Were the ropes that bound her to the quay keeping her afloat? That bolted hull was all that lay between a better future for us and the green and icy brines of damnation. I must admit to being a little nervous.

Despite the boys, and the anticipation, I felt alone. The unknown was a great fear for me. But I could not turn back, for the only path left in Camborne now was the one to the work house. The work in Cape Colony had to be the beginning of a new life. I had to keep the resolve that had presented me with this glimpse of freedom. I was close enough now to see it through the crack in the door.

We walked up the wooden planks and on to the deck. The African smelt new, like the hope she carried. By sunset the large thick ropes had been released, our bunks claimed and the screw steamer's engines had rumbled into a full throaty roar that made the air hum and the boards of the deck rumble.

I stood out on the long poop when I could. On that first night I gripped the smooth rail in the darkness and breathed in the cold air, saying my good byes to the dark shoreline, relieved when we passed the Manacles and the vigilant Lizard Light. Cornwall and I had not turned our backs on each other. We just had some matters to attend to.

It took us a few days to find our legs as our stomachs lurched each time the African sliced up and down, over the crested waves. What sorry Cornishmen we were. That is, apart from Richard and William, who both ate heartily at every meal time. They ate as though each cutlet was the first, and the last.

The meals were generous and for me, unused to such bounty, eating breakfast, lunch, tea, dinner and supper all a matter of hours apart was not a good habit to fall in with. What wretched luck to find such fine trimmings when you had no stomach for it. Oh, for such riches a few years ago! I found myself saving items like currants, for they would keep long enough to be treats in the first of the flour foggins when we were safely back on dry land again.

A few days in and the African paused to take on coal at a small island called Madeira. It was but a green, leafy foothold with nothing but salt water around it for as far as the eye could see. It was as tall as it was long, towering up out of the fathoms like the last outpost on the edge of the world. An obstinate mist clung moodily to its dark damp cliffs. We stepped ashore for the first time since Plymouth and laughed at the absence of swell and the struggle for balance in our legs.

What a strange world we had arrived in. Red cloaked ladies with their black hair tied tightly under stalked caps offered us bright coloured exotic flowers for a penny or two. Their striped dresses swirled in tandem with the mimosa and warm sunshine. What they made of us in our plains I could only speculate upon. I am sure they felt sorry for our pale unwashed skin and sea sick eyes.

We cheered up with a glass or two of tinta negra in the lengthening shadow of the Pico fort. It was my first drink in a while and I was soundly asleep back on board by the time the African was again turning its screws towards open water.

I had to become used to those wide waters and fresh breezes. When the swells were kind I took long walks up and down the area of deck that was set aside for passengers in our class. It helped to pass the time. I had walked every day of my life and needed to keep my feet occupied. A fight might break out in my boots if I didn't keep my toes moving. Should they seize and say they preferred comfort from now on then I would soon find myself unprepared for the toils that lay ahead.

On one of my walks I asked one of the crew men working on the ropes near the prow why the sea was a deep dark blue. 'It is because the ocean's floor is a long way down' he had replied, adding that 'It will take a full day to sink through the brine to the silent weedy bed'.

'I prefer the rock of a boat and to catch my breath from the passing breeze' I had continued. I could not swim with any confidence. I would surely meet my fate quickly and sink like Nicholas's prong which he had dropped in error over the side three days before.

'If you do slip and take a tumble into the sea, swim in that direction' the mariner had said, pointing towards nothing but a sea filled horizon. 'When you come ashore hide well, or be prepared to go in a pot, and for your bones to be picked clean by hostile, hungry natives. A white man is a delicacy in that part of Africa'. He gave me a smile and I thanked him for his warning. I went below to find the others to share the news. As I thought about the choice between drowning and being eaten I consider he was either too jovial about it or he had taken me for a thickerd.

The weather had thus far been kind to us. For a new vessel the African was making good headway and encountering no trouble. It had two masts and one stack for the smoke coming from its twin engines below deck. Its front mast was substantial and able to support a full sail. When the canvas was out, the wind four square behind and the engines at full throttle nearly three hundred miles a day could be conquered. I could see that no time would be squandered.

Our next sight of land was at St. Vincent. Far bigger hills than Carn Brae stretched out before us although, again, these were a small collection of islands.

It was a delight to see land once more and the change of view enlivened the mind. The colour of the sea brightened to light blue and white sands shone under a dry warm sun. Clouds lay scattered in the sky and the brown empty island earth lay captive, burning beneath it. Bells tinkled as they hung from the necks of whinnying goats that roamed freely, snatching hurriedly at parched scrub as they went. It was altogether different to anywhere else I had seen.

Although we were but halfway on our journey to Table Bay, our stop was long enough to take on provisions which would support us through those remaining three weeks on the African. The port was busy but its trade was humankind. Lines of naked black men in chains, dejected and in silence, were being taken aboard vessels lying alongside us. They had given up waving the flies away. 'Slaves' Nicholas said. 'I heard from a fellow in the crew that they are taken from their families and clamped against their will. They are bound for work in Portuguese lands as far away as the Brazils, transported and treated no better than a cheap cargo of jute'.

The sight of those wretched men, deprived of their freedom, put me in bad humour. I was almost fifty years old and had endured tough moments but nothing had prepared me for that. It was a long way from the sheltered water line of Porthalloe. I had always felt that labour should be freely given but not given for free. Any society that thinks it should is not a society to be a member of. You may be thirsty, hungry, without shoes or hope but, if you had your freedom you still had your free will and the will to work. Whilst you had your free will your soul could flourish, like a vibrant bloom under the spell of a splashing rain drop.

I gave thanks for my boys, and Ed. We had each other and that made us stronger.

We spent a plentiful number of hours together on that journey to Cape Colony and talked over many thoughts. I knew their dreams and desires were for a better future for both them and their families. I also learnt the weight of their fears and, as their father they looked to me for guidance. I could not show my fear. All could be lost if I did. Instead I said 'Keep your heads down, do the work, stay out of trouble, and all will be well'.

William and Richard hadn't always listened to that at home and could both sometimes let temper and drink get the better of them. They could rouse a fight between two empty sacks. I hoped they would see my view now and agree that it had some merit.

There were still arguments, usually over a hand of cards craftily dealt. Nicholas lost his knife in one game. It was not as a result of threat but as a result of an overstretched gamble to win back the money he had already lost. To pitch in your last eating utensil over a pair of jacks was a desperate act. As he had already lost his prong over board he was reduced to eating with his hands once again. It did not hamper him and he still finished off anything that had been left over. Sometimes that was before the owners of the food had decided it was left over. I sometimes wondered if that journey was a little lengthy for him.

Of course we missed home and every one we had left back there but our skills were no longer required at a rate of pay we needed in order to live. Those skills were required in other places where the frontiers of the Empire were being pushed further and further and where there was an unquenched demand for the skilled artisan and willing worker. We had to chase it. We were not masters of our own destiny. Our lives had changed beneath us and would never be the same again.

After St Vincent we spent a number of days below deck. The weather took a turn for the worse and the poop was no place to be in a showery squall let alone a howling gale. The sea changed from a flat calm to angry surges that broke across the deck as the bowsprit plunged into its midst. The African groaned as she rose and fell. We took to our bunks, subdued and pensive whilst she took and withstood the beating.

William needed calming for he had visions of the wrecks along the Cornish coast line. He recalled the second hand stories he had heard of those who had perished, the torn sails, the wet barrels rolling in the surf and the clasping tentacle of a hungry sea creature upon a Cutter's splintered mast.

Richard worried about an ancient story he had heard about an old witch who had a short white rope for sale with three knots in it. When asked by a passer by, she had replied 'Why, I'm selling the wind to sailors so they will have safe passage, of course. They pays good money for a good row of tidy knots'. That may have all been very well but later, after nightfall, she had been spotted again, selling another, darker rope with not three, but four knots in it. 'What are you doin' now?' the same enquiring soul had asked as he ambled past the same corner on his return home. 'I am selling powerful storms to those who 'ave a mind to go a wrecking'.

I urged the use of prayer.

Nicholas said he hoped a wave would toss his prong back out from the depths.

Once the storm had passed the rest of our journey on the African passed without further incident. That is if you discount Ed's snoring. I am sure he could add a few knots to a favourable wind. God bless my daughter Margery Ann with patience when she arrives if that is a noise she will have to endure for the rest of her days. Maybe a witch will some day sell her a rope for that.

We knew we were close again to land when birds began to follow in our wake. After over a month at sea we pulled in to anchor at Table Bay and were happy to be safely ashore. We had travelled nearly six thousand miles and grown used to the murmur of the timbers and the groans of the hull.

All ports are busy ports but this one was full of different accents, most of which I struggled to understand. I'm sure no one had trouble with mine. Perhaps it was of no consequence for this was a meeting place for people from all corners of the globe. They crossed paths here on their way to a multitude of other unknown destinations and the air was full of eager chatter that recounted their diverse experiences. To a man they spoke with the intention of achieving prosperity but some looked relieved that they had survived a scare or two to get this far.

We could have been enchanted there and we might have slipped into easy ways and drifted into casual work and settled for the local attractions. Had Richard been a horse all we would have needed to do was give him one firm slap on his haunches and he would have been loose, galloping aimlessly away, never to be seen again. Instead, we kept his blinkers on.

We could have fallen prey to gangs of sharpers there, too, so we did not stay long enough for any one to firm up an interest in what we had which might be to their liking. A slip of the tongue and our coins might have been forced from us by the threat of a sharp blade across the throat. Mind you, there would be no point in stealing from Nicholas. He had already lost everything he had on the voyage out, apart from the clothes he stood up in.

In any case, we were hurried by time, anxious about the unfamiliar surroundings and bothered by the flies and warm weather.

We found the offices of the Union line where our onward tickets were presented. 'See that smart little steamer over there, with the thin black funnel?' the clean dressed clerk in the office had said. 'Make your way there and present your papers. She sails tomorrow. If you miss it there is a two week delay before the next one'.

The Namaqua left port at the beginning of May and we were on her. It was a much smaller vessel than the African. From memory I would say the Namaqua was about half the length, that is to say sixty paces from bow to stern. Its deck still found room for two masts and one stack. We could see the captain standing on the bridge, in his peaked hat, gold braid and smart tunic. He surveyed the waves with his eyeglass and instructed the wheel man at regular intervals to turn this way and that. All it took was a point of a finger. What a mysterious wonder the art of seafaring is.

The journey took three days and throughout the weather was warm and benevolent. Namaqua skirted the coast staying in sight of land so in daylight we had good views of the new province as we steamed up from the foot of Africa. The low hills displayed only the occasional sign of life, possibly settler's farms, and apart from that the shore seemed very bare.

On the day we reached our destination a lazy fog came down, shrouding the Namaqua in a thick white mist. The air was silent but for the toll of a distant dull bell, which rung out at monotonous intervals. Was it a chapel calling tearful mourners to our funeral?

You could hear the sound of water lapping gently against the hull as the steamer slowed, exercising caution. For a moment I felt like I was back on the slopes of Penare, looking out across the clouded mouth of the Helford. Not even a gull would stir on those days.

On shore we hoped that John Henry and Zeb were waiting. I was eager to see them. Somewhere in that gloom lay our new quarters and our new lives. We could see nothing so there was no easing of our fevered speculation.

The Namaqua came to a halt and the anchor was dropped with a violent clatter and splash. It broke the hushed silence. If it were in the middle of the night it would have shaken us from our beds. Then a deep calm fell across the lifeless sea again.

'Climb aboard the whale boat' the deck hand shouted out, pointing to the small timbered rower hanging by two pulley ropes at the side. We all took our places on the slats. Mr and Mrs Jane were the only other passengers with us. After what seemed a long pause the ropes were slackened and the small white boat winched its way reluctantly to the murky water line.

Richard and Ed sat on the thwart. They took an oar each and, once the ropes were released, the crew steered in the direction of the bell.

Were we heading for the river Styx and the ends of the earth?

A whistle then may have summoned an evil spirit to submerge us but, as we lurched through the grasping fog, no one spoke or made a sound.

All thought remained unheard.

It was the 5th May 1873. We had arrived. We were in Port Nolloth.

14. News from Home

In those days Port Nolloth was but a speck, on the edge of the shore line, clinging like a barnacle to the hulk of humanity.

A man could think, on arrival, that it had been a long way to travel in search of satisfaction only to find oneself in the clutches of despair.

Once there, your spirit could plunge and all hope be dashed, sunk like a brig caught on the sharp teeth of 'old Port Jolly's' hidden reef.

'What happened to Mr Pearce?'

'Oh, he went off, his sails full with the hot breath of hope. His ropes must have frayed, and snapped, stranding him somewhere between hell and damnation. He will rot there, waiting in vain for the uplifting hand of a passing Samaritan. I think someone said he was last seen heading for a place called Port Oblivion.'

But, you soon get used to it.

It is true, at first you feel like a corpse slipping over the side as it is buried without ceremony at sea and I do not expect Queen Victoria to ever trifle with an excursion to this extreme frontier of her Empire. However, it is not all bad. Compared to what I have been used to, the pay is good and no good Cornishman ever complained about his suffering.

In the morning the fogs usually sit in silent gloom, shrouding the small row of shanties that jostle along the shore in a stubborn line. In time, the chill in the air is burnt away by the growing heat of the sun as it fights to peer through the mist. Then, the wind begins to rise and the powdery white sands that continuously threaten to engulf the town start to swirl in little eddy's. If the breeze decides to exercise its lungs it will blow grains into every corner of every shack. If you are still, sheltering briefly in a borrowed shadow from the rising heat, expect to be betrayed, for you will almost certainly emerge covered in a fine layer of all kinds of dust.

My boy Zeb had grown into a man. I had last seen him when he was twelve. Now, here he was at almost fifteen, tall, lithe, healthy and proud. He had changed from the quiet Camborne boy I had last seen and I may not have recognised him had he not been with my eldest, John Henry, who had looked after him well. I was proud to be their father.

It was a long embrace, although I had almost no time to enjoy the relief of seeing my sons John Henry and Zeb again for the Cape Copper required us at work almost immediately. The company wished to connect the port with the mines inland at O'Keip, Concordia and Springbok.

As copper ore production grew, the hard eighty mile six day wagon trek over rough tracks and through sand became far from adequate. Oxen and mules had been used, and local farmers employed, but this meant their farms were neglected. Droughts blew in, bringing punishment for their absence. The climate, a lack of food and water and a wastage of ore lost along the way added to the problems of the diminished souls charged with the task of transportation.

A rail way linking the mines to the Port was put forward as the resolution of this misery by a Mr Hall, Engineer, late of Falmouth. Such a wonder that I should come all this way to find work on a rail way planned by a neighbour that I could almost have seen as I grew up across the bay in Porthalloe.

Construction on the rail way had started from Port Nolloth in September 1869. When we arrived in 1873 just over fifty miles had been laid across the sand belt and up into the mountains as far as the Nonams springs at Anenous. The Cape Copper had worked this new line successfully and money was therefore available to build another twelve miles of track over the daunting spiral of mountains and through to Steinkopf Mission Station.

That was what the Cape Copper needed us for.

We had been brought up in the train from Port Nolloth and stayed in makeshift shelters along the line as it was constructed. The shelters were sometimes dome tents made for us by the local natives, who were called Hottentots. We started work early in the morning and laboured under the growing heat of a bright glaring sun as it rose into a blue eyed sky. The sweet air at altitude did refresh our lungs and our reddening scalps had some shelter under wide brimmed hats made of animal hide. The weather at this time of year was at its coolest and the nights were cold. There could well be rain during the day but, other than to make the mountain rocks slipsey like a Porthalloe path, it did not hamper the work too much.

What did hinder us was the climb of the railway, rising over one thousand three hundred demanding feet in seven and a half miles. We cut a path into the side of the mountains, with picks, hands and shovels, on a steady incline up towards the plateau. We clung like goats to the edge of the rock face, chipping away at the slopes, laying rails and sleepers on the narrow flat road created behind us. Danger crouched, salivated, and lingered, ready to pounce on the smallest of our errors. We all had to stay alert.

Richard did not take to the work. He was often left clinging to wisps of vegetation as his feet slipped. After being rescued he would wipe his bloodied hands down and complain that the pay was not sufficient nor the food ample enough for his neck to be risked in such a manner.

There was reason to his view. At times it was a long way down. If you went over the side it would be a long climb back if you had not succumbed to the fall of rocks that followed you as you fell. I told him it was far better that you die with your stomach full of beans than to die with a stomach echoing to the ring of the starvation bell and that he should labour on. 'Be grateful for the work, Richie!'

My work on viaducts near Hayle gave me knowledge of the viaducts we had to build here close to Anenous. Set on stone footings, the large timbered legs on which the rails sat were like the trestles of tables laid for a sumptuous celebratory tea. What pride, what satisfaction, to see such a vital work set in such a wild place high above the desert plains and sea. Man was imposing his will even in extreme places. Brunel would have been impressed with us. No one waved to me from below this time. Those ravines sixty five feet beneath my hammer were empty but for the moan of a restless wind.

We did loose a man there.

His name was Jack Collick.

A metal nut dropped from the grasp of a colleague as he worked on the viaduct. It fell, bouncing on a wooden bridge support on its way down, before striking Jack hard on the side of the face as he looked up in response to the warning cries from those above. As he recoiled, he fell and hit his head again on a sharp rock before slipping twenty feet down a bank in a dust cloud of shale. Grazing gemsboks startled and scattered. They had grown used to us even when we were shooting for the pot. Silence cut across the warning cries and the tumbling grit finally came to rest.

Work stopped and, for a moment we waited and watched to see if Jack would stir. But he never did. He just lay there, as if asleep in the scrub below, with his sandy hair blowing serenely in the light breeze.

We recovered his body and we dug him a grave. The gang master gave us an hour. When the scraping shovels fell in to silence, hats were removed and we gathered round for a prayer. Its words were recited from memory. Dust to dust was never more truly felt by us all.

The small wooden cross that was hastily nailed together must still stand faithfully at the head of Jack's grave. He lies a long way from home but no one will ask any more of him or disturb him there as the sun sinks and the shadows lengthen each day. It is a final resting place with the back drop of a magnificent silent valley. Jack's soul can cast a reflective gaze over the blue and grey haze of the views around him, lit by the shafts of light that penetrate through the brooding clouds. He should always be at peace in that lonely, heavenly place.

There could be no further delays. Our work gang moved on, eating away at the slope until we were out of sight, around the next tortuous bend.

On the return to Port Nolloth, or Port Jolly as we began to call it, by train, for a few days of rest, it fell to me, an older man, to speak to Jane Collick, Jack's young widow. She guessed something was amiss as soon as I came to call on her tidy little cabin, one row back from the sea front. I had brushed up and changed my clothes after splashing the contents of a pail around until the dregs were brown with silt.

She cried and sobbed, her body heaving with the awful despair of my news. Tears streamed down her pale pretty face. She was small, perhaps five feet and an inch or two, with ample round shoulders and a full face. I guessed she was in her thirties. I offered to help her in any way I could. She was alone, Jack's pay now cut from noon on the day he died. 'He did not suffer' I said. Mercifully there were no children.

Towards the end of 1873 the first news reached us from home. John Henry could read it. He seemed happy enough to relay time and again what the scrawled words in black lines uttered, until the paper was creased and the ink had faded.

'My dearest boys and Zeb,

W T, Nicholas's son, who is now thirteen, has kindly written our thoughts. It is October and we write with hearts that are both heavy and light. We miss you all so much and ache each day to see and touch you. We have had your letter and are pleased that the work on the rail goes well and that you have not been eaten. We hear tales of lions and missionaries. Elizabeth, Ann and Christiana and all the grand children are well. Little Annie is now two and she is up to mischief each day. We look forward to joining you soon, now that you have all decided to stay. Mary Jane will not be coming, for she has married and wishes to remain in Cornwall. Do you remember William Harvey, the boiler boy? Well, he proposed in May and in June they were married up at Redruth. Why the hurry? I dare not say in front of W. T., for he is a sweet boy. Mary Jane is happy and the skill Willie Harvey has was much in demand at Dolcoath where he has worked as a riveter. They talk of moving to be closer to his family over at Perran before the baby is born and now that the workforce at Dolcoath is being cut it might happen soon. It is a shame you were not here to give her away but Tom Hill, your friend, colleague and neighbour, was happy to oblige. He says the rail way goes from bad to worse so please have no thought of returning. Stay and make your way, despite the sacrifice of a family life. We feel it is best that you are not here to bear the grief of it for Camborne has had its fair share of trouble since you left. Work is scarce and pay is poor. There is a belief amongst the miners that drunkenness and fighting is the answer. Mr Smith's son, William, the magistrate, was hit in a riot as he attempted to dispense justice at the Court house and the police were set upon. Fighting broke out in the streets of Camborne. Red Jackets from Raglan were sent for in order to calm the anger. As luck would have it the trouble was over when they arrived so there have been no deaths. There is damage and mayhem to clear away. Do not worry, whilst we are fearful of what might happen next, we are safe and we hope that order has been fully restored.

We all send our love and long for the day when we will see you again.

Mary Ann, your loving wife and mother'

I now know that Mary Ann wrote about the riot in Camborne in October 1873. I was later told by one who was there that Jimmy Bowden had been the spark, aided by his brother Joe.

At times Jimmy really was a saffron bun short of a tea treat.

The temper of the people exploded like gunpowder and all attempts to keep the peace were buried under a shower of stones, sods and bottles thrown by the angry mob which had gathered. The Police station had paraffin and paint poured over its contents. The Reynolds was ransacked for its smuggled spirits and the windows were victims of some sharp decanter throwing. For a day and a night there was threat and menace in the air. The aggrieved men went looking for a victim to bear the brunt of the trouble and marched up to the Smith's house at Trevu but George, a son of the much admired but now deceased Mr Smith, and a brother of William, the magistrate, quelled the riot with some forceful and thoughtful words. I recalled our days at Stray Park and always knew, even from when he was but a boy, that

George would be a fine man of solid principles once he had emerged from his studies.

I have to smile to myself when I think of the Red Jackets. I heard they believed that they were going to Africa to fight the Ashanti. What must they have thought when they stepped out of their train on to the platform at Camborne station with orders to shoot. How odd it is to think that such a wild place as Africa had to wait whilst the natives of Camborne were filled with buck shot and put to the sword instead.

At the end of January, 1874, another letter arrived on the Namaqua, this time for me. I showed it to Jane Collick who had decided to stay in Port Nolloth and take a lodger or two. I was one of them and she had looked after me well. As she could read I was happy for her to take the letter and share its content. There was nothing I had to hide. As she opened the envelope she looked across at me and said 'it looks to be hastily written'.

'Dear Zeb,

It is your brother Nicholas here, writing through W.T. I am sorry but I have some bad news for you. Mary Ann has had a bad seizure. Elizabeth said that for a month or two she had been suffering from headaches and was having trouble with her vision. After a couple of falls and convulsions her health declined further until, after the last seizure, she was unable to move or care in any way for herself. Please do not come home. Carry on and finish the work required of you. The girls are caring for her and provide what she needs. We did call the doctor and he has said that she might recover. We cannot afford to keep asking him so trust his opinion to be right. Please send word back for if she has news of you then that will surely give her hope.

Your brother, Nicholas.'

Jane finished reading, looked up and put a hand on my shoulder. It was her turn to comfort me. She folded the letter away. I felt I would not see my Mary Ann again. I felt helpless there, miles from my love, the mother of my children and my companion. Where was I when she needed me? Here, in a wild frontier town, digging for a pittance, escaping the duty of a proper man.

No day of mine would have even the glow of moonshine to it now.

Mary Ann and I had been through it all. As I lay that night, unable to sleep, before a return to the mountains, I thought of the squeeze on food that we had back then. I don't know why it was that thought which crossed my mind. Maybe it was because I could not have lived or survived without her.

Mary Ann had made the scraps and leavings last for ever, pushing every ha'penny as far as she could. One day she'd say to us all 'We are having tater and leek pie today'. 'What are we 'avin tomora ma?' the nips would shout excitedly in reply. 'I think we'll have leek and potato pie' she would say with a hint of intrigue. They would consider this for a moment, then their faces would light up and they'd say with a great deal of excitement 'I can't wait! That sounds delicious.' I smiled quietly in the dim glow of a single lamp. If there were a dozen ways to serve a potato, she would know them all.

Mary Ann and I had been married for over thirty years and had shared eight children. We had held hands amongst the snowdrops and we had held hands amongst the snowflakes. She had followed me loyally. She had given up any thoughts of her own to be with me. At times we had nothing but each other. Despite the unending hardship she did not complain. She kept a faith in me that many, including my father, had said was unfounded. At times not even I had faith in myself. We had sheltered in each other's fears and stirred ourselves up with a sharp dose of courage. She pushed me back up and she asked for nothing for herself in return.

We shared many moments no one else would ever know the truth about. Our thoughts could be there for each other simply from a look into each other's eyes. Eyes are such open books. All you need to do is learn to read. She saw my soul, and she stayed with me. Yet I had rewarded her by taking all the boys and going to Africa.

I stayed with Jane Collick in Port Jolly. The rails to Steinkopf had been finished and a hotel was being built at

Klipfontein where the engines would rest over night. Further work to extend the line as planned to O'Keip was announced for 1875. Local labour would be used for that to keep costs down and I was one of the men charged to over look. It would be a more straightforward construction and nothing like the last difficult two mile stretch over the mountain that we had just finished building. In the meantime, as agreed, I worked as a platelayer and overlooker for the railway along the length of the sixty miles of track that had already been laid. It would pay for Mary Ann's care. I owed her that.

I buried myself in work and tried hard to forget home as I travelled up and down the line. I was able to escape into the wild magnificent solitude of those wide open spaces. The land was empty but for the gemsboks, the rugged rock and the views down across the sands to the coast.

In October of 1874 I received another letter. It was one that I had never hoped to receive and it lay waiting for me like a coiled desert snake when I went to the office to collect the balance of my pay that was not, as usual, being sent home. I asked Bill in the office to read it to me.

Before he had slit the lid from it I had been hopeful that its notes would sing a soothing tune of good news about Mary Ann but, alas, that was not to be.

'Dear Zeb,

I am sorry to have to write this letter to you, my beloved brother. It is sorry news I have for you. Your wife, Mary Ann, passed away on the evening of the 25th August. She has been troubled for some time as you know but her breathing had begun to grow weak. We had all become anxious for she seemed lost in pain. I think at the end it was a merciful release. Margaret, her nurse, has carried out her duty as best she could and stayed by her side as we all have done when we could. It has been eight months, Zeb, and she had shown no signs of recovery from her steady decline.

We have buried her for you and she lies at peace in Camborne. Her soul must surely be up in heaven so look to the sky and see her there. She is released from her mortal shackles. Do not come home, Zeb. Stay there and finish the work. I have talked to your daughters and they plan to follow now that you are all settled and the work there is regular and profitable. They are closing up the house.

Your brother, Nicholas'.

15. A Great Force (God)

The climate in Port Nolloth is warm and the sun shone with a brightness that made me shield my eyes from its dazzle.

The white sand, hot to the touch, does nothing to dampen the searing rays as you attempt to go about your business. I could almost hear the sweat that dripped from my forehead sizzle, as it hit the ground.

Above the heat, petrels swirl in and out of the blinding glare of the sun, chasing each other in tight swooping curves.

From here the mountains inland are shrouded in haze and barely able to be seen. There are no trees. At home every lush ancient green field had a name. In Port Nolloth there was no green to be seen and there were no fields to be worked. Everywhere that stretched before me was dry, uninviting desert. No rivers ran giving succour to their banks or drops of cold water for the parched lips that passed by in search of relief.

Food had to be brought in by steamer from Table Bay. Even the hay for the rail mules came that way.

When I walked inland, checking the joints of the track and brushing sand with every step from the rails, the line was joined on either side by a low lying ashen scrub. Here, early morning dew is sucked up by the arid vegetation long before the sun has been able to bloom fully over a new day.

Further on, past where water is collected for the town, the rail way runs through a thicker more prosperous form of plant life and is bordered on either side by sand stone hills as it curls its way through the landscape. It stretches through a valley and across more dried river beds, where water no longer cares to run, before meeting the rise of the mountains.

The rail way then twists through the range and climbs up into its heart until you are surrounded by towering peaks of blue and grey stone. The air freshens and you can sit amongst the jutting crags, once the day's work is done.

There, you are isolated from the world and its noise and can look out across a mixed view of different greens, browns, blues and greys that merge into one with the fiery twilight of the sky in-between.

This became my life.

At first it was an ordeal, but I learnt to savour the wild beauty and tolerate the blistering, burning heat. Strangely, the rails carry you beyond the hardships.

After Anenous you arrive at Klipfontein, some fifty six miles from Port Nolloth. There, in the desert, and only in September and October of each year, a carpet of flowers flourishes briefly on the dry slopes and flat plains.

It was to there that I walked, punishing myself, when news of Mary Ann's suffering, and her death, arrived by letter.

I went to find a thought, a reason, and to lie undisturbed, wrapped in the barbs of my own blame. I found solitude amongst daisies and flowers of every colour and shade. I found myself staring in wonder at more colours that my eyes could digest. The celestial sprays of yellow, orange, azure blue, pink and crimson danced before me under a light valley breeze. The brightness of the sun is welcome here for it brings out the sharp soothing colours of every petal.

Every colour in the world must glow there in that peaceful meadow, cascading and tumbling in splashes which clamour silently, trying with every fragment of their existence to catch your eye.

You have to come through hungry desert and then a tough muscle sapping steep climb to reach it. It is a thirsty journey you have to endure. Every joint and sinew aches. Every freckle has been earned and every bead of sweat is rung from your flesh as you place one step in front of the other.

As you walk you are constantly reminded with each breath of how big the world around us is, and how small the part is that each of us plays in its temperamental backdrop.

And, as you dream about the miracle of water, you have to keep on walking towards the mirage, determined to keep putting that one foot firmly in front of the other because, the further you go, the more rewarding it gets.

It took me a long time to reach that zenith for I had not seen the signs, only the blind bends, and so I had been unable to choose where to take the right turn.

Life, up to that point, had been but an outline sketch.

Then, there in those secret meadows, the heavens opened and I discovered God's palette.

And it saved me.

It is a place that enjoys a sharper light. It is a place surrounded by an infinite splash of colours that wash against your drained face and dry lips, and stretch as far as the eye can see.

It was where the colours for God's world are mixed before, with a dab of his brush, he applies a fresh hue in one glorious corner of his Kingdom or another, easing the anguish and sorrow.

It was in a moment there, amongst the intense bands of unified garden shades, that I heard him speak to me in a gentle tone.

'Do not worry, Zebulon. Be calm. The rails have guided and brought you here. Everything will be alright. You have had a long, tiring journey. Lie here and let all this infinite wonder in. Let my colours enrich your soul and gently soothe your fears. Be at peace with yourself and everyone around you. Mary Ann is fine. Renew your purpose here. Be fortified and stride back down the mountain and put to good use all that you have become.'

I remembered the daisies back home. They clustered amongst the grasses, stretching white petals out from their yellow faces to catch the warm glorious light of the sun. When the cows or sheep ambled through, snatching at the ground with their mouths in a constant search for food, the little white flowers would disappear under a grind of molars.

It would amaze me that the following day I would return to the same place with the animals and there, once again, more white petals lay, renewed and hopeful of a passing glance from the sun before being snatched up into greedy wet lips.

No matter how much the livestock ate, those flowers would be back the next day, with the courage that this time some of them would survive and be able to bask in peaceful glory. They did not hide until Mary Lou or Trumpet had passed on to a more inviting pasture. They stood firm and the small golden seeds in their centres would caress the feet of passing black beetles no bigger than flecks of soot. Together they would continue nature's dream, filling every forgotten corner of the lea with a shower of silver and providing precious sweeps of colour for all the seasons that followed.

It was a spirit to fortify the most doubting of souls that you should rise up and fulfil your great aim, whatever force for good that might be. If you are cut down, rise again and have faith that God has a purpose for you. Indeed, for us all.

If you lift up your eyes and open your heart no man is ordinary for life is an extraordinary thing.

Arrangements were concluded for the wives and families of John Henry, Nicholas and Ed to now come to Port Nolloth and settle with us. We had suffered more than a year apart. My daughter Mary Jane was to stay in Cornwall. She was not strong enough to endure the climate and her first child had just died at birth. Elizabeth, my youngest daughter, had planned to come but she had met a shoemaker from Mawgan, called John Julian. He was a slight and gentle man who took pride in the craft and detail of his work. The boots he turned out had a reputation for solid stitching and Elizabeth said she believed their sturdy leather frames would outlast their owners. She saw her future in Camborne with him.

Most of my family were coming, and they would be with us by Christmas 1874.

The chapel we decided to build would be ready by then. We had felt that God should have a place in that flat valley which was his own. We desired a location where he could rest on his travels across the troubled plains and we could also shelter and discover his peaceful glow. There we wanted to share our thoughts and hear his messages, each like the purity you discover at the source of a gurgling spring.

It needed to be a special and glorious place. He had shared with others in Port Jolly in a building where formal meetings about money were held and informal deals over alcohol were struck. He deserved better. Even a barn would be more fitting. Why had we not provided that? Were we not civilised here on the boundary rope? It had to be put right. I had seen that it was for us to do it.

The Cape Copper agent said we could build on a thin neck of sand next to the club. It occupied ground in the front row overlooking the sea. If we squeezed hard our ambition would fit. No bricks or stone could be found but a small gift of wood and corrugated iron came from the company and a spare engine bell was found in a dusty corner of the blacksmith's stores. The rest, including all the nails, would have to be made or paid for by ourselves.

We were a small band and we did not try to build a towering spire, for we stood on swirling sand. We would need room for extra chambers, like a vestry. Plain glass came from Table Bay and we cut it, coloured it and leaded it into a neat row of windows to shine a rainbow of light upon the altar.

It reminded me of all the daisies up the line.

On spare days away from the rails, my sons and I helped to create this small sheltered space where praying and singing could take place. The corrugated iron was used for the roof. The planks of wood were used for the walls, floor and doors. It was surrounded by a picket fence. We placed two crosses above, on the entrance, and on the front part of the roof, to greet those who would come to worship. The engine bell, saved for this highest of callings, swung from a small metal frame set in a neat corner of the yard. It chimed out across the shore line.

If you came across St. Andrews chapel on your travels you would barely notice it or remark upon it. In no way did our building compare to the grey stone statures of the churches at St. Keverne or Camborne. But, you would most certainly be welcome in it and we were the proudest flock on earth to have had a part in it. We had made the best of truly meagre resources and our hearts and souls had gone into the tongue and groove, the stained glass and the humble arch of the entrance.

Even in a storm, it was a fine little chapel.

On the day the family arrived the sun spilt through the mist, like sour milk. A silver glare spread across the flat bay and the kelp lay uncollected amongst the foams and wet shingles.

But it turned out to be a good day. It was a joy to be reunited with my ten grand children. There were now seven girls and three boys. The youngest were Annie

Burgoyne, Mary Ellen Pearce and Laura Pearce, who were all three years old. They formed a gaggle of tired confused tots on the quayside. I ran my hand across their brows, giving them all a grandfer greeting. It was like brushing the heads of a row of towselled boys fresh off the beach.

It was uplifting to see my daughter Margery Ann and to see John Henry, Nicholas and Ed surrounded by their families. William, Richard and Zeb Junior had come out to greet them as well.

We had canned pilchards as a treat for tea to remind them of home.

Only Elizabeth, Mary Jane and, of course, Mary Ann were missing. We paused a moment to give thanks for our fortune in meeting again and to the memory of those who could not be there with us.

Ed, Margery Ann and their three young girls were soon on their travels again. They were settling at Anenous station, in the cool of the mountain plains where Ed was to continue his work as a platelayer. There the engines could fill their water tanks when they ran and mules would be changed and rested. Everyone who travelled the rail way was able to pause for a drink and to reflect before they went on their way up or down the gradient to somewhere else not quite as perfect.

A new town was planned at Anenous. Those going went full of hope. It would be a safe, quiet, undemanding place to raise a family. Apart from the daily train, and the momentary burst of frantic activity it brings, their new home would be an escape from the beaten track and a chance of prosperity not often granted to folk like us. Margery Ann intended to provide meals for those who came on the train. 'Maybe even a pasty or two' she had said, smiling across at me.

John Henry and his wife Elizabeth and their four children were settling in Port Nolloth. So was Nicholas, his wife Christiana, and their three children. I worked with John Henry and Nicholas. William was good with his hands but had not settled. He always searched for something else. If he had known what it was that he was looking for then that would have helped us all to help him. Richard was the same. Always restless, always feeling something somewhere else would be better. For now, they both worked in and around Port Nolloth. It was merely a matter of time before they were busy drawing up another wretched plan.

Zeb junior was happiest in the Port Jolly engine shed making things limp on a little longer, adapting the ideas of others and improving upon some of them. He was never more complete than when he was surrounded by dozens of orphaned metal pieces. Richard would ask 'What are you going to do with that pile of rubbish?' Zebbie would just smile, blink, pick up a rusted scrap and turn it into a useful tool which made his day by day work a little easier.

Over those last few months of '74 and the first of '75 I became much closer to Jane Collick and she to me.

I continued to lodge with her. In our individual grief at the loss of our spouses, we had become easy companions. The arrangement was less formal than our neighbours might have expected but we were comfortable with the tranquillity it brought to us both and we sought no reason to change.

Besides, I needed somewhere to live and she needed a living.

She led a simple frugal life and took pleasure in that and her strong convictions. What she did not have she did not need. What she did have she cared for, and made it last for an eternity. What she had but no longer needed she kept, stowing it in a safe spot in case she would one day find a good use for it again.

I sometimes feared that I fell into that last pigeon hole, neatly tucked away like a railway ticket for a station no one ever travelled to. Gwinnear Road used to be like that as well. If Jane were a ticketing clerk, one day someone would come, shake the rain from their umbrella and say 'A single to Gwinnear Road, please' and she would be able to reply 'Ah, Sir, I have just the ticket waiting here for you!'

She brought out my thoughts.

'See God in everything' she had said before adding 'He wants us to help each other. He sees it as the best way of getting his work done for the benefit of all'. I remembered her looking up from her needlework when we sat together in the evening and she would say 'Give people your time. It will be the most enjoyment you will have and, like the daisy fields at Klipfontein, it will be the best journey you will ever go on.'

'What do you want?' she had asked me.

It had taken me by surprise. No one, apart from Mary Ann, had ever asked me that before. Everyone had always wanted something from me. Quite often they gave nothing in return.

As I thought about it she had added 'I will help you achieve it'.

'Thank you, Jane' I replied, 'I will think about it as I dream tonight'.

Later, I stepped outside for some cooler air and a pinch of fired tobacco. As my smoke rose, a full jasmine moon hung in an unblemished night sky. It lit the breakers as they ceaselessly rolled towards an unyielding shore. I hoped my thoughts about her offer would be as clear. I drew away from the thought that she had prepared a single fare for me as far as Gwinnear Road.

As morning broke, I rose for work and gave her my answer.

'I would like you to teach me to read as you do, so I might view the Bible from its written word' I said. She stopped what she was doing, looked at me, paused and said 'It would be a pleasure, Zeb.' There was no emptiness in her words. I knew that she meant it and I set about my day replacing rail near the port's sheds with a big smile.

As Jane delivered her gift to me of learning to read and write, and the days turned like the pages of the Bible in front of my eyes, my feelings for her began to deepen and grow.

She had struggled all her life but would always rise with 'its going to be a lovely day today.'

And, each day, she would fill me with beautiful reasoning.

'Why fear?' she once said whilst clearing the sand from the house. As she emptied it in a pile outside the back she would add 'Most of what you fear and worry about will never happen'. I could see that the sand did not worry about being thrown out for before she had finished speaking and shut the door most of the grains had flown back in again.

Another expression of Jane's that I liked was 'Love everyone and do no harm'. As I laboured over the crowded lines trying to read the Bible she would always have words of encouragement for me. She failed to be as frustrated as I at such times and she refused to say 'enough' if it was I who wished to carry on learning a little deeper into the night. I needed what she gave me. I believe only she could have succeeded with such a hopeless pupil.

We shared our thoughts about the Bible's passages. Its wisdom and her help formed cornerstones in my mind which have remained there ever since. So, I have tried to forgive and I have tried not to judge others too harshly. I let them be and I lend a hand if I can. I have even tried not to be too severe with myself, to feel good about qualities Jane said I possess and to see a place in the world for me, as well.

We accepted each other as we were.

She told me about the four wise monkeys. I do not know where they came from but I liked them. It may have been a story her father had told her in her childhood. But, she was gifted with words so the letters in them may have drifted on the wind, perhaps for centuries, seeking a messenger like her who could put them in the right order. Jane had plucked them like ripe red cherries, from a tree of knowledge, where they had rested on their long searching flight, and placed them in to a story which all could understand.

The monkeys were called 'Hear No Evil', 'See No Evil', 'Speak No Evil' and 'Do No Evil'. From the story she told my son William carved four statues of the monkeys for me in a lovely solid dark wood. One, 'Hear No Evil', holds its paws over its ears, the next holds its paws over its eyes, the third holds its paws over its mouth and the last, 'Do No Evil', has its paws folded across its chest. They all sit comfortably on sharp rocks. I like it that they are all different sizes. See No Evil is the largest at just over four inches but they are all the same to me. Bless you, William.

They went by my bed, next to my Porthalloe pebble. 'See' and 'Hear' are so that evil does not become part of us. If we follow their advice, the outcome is that we 'speak and do no evil'.

But, my monkeys can sit in any order. They can face the wall or the window. They can all face the same way or each point in a different direction. Sometimes Jane would place them so they pointed towards me. I knew when that happened that it was time for further reflection down by the clear waters of the ocean, under the cooling rays of the setting sun, and on my own.

Amongst all Jane's words, the one I shall remember the most from that time was 'Yes' when I asked her to be my wife. She was thirty seven and I was one over fifty.

I missed Mary Ann. I would continue to miss her. I had thought my life over, too, when she had died. Now, instead, here was an undeserved blessing and the promise of a new beginning.

I wanted to give Jane my remaining time.

We were married, in the small tightly packed chapel of St Andrews, on the 21st March 1875. Even the Hottentots came to see and to celebrate. Thanks to Jane, I was also proud to be able to stand up, read a favourite passage from my own Bible, and sign my own name.

16. Copper

We are all different, like the array of pebbles lying there on the beach back home in Porthalloe. Different shapes, sizes and colours. We are unique, no two quite the same.

And we all enjoy glorious moments and spectacular failures. It is what makes us human and we should see beauty in it all. Each pebble, however plain it may seem, has at least one wonderful feature when you take the time to study it closely.

There, in that wild and raw wilderness, many races and creeds had all been thrown together in to a sweltering melting pot. Many had sailed across mean glassy seas, like us, to earn a penny or two more than they might have done back home in Norway, Germany or Cornwall.

We had to learn to accept each other in that isolated outpost, with all our odd habits, customs and foods, and to live together.

A pecking order had been established on the shoreline where those with the most faced the sea. They provided the brains and the wealth, leaving the desert to others. Behind the influential's, in the next row, lay the corrugated iron shanties of those that applied their skilled brawn to every task. Finally, obscured and forgotten, you would come across the scattered tented village of the local natives. They existed there on nothing more than miserable scraps. Their whole lives had been like that so they expected nothing different. They did all the hot sweaty work that no one else wanted to do. They did all the gruelling work no one else was able to do and they did it all under the glare of a searing noon day sun. Jane had said that if God's world were a ship, those poor natives would have spent their whole lives below deck, searching for a glimpse of a soothing light from the cracks in the deck above their heads.

They had settled for the role of fourth spear carrier in Hamlet in a society where most desired to be Hamlet. But, they carry the scene because Hamlet, if he were the only actor upon the stage, would not make a superior play.

To me, the native Hottentots were also a reminder that there were always people walking this earth who were far less fortunate than I had ever been. I tried to help them, where I was allowed.

One reason alone brought us all together in Port Nolloth, like flotsam washing in the tide against the damp legs of its jetty.

It was the Cape Copper Company.

They were a fountain in the centre of a town square. They were the only source of all life, in that most arid of places.

We all worked for the Cape Copper and everything was controlled by them. Everything you ate, when you worked, what work you did and what messages you could send back home. We were firmly in their grasp. If you did not speak out of turn and did what you were asked to do, they would look after you. 'Keep turning the handle as required and our lives will be as golden and smooth as freshly churned butter' Jane had said.

The transportation of the ore to Wales flowed evenly that way. Whatever of value was dug from the ground our little daily train dutifully brought down the mountain where it was loaded, at the quayside, on to patient trampers bound for ports like Swansea. The blackened smelting plants there were hungry for ore and they could not consume enough of it. There was money in copper and the Cape Copper Company knew that well. The five hundred mules used along the line was testimony alone to that.

In return, our pay was on time. John, Nicholas, Zebbie, Ed and I all got on with our work, grateful for it and fiercely protective of it. William and Richard were happy with the money but less willing to fall in line. William never did like mules, but, sometimes in my darkest moments, I think he and those mules were too alike.

Everything that we needed came from outside and was provided by the Company. Coffee, sugar, sago, split peas, sweetmilk cheese, candles and soap was made available in the store. We had money to buy it, if we could change our frugal ways. On a delivery day, the brimming store shelves were a guilty release from the barren, anxious days of our pasts back home.

Even the medical care was an improvement on the outside world. I suffered from headaches from the heat and my skin had soon flaked and freckled beneath the sun's furnaced glare. Indeed, the freckles had soon joined together and baking like a browning oven bun was something I could never avoid. There was no shade as I walked the sleepers checking the nuts and bolts, repairing collapsed sand banks, and replacing buckled irons.

Yes, the Cape Copper's firm but calm hand on my shoulder meant we no longer fended every minute and every day for ourselves, as we had done all our lives.

We had time left over for thinking, reading, music, opinions and imagination. I lost the opportunity there for monotony, for I had found God there. In turn, he helped me to find myself.

'Zebulon, you are a quiet, unseen mender of the rail so others might pass safely along as they, in turn, discover their way'.

The glow, of a knowing I received from that gave me thanks enough.

Not long after Jane and I were married, Jane fell with child, despite saying that she would never be blessed with mother hood.

She followed Christiana, Nicholas's wife, and my daughter Margery Ann, Ed's wife, who both came off the Union steamer and immediately fell pregnant. News came from

Cornwall that my daughter Mary Jane was also with child again and that Elizabeth had married John Julian, the shoemaker. I saw him in my mind, surrounded by tools there in his alcove, making a dozen pairs of boots in a much smaller size. No doubt he would receive orders all the way from Port Nolloth and spare some for children of his own.

The Cape Copper pressed ahead with plans to lengthen the line from Steinkopf as far as the O'Keip mines, and to add a strand of rail across to Nababeep. In all, this was another thirty miles of track. It took my boys and I away from Port Nolloth, for we were employed as overlookers and experienced labourers in charge of the new native teams as we carved our groove across unblemished soil.

The landscape between Steinkopf and O'Keip formed a series of sandy valleys, flat in the middle but flanked by unforgiving grey granite rock. There is little sign of a tree there and those there are have smooth white trunks instead of bark and are topped with green fingers, like spears, instead of leaves. The ground is covered with a sparse scrub that licks and bites hungrily at your ankles as you brush through it. Sometimes a plant can scratch and claw at you or send a piercing needle into your flesh which leads to agitation until either you can dig it out, like a splinter, or your skin is able to expel it by its own remarkable means. Insects gathered to welcome us as we would welcome a side of hot roasted beef and gravy after going hungry for a month. As we pressed ahead across this virgin country I thought of Jane. I missed her terribly and longed to see the swell of her belly and to share our joy at such unexpected news.

By the time the line was ready to open along its full length, two grand children, Albert Henry Pearce and Albert Ernest Burgoyne had been born. Fresh young lives thrown in to this new land of great hope, I thought. They will love Africa as I have loved Cornwall. I wondered what the future held for them there in Africa and resolved to guide and help them gain a trade as they grew older.

As the new part of the line opened, the loyal engines being used had to be withdrawn. The engines were gasping for water, which was as scarce in those sweltering parts as a freshly landed pilchard. They had choked on the sand, and suffered constant mechanical failure as the grit blew everywhere, wearing their wheels and pistons into submission. Zeb, my son, and others, had been unable to do any more to lift the fatigued mood of the steam.

The engines were replaced by teams of mules which pulled the ore wagons, and by daring brakesmen, who became skilled at shepherding the wagons through the gradients and mountain curves as they rolled down from the pass at Anenous. They used nothing more than a brake and God's benevolence to control those descending trains.

I once rode with a brakesman, to save my legs. All the way down through the difficult echoing peaks he laughed and shouted out across the valleys like a mad man as he banked through the inclines. My eyes watered, my fingers gripped and went white, and I lost my trusty gemsbok hat to a forgotten nook.

Better not to loose my legs as well, I thought, so I never took that ride again.

Later, well into 1876, sad news came from Cornwall that Mary Jane had given birth to a son, her second, who had died after only two weeks of life.

My wife, Jane, then suddenly went into labour. She was helped through the birth of our child by Elizabeth, the wife of my son John Henry.

But, it was to no avail. The baby, a son, was stillborn. No life came to his fine hazel eyes, even for a short while. He had moved quickly and peacefully on with his own journey. I held, and kissed his little hand. Had he lived, we would have called him Thomas Samuel Pearce, after my father and my two eldest brothers.

Another baby did not come and as time passed Jane and I settled again to our life together. But, she felt that she had failed me. I held her hand, kissed her, and told her every day that she had not. She meant everything to me and I did not wish for her to be sad on my account when she brought me such welcome joy. My life with her was calm. Her daily beams of wisdom shone through into the deepest marrow of every bone I possessed. A child between us would have been miraculous, but, it was not meant to be.

Besides, barely a month passed without the arrival of another grand child so, whilst we do not forget, life promised to keep us occupied.

Time marched on and the years slipped by, with a brakesman's gathering speed. It is inevitable.

We always had plenty of work to keep that rail way going. That was vital. Everything would come to a halt without the coal going up the line to fire the mines and without the copper ore coming down the line to turn a profit. Each chain link of the Cape Copper played its part but that rail way, the men it relied upon when a sheared bolt had to be replaced at the remotest place along the line, and their mules, had to be amongst the strongest.

As industry gathered pace, in 1878 the 18lb Brunel rails were replaced by sturdier 32lb rails. It brought Ed, my sons, and I together again as this meant much more work, heavy, hard, but satisfying. They were good times and we could all be proud of what we had achieved in that hostile, marvellous corner of the globe.

Materials, men and animals could sometimes be lost, often at the unmerciful hands of a gale coming in to port from the cruel Atlantic Ocean. I remembered the whole town came out to see a barque, the Gleam, being ripped asunder in less than five minutes on Jacob rock in 1882 after her anchor chain had snapped. She had drifted to a violent end, under the watchful glare of our all seeing God, whilst we prayed in the icy, whipping rain.

There were many other wrecks and their skeletons lie broken, and scattered, in small pieces, across the sea bed. The wet tangled salvage was a daily reminder that you cannot take nature on. You have to bow to her, value her and blow with her.

When out on the rail, the vast empty loneliness all around me became my rich solitude. I loved to stand looking across at the power of lightning in a swirling sky or up at the clear sparkle of a thousand thriving stars. I started to have vivid dreams, and some wonderful things happened.

Once, after a morning walking the line, I came across a place I had always liked and decided to rest a while with my keg. I would take a bite there too, I thought. A springbok stood where I wanted to sit. I was surprised, for they, like other boks and the darting lizards, would normally scatter and hop off across the bush at the first glimpse of a platelayer. This bok stood there calmly, alone, looking at me.

Springboks are magnificent creatures and some folk, including Ed, would shoot them with no more than a passing glance and feast wastefully only upon the best parts. They would leave the remains of the slaughtered animal to rapacious scrub flies and other lurking, unseen scavengers.

I waved my hands but the springbok still did not move. His large eyes shone a peaceful glow, speaking in silent words. His ears, like gloves, stood alert. The boks two horns twisted up above his head, thick, black, strong and dangerous. His black striped flank and tanned back moved in and out as he drew each desert breath but still, that lovely beast remained steadfast in what I had decided was my resting place for a few minutes that day.

So, after a while, I changed my mind and choose another place nearby. As I settled I looked again towards the springbok and noticed a movement below his white belly, close by the rock on which I had wished to rest. A mottled shape slithered across the stony ground and, after lingering with some regret at a now lost meal, it spat a forked tongue towards me and was swallowed down by a dark hidden gully. The snake was a puff adder, whose bite could silently kill a man here, before claiming him by coiling itself in and around his limp limbs. The victim's last lonely moments would be spent beneath untroubled whispering winds and passing carefree clouds.

It would have been days before anyone came or, may be, even longer than that.

The springbok had saved my life. I took my hat off and placed it upside down on the ground. Then I filled it with water from my keg and stepped back, inviting the bok to drink. He came forward, looked at me again, lowered his neck to drink from the water in my hat, and drank well. He must have been thirsty. Then, he looked up, startled, as though surprised to see me, and galloped off across the sands.

Perhaps I, too, had saved him, with that sip of brackish, but welcome, water.

One dream I can remember was of a dark empty pasture, squared in perfect Cornish hedgerow. The farmer, who was dressed in a white robe, and wore a miners' pressed felt helmet with a burning dip to light the way for him and others, had said to me 'I would like you to plant an orchard'.

'What kind of orchard shall I plant?' I had replied, seeking to be guided. The farmer, whose face I could not see for the glare of the dip, quietly said in a lower voice than any master I ever worked for or knew 'Plant YOUR orchard. Perhaps apple trees, and many kinds. The blacksmith is a good one, and so are carpenters, builders and Mr Smith's. They are strong when it snows and the frosts bite, they bloom well in spring, and their bountiful fruits will grow for many summers, feeding and sheltering all those in dire need of their help. In autumn their leaves will gleam with golden colour before they fall so your soul will be warmed for the coming of the chill. Care for them well and your apple trees will thrive, long after you have moved on, along the rails'.

The farmer paused, perhaps to see if I was listening. I was, and so he continued 'Devote good time in your orchard and do not begrudge that. Take good care of the roots and let them grow deep. Water your trees with kindness and correct them gently and often so that the branches are strong, and laden with sweet purpose. Your trees will repay you for your faith, over and over again'.

I had a question for the farmer and so I looked up, but he had gone. The sun was stirring from its nightly slumber. As it rubbed its eyes, sending a glint across the dew, and stretched its rays above its head, I saw that the trees were already there, all around me, waiting for me to plant them. I had wanted to know what was meant by the trees but then I also woke. Somehow, I already knew the answer. They were my family.

My son Zeb had a trade, as a blacksmith, and was producing a good crop. It is true that in darker moments he could be bitter for having to leave home so young in search of those skills. Best, I think, in those moments, to let the apples stew. But, I can see that they serve him well now and he has the gift of invention and creativity. All my family deserve their chance to prosper, under the kind farmer's shine.

Then, almost the next night, I had another dream. I was walking and a bleak wind was blowing dust into my exposed face. My eyes were sore from the powder. I came across a pond and there I saw a frog. It sat on a boulder at the edge of the pond. I could have left the frog undisturbed or even frightened him away. I could have washed the dirt from my eyes, taken a cupped sip to soothe my throat, and moved on.

But the frog said to me 'You will not be able to do it'. I looked down at his scarred green and yellow face and replied 'Do what?'

He blinked and said 'You will not be able to throw this large grey boulder that I am sitting on into the middle of this pond'. Again, I replied 'Why would I want to do that? How does that benefit me?'

Again, the frog blinked and tilted his head before saying 'Because, even though you cannot see it, your good deed will be of benefit to others'.

In my dream I thought about this and decided that I was not strong enough. 'Of course you are!' said the frog, without me speaking. So, after what must have been an age of doubt, I bent down, on to my knees, strained, and lifted the boulder up. It was not as heavy as I had feared or thought. With an almighty heave I threw it into the middle of the pond, where most of it sank. 'There', I said, 'I have done what you asked though I can still see no reason for it'.

The frog pointed to the ripples as they curled outwards in widening circles, long after the boulder had sunk into the mud. 'Everything you do has an effect, and for a long time' he said before skipping into the water and swimming to the small part of the boulder that still jutted above the lapping water. There, he climbed out and lay on his back, basking in the sun, on the side sheltered from the dusty wind. 'Here, I am at last safe from the dust and from being eaten' he shouted across the water with a smile. 'I would like to thank you, Zeb, for that was kind of you to put the needs of others before your own'.

I awoke, it was almost dawn and Jane was snoring soundly. My pebble was not by my bed, as it always had been. It lay in the corner on the other side of the room. I do not know how it found its way there.

Outside I could hear the Hottentots as they began to stir. I decided again to help them where I could and to show kindness where none was asked for, nor expected. I decided to do that even though others might not like it or approve.

When laying new sleepers and rails we were helped by the Hottentots who received even less recognition than we did. I felt this was wrong. I did my best in every way to help them, without rocking the boat. Yes, that was all. I sought no power over them. My power was in the giving. It was not in using power to have yet more.

Serenity is to be recognised, and enjoyed, for its brief blissful flicker will always fade.

And, everything changes in a rain drop.

Having found yourself drifting peacefully across the sky, all of a sudden, with a growl of thunder and a flash of lightning, you are cruelly pushed from the comfort of your cloudy bed and find yourself falling.

It is rapid. You are plundered as you plunge. When you hit the ground, everything shatters and, for what seems an eternity, you cannot gather yourself up.

In late December 1889, such a rain drop arrived in a Christmas letter from home. In the letter my youngest daughter Elizabeth, though the help of another's written hand, explained that my daughter Mary Jane had died on 16th Nov 1889.

The death of a child, however young or old they might be, is a hefty hammer blow across the temples. Mary Jane had been widowed three years earlier, on the 8th June 1886, when her husband, William Harvey, had died from epilepsy at the age of thirty seven. His body and soul had over time succumbed to exhausting daily fits. He had suffered a long decline, losing his health, his employment at Perran, and his dignity. Now Mary Jane was gone, claimed by the red rampage of lupus whilst still only thirty five. She had been ill, one way or another, almost all of her life and had also endured the birth of three children who had died within moments of their first glimpse of breath. At last, a cherished daughter, Mary Elizabeth Harvey, had been born in 1879. We called her Bessie. She was followed by Albert in 1881 and Zebulon James in 1883. It had seemed that life was turning for them and heading towards calmer waters.

Now, those three young children were alone.

My daughter Elizabeth explained that she had taken Bessie back to Camborne where work could be found. There was no room, or money, for two small boys who could not earn their keep. They were given up by other family members to a workhouse.

I was deciding what to do about this when Jane, my wife, fell ill and took to her bed with an uncontrollable sickness and fever. It was a bad turn, another rain drop. There, my bright sun lay dying, plucked from the sky. Any shadow she had cast after shining on me was always my own. Nothing I did for her was of help, even the hourly pleas to God that I should be taken instead.

Over the years that we had been married our souls had blended as one. We had lived, like Porthalloe pebbles, in each other's pockets, and we shared the same view like two laundry pegs holding up the sleeves of a drying shirt as it swayed merrily in a breeze out on life's washing line.

I sat still beside her for a long time, willing her to fight the fever off as I picked aimlessly at my cuffs.

As she grew worse, a weeping moon hung its head, low in the pale night sky, and a passing strand of cloud wiped a tear from its face.

On the 8th January 1890, Jane slipped away below the waterline, whilst in my arms. Gone, for ever, my friend, my soul, my heart beat, my essence. Gone, Jane, oh Jane, the very person who knew my thoughts, before I knew them myself, and who had made me so complete.

Gone, every morsel of serenity, smashed to atoms in the thunder of a few vicious seconds. It lay, like the Gleam, amongst the cold colliding spray and spume on black Jacob's unmoved razor sharp rock.

17. Elizabeth Ann

Some fortunate people live exactly where they want to live. They are where they have always wanted to be. They know it soundly from the peace that washes through their heart whenever they are there, and from the wars that rage in their mind whenever they are not.

They hope for nothing more than to always be in a harmonious balance with their fate.

I found that peace in my heart, too, when I was in Porthalloe.

But, my dreams had trickled down the blue stream there and disappeared into the sea. If I wanted to keep hold of anything I had to leave. I had no alternative and, when I left, it had been for good.

I had felt I would never get back again, as though washed overboard and just out of reach of the life saving rope thrown after me by a despairing crew. There, in the angry brine I floundered, unable to quite grasp again that elusive golden thread of what makes our lives whole. I felt I would never be able to fully recapture that exact moment of calm excitement when you know that you are somewhere you truly, truly belong.

I had to settle for a life of compromise, exchanging money for the pure happiness of living as a man in the place where he had grown. I had to chase work. For over forty years I did that. The last fifteen years had been working in Africa where, in exchange for my time and my life, I had been looked after, pampered and beguiled. Africa is beautiful and I have learned much from her. We had made the best of it and accepted each other. I had grown used to her and she had grown used to me.

There have been other glorious rewards. I was blessed with a family and the love of two loyal wives and I have lived a good life. God has been kind and shown faith in me and, in Africa, he gave me my purpose. Amongst those glorious Klipfontein daisies I discovered that.

God had said 'I am the soil for the keeper of the pasture. You, Zeb, can give those you love the skills and knowledge to tend the pasture well'.

Jane had said 'You have gone to a place where most would fear to tread but you found your inner beauty there.' It has been the greatest gift of all and I have continued to fulfil the purpose set for me ever since.

But, throughout 1889, at the age of sixty five, I began to pine again for Cornwall. My heart was saying it was time, at last, to go home, to rose petals, honey bees feasting on July clovers and the smell of hot freshly cut grass being turned as it dries on a warm day. I missed the tales of shipwrecks in furious seas, told by the light of a candle over a draft of amber ale, the superstitions, and the folklore of home. I even missed the yellow lichen doilies that bask on finely cut grey slate roofs and the fall of buttered and bronzed leaves as autumn's flakes begin to swirl around you.

I had often thought of those ancestral paths, guarded by crusted oaks with their knuckled roots gripping the banks, and those sloping fields where seagulls chased worms churned up behind a ploughman's line. I wanted to once again see the frothing white bubbles of the breakers as they fizzed over the mustard sands on a windswept bay, and the moss covered trunks snoozing by streams in the shaded forgotten woods of my youth.

During those dark and silent African nights I would lie awake, watching the net curtains billow gently in a lingering breeze which carried the aroma of roasting meat, and remember the days that had been lived. I fondly recalled those who had passed, like my grand mother, Margery.

She kept a few raspberry canes down in one dappled corner of her yard. As a treat, when they were in season, she gave us each a daily allowance of one ripe raspberry, until they were gone. What a taste it was. I would look forward to it all day and then savour the sweet warm juice as the raspberry splashed the insides of my young mouth with flavour. We brothers would all sit round licking our lips, picking at the pips caught in our teeth and looking forward to 'another treat tomorrow' no matter what the day itself would bring. We were happy and grateful for what we received. We did not argue over the size of each raspberry and feel our own gift had not been evenly matched.

One summer, when I was about six, I was given no raspberries for a week after I put the knees out of my britches scrambling amongst the shales at the shore line. I did not sulk. Instead, I tried to make it up to my grand mother by collecting extra snails for the pig's suppers. On that occasion, I wasn't able to melt even her soft heart. I loved her more for it. I have always known that she wished nothing but the best for us all.

I had told Jane of my childhood and she had said 'It sounds wonderful, Zeb. I look forward to being there, with you, eating raspberries'.

It was too late now, for Jane.

But, maybe, it was not too late for me if I followed the call of my heart.

So, after Jane's death, I decided to go home.

You have to know your place in people's lives and I had felt, if I stayed, that my cold wind could ruin the fruit blossom.

My own flower had lost its bright scent. There were now other, fresher blooms to attract the honey makers dancing in that meadow. There, in Port Jolly, I felt my work was done and the chapter was closing.

And what of my family, there in Africa?

Well, they had each other and their own families to care for. They now had a future. I was the past, like the pod left behind after its young vibrant seed had sprung forth. I had helped them as much as I could. The orchard was ready. What was left for me to do there? By going home I could be of use to those who had stayed behind all those years before and who were in the midst of their own troubled, icy squall. That was my purpose now.

So, home I was going to go.

My recently orphaned grand daughter Mary Elizabeth was twelve, lodging in Camborne with her aunt, my daughter Elizabeth Julian. Mary Elizabeth had to take work as a bal maiden, at Dolcoath Mine. There she broke rocks on the surface all day and in all weathers. The money she earned gave her enough to eat and her lodgings were in exchange for helping her aunt with the family chores. Her two younger brothers, grand sons of mine, were still believed to have gone in to one of the work houses. They were lost. I had to find out where they were, and I had to help and rescue them, if I could.

Then there was Christiana, my son Nicholas's wife. She wanted her three daughters and two youngest sons to have professions. Port Nolloth offered them a chance to learn, but not to progress. They would come home to Camborne after me and the two eldest girls would be employed in dressmaking and tailoring whilst the eldest of the boys, Albert Henry, was to become an apprentice blacksmith. Nicholas would stay in Port Nolloth and send money home.

Then there was my brother William's family. William had died in the fertile Cornish fields where he had spent most of his life, at the age of fifty two. He left Ann, his widow, five surviving children, and no money. It was not his fault. He worked hard. They needed every penny he earned from his work in Flushing to get through each day. Nothing could be kept by for days not yet dawned. The youngest, Maggie Jane, was only nine when William died. The oldest son, Samuel, was deaf and dumb but as skilful as anyone I had ever seen in the fine art of tailoring. Samuel could work but he needed to be employed and I helped the family move to Camborne where they could depend on his income. He would work with Christiana's eldest daughters.

Then there was my brother Nicholas's family. His coal business had collapsed and he had left town, owing money to many and leaving his wife, Teresa, and his five children, destitute, and in Camborne. He sent letters, and some money, from a place in the Americas called Ishpeming. Then the letters, and the money, stopped, and nothing else ever came. For many years I had posted money home earmarked for William Thomas, his eldest boy, to gain a trade. He also worked in clothing, as an outfitter. George, the second son, had trained as a boot maker, with John Julian. It was my turn to look after his wife, as he had so dutifully done for mine fifteen years or so ago.

Then there was my daughter Elizabeth Julian. Her husband John eventually had to give up shoe and boot making. His work was so careful that no running repairs were ever needed. Soon, people no longer needed new boots. They found that if they looked after the ones they had then they would last, just as Elizabeth, my daughter, had always said. John gave up or gave in, and went down the mine at Dolcoath to escape the sharp blade of the workhouse. They had five children by the time I came home. Four daughters and a young son, called Wilfred. I helped with medical bills for the youngest two daughters, Beatrice, aged nine and Mabel, aged eight. They had suffered with illness which had made them homebound all their lives.

Should I continue? I felt it was my purpose to provide the difference for them. For the young men, and women, that meant an apprenticeship and a trade. For the women now at the head of their families, that meant enough to keep them out of the clutches of the work house.

They were all my dear apple trees and they all needed help to deliver a strong flower and fruit.

The only ones not in need were Avis, my brother Sam's wife, who together with her one surviving son, their fourth child, also called Samuel, had left for America to join up with my brother. There, I hear, they had another daughter, called Minnie.

I had heard little more from them since, and I won't hear from my brother Peter either, who had died in a blizzard near a place called Houghton in 1885.

He had met a Cornish lass, had a family with her and was working in the Americas as a dock man and as a sheriff. He had escaped from under Hannah's feet, and from those grasping holes in the ground. He had been set free. Free as a bird, in the great wide open scapes of spruce and green grass, swathed beneath a canopy of roaming, ragged clouds. By all accounts he had seemed happy and settled, and where he had wanted to belong, until that sad tragedy had struck him down. Knowing the fortitude of my brother Peter, I expect that, right up until his last moments, he had viewed the blizzard that had claimed him as 'nothing more than a light flurry of snow'.

In March 1890, I therefore left Port Nolloth, for good.

I was alone when I stepped off the jetty into the loading basket. I had already said my farewells to family and friends. They all had work and had to carry on, as every day before had been and every day after surely would be. William and Richard had given up the rails and had moved on to O'Keip, where they were now mining in the bleak suffocating heat of a lawless town and keeping questionable company. I had taken one last journey to see them. I doubted I would see them again, and there were tears. I hope they catch nothing there but prosperity.

Jane lay under a newly carved gravestone, amongst a crowd of wooden crosses, in the drifting sands of the town's gusty, expanding cemetery. Before the coffin lid had been nailed I had folded her arms across her chest and placed my Porthalloe pebble in her sweet lifeless hands. Those hands had held me so tight. They would continue to hold my heart.

As I stowed my case, the steamer fired its boiler, raised anchor and slipped quietly on the tide, over the bar, beyond the reef and out of the bay. I then sat on the deck, bathing in the sun, hair ruffling in the breeze, and watched the barren brown shore wash past. As the thin plume of dirty smoke from her stack trailed behind us, I raised a glass of clear clean water, my first in months, up to the heavens, and hung on for dear life to the rope I had been thrown.

I arrived back in Camborne by train in April. The grey platform was damp with the shine of a morning's mizzle and the air thick with the smell of coal dust. In some ways nothing had changed. The ghosts of those departing for good to far off shores still hung from carriage windows in the silent wet gloom. I remembered the many tears, and the jokes, as the guard's whistle shrilled another departure signal.

I had arranged a long term lease on two properties, side by side, in Dolcoath Road. It was still close to the clatter of the railway that carried so many of my memories.

Elizabeth, my daughter, already had the keys. The houses were secured from the Basset estate for the use of the family well beyond my lifetime. If anything happened to me, as it surely would one day, they would not want for a doilied roof over their heads.

Compared to others I suppose I had come back 'made'. Despite those I had helped so that they could help themselves, I still had some money saved. I also had all that Jane had bequeathed me on her death so, compared to most folk, I was comfortable.

My new neighbours quickly saw that. 'Hark at moneybags' they would whisper jealously in huddles as I walked along Trelowarren Street. 'He would still be a catch with all that gold on 'im,' the chars, including Elizabeth Ann, would say as they dug each other knowingly in the ribs with their elbows.

'He be too big for those boots of 'is since he cum back 'ome' Dickie Prisk from Skew Bud had said.

'Don't he walk awkward? He won't want to know us no more with his toes all pinching up' Mrs Polkinghorne had said, waving her left hand about all laardy da.

'Can't Lordy Pearce afford a new pair of bigger boots with all that jangle about him?' Tom Trythall had remarked.

We are all judged by what is in our pocket and on our feet rather than what is on our mind and in our soul. I had resolved to ignore them, use the money well on deserving causes and not to waste it on idle frills and fancies.

My only luxury would be a housekeeper. Whilst I could do most things for myself, I preferred help and the company of someone that I trusted. Elizabeth, my daughter, remembered and suggested Elizabeth Ann, whose son had worked for John when he was boot making. 'You know her already' she said, in reply to my raised eyebrows before adding 'You have known her all her life'.

In July of 1890, I met Elizabeth Ann again.

Elizabeth Ann was the daughter of Willie Tripcony and Ann Michell. Willie and Ann were from two St Keverne families that both stretched back into the mists of time, their histories twisted together like dense forest twine.

She was one of at least four children and she was born twelve years after her brother John, the eldest, and ten years after her sister, Annie. It was difficult to tell if there were more children after Annie and before Elizabeth Ann was born because Willie was always evasive about his early life and the time he spent working away in Devon. No one ever spoke much about it and when you dared to ask, the answer nearly always drifted away like smoke on the wind before a prying ear like mine could catch it.

There were rumours that Ann never had children when she was faithful to Willie and that she was always fertile when the handsome Anthony was home. Anthony was

Willie's elder brother who had chosen Mary Champion to be his wife but couldn't leave Ann alone, or other ladies, for that matter. He was a tall, handsome charmer, with broad shoulders, a big mop of black hair and a permanent wink in his left eye. He was accomplished in all he did, be it labouring, fishing or maintaining the thatch of the cots of lonely women in the area. Willie was smaller, and had never grown far from the ground. He lived in an adjoining cot and in his brother's wake. Eventually, he had tired of the fixed shadow cast over him by Anthony's long, dangling nose and took Ann away to Ide, near Exeter, in an effort to put a stop to the lust and to save two marriages.

Willie did once tell me that in Devon he had said to all who asked that he and his wife could no longer have children. This way I suppose he thought he would prevent further infidelity. But, Elizabeth was born in Ide in 1838, the year my mother died. I'm sure folk all around were wide eyed in amazement at the little miracle before them after such an affirmation of barrenness. 'Has someone been sowing their wild oats in your field whilst you were dozing?' they had said to him teasingly whilst gathered on soaked afternoons to sup their flat ciders. When Ann fell with child again, Willie packed the family back up and came home to St Keverne, hoping to prevent the new found fertility from swelling into public view once more.

Like a fisherman patching the bottom of his boat to prevent further leaks, this only worked for a while. The chatter, like water, threatened to pour into his overwhelmed sloop at any time and sink him for good.

After Francis, the youngest, was born, they moved to Mellanoweth, near Angarrack. They changed their name to Tripp and Willie gave Ann, his wife, a final warning. There were to be no more oats and from then on he would be sleeping with his right eye open.

Willie was the kindest man you could ever wish to happen across. He was one for a story, it is true, but he would offer a helping hand, hospitality and a word of advice to deserving folk in need. All he asked for in return was kindness and no judgement. It was not always what he received. Others did take advantage of him as I suppose they do of anyone with a good nature.

Elizabeth Ann said that Willie loved children. When I think back I know he must have done, for I believe he raised other people's children as his own and he stayed faithfully with his wife, Ann. He took her back time and again, like a swinging stable door would the wind. He was always too loyal for his own good.

He treated Elizabeth Ann like his daughter and she treated him like a father. In their eyes it was the only truth and they silently agreed never to speak of the past.

You will remember that I stayed with them when I left Porthalloe, and my children also stayed there when I had trouble and no room was offered by members of my own family. Willie and I would laugh together, full of devilment. He was like a father to me during those times. I remembered Elizabeth Ann then, how she cared for my young boy Nicholas, and how she bloomed into a beautiful young woman.

In 1856 Elizabeth Ann had met John Scadden, a miner from Gwinear, who was living in Angarrack and working at the Alfred copper and lead mine near Trepuska. He had worked in and around mines since he was seven and so knew of nothing else. He was from a long line of scrapers and scrappers and as reliable as wet gunpowder once he had a drink inside him.

By Christmas of the same year they had married and moved to Camborne. There, the first child, a girl called Eliza, was born. Money was tight, but tighter than it need have been for John spent his wage on beer and chasers as soon as he had received it from the purser at the counting house. He never had a use for pockets.

Always short for the rent, they were forced to move back to Mellanoweth. There they stayed with Elizabeth Ann's parents. John fell out again and again with Ann and Willie, who had not seen eye to eye with him on any matter where the welfare of their daughter was concerned. So John, who spoke in grunts, again moved his young family to Camborne and once more went in search of mining work. But, there was no getting away from it. Elizabeth Ann had married a bit of a ducker. When drunk he cursed his miserable life saying he had not asked to be born and that his life was nothing more than a desolate circle leading him nowhere. All his time and money was spent only making matters worse. Elizabeth Ann said 'He added salt to the pudding instead of sugar and made it bitter to the taste for everyone'.

Within ten years John was dead, the victim of a breathing disorder which afflicted many miners. If that had not claimed him, drink would have. Elizabeth Ann was left a widow, at the age of thirty, with three young children to care for and no income. Just like my daughter Mary Jane. To avoid the workhouse she moved home and made her peace with Willie. He wrapped his protecting arms around her and forgave it all.

By this time Willie was himself down the mine at Alfred, forced from the fresh air and fields he'd loved all his life at the age of nearly seventy. When Alfred yielded nothing more of value in its shattered rocks to all of those that worked there, the family moved to Brea, close to a small mine by the tracks of the rail way. Elizabeth Ann's two boys, John and William, both went down the mine there with Willie. Whilst living there we crossed paths once again for at that time I was working along the lane at Burn Coose for Mr Burgess. It was just before I went to Africa.

Sometimes I came across Willie up on Carn Brea. When I enquired he would say he was wondering what might have been and dreaming of what was never going to be.

He was missing the things he never had. Looking out across the fields and mines below helped him to think, he said. We did do some talking up there. He was always proud of Elizabeth Ann, whatever else in his life, and hers, had not quite been as he would have liked.

'She never gave up' he had said. In that, Elizabeth Ann was very much like him.

At Brea she had work as a laundress and became very good at looking after others besides her own family. She stayed with her parents and the three children were brought up there, with Willie's help, guidance, stories and love.

On one windy day back then, when I had met Willie Tripp wandering up on Carn Brae, we both had time enough to stop for a talk and a smoke amongst the shelter of the proud undaunted rocks that looked down towards Camborne. We had not seen each other in a while and he was in another pensive mood. He was a wise old owl and clearly had a story he wanted to tell.

He told me that day about a dream he had the night before. Well, I suppose it must have been a nightmare.

'I were asleep and dreaming that I were asleep' he had said. We both laughed at that.

'Then, of a sudden, I woke in my dream. I looked across at Annie, my wife. On the other side ov 'er there was another man. They was both awake, looking across at me, looking across at them'. His eyes looked up at the gathering leaden clouds and he took a suck on his clay.

'I told 'im to get out and be gone. He collected up his testicles and trousers, and scrambled from the room. Annie said she did not know who 'ee was. I accepted this and, in my dream I gave it no more thought an' went back to snoozing'.

After a pause, Willie continued 'In the morning, still in my dream, the thought struck me like a bolt of lightning and I went all rigid'. He paused, looked at me and said 'No, not like that, Zeb'

I had said nothing and he continued, after being assured that I did not have any untoward thoughts in my mind.

'Annie had been awake all along yet she 'ad not told me about the other man next to her, preferring to let me sleep on, like the foolish old exhausted hound I was.'

There was a silence whilst Willie thought through the moment again before he concluded 'Still ….it were all but a dream'.

As a puffer pulling a long line of coal wagons strained past on the rails in the valley below, smoke belching from its overworked stack and pistons punching sound into the banks on either side of the track, I said to Willie 'Well, who was the man in your dream? Do you know?'

I will never forget his reply.

'You build your life, day by day, stone by stone, like a good hedgerow. You chisel the stones into shapes that fit. Then you pack it down, solid. Why?' Willie paused, not expecting a reply, before continuing 'You do this to protect your crops, so that the wall might stand the test of time and remain firm against the buffeting of bad weather and the rubbing of irritable cows'.

On he went. 'Should the wind eat into your wall, rebuild it again. Keep watch, and build your walls deep, broad and high. Otherwise that mole, that weevil, that stoat, will ruin your crop and have your lady down from the tower. He will burrow, silently, under your ramparts, until there he is, in your castle, flying his own colours. It seems I did not take care of my wall and he did not care to tell me. All along I had welcomed him and treated him as my friend. I even bought him cider but, all along, he was plotting for what he alone had wanted. It was, in time, to breach my wall, have my life and, most of all, my wife'.

Willie had paused again, looking up at me. I remember him tapping out his pipe on one of the rocks before he said 'Whilst you sleep, he is at work. Beware, yes, beware of the quiet usurper, Zeb, and damn my brother, yes, damn him for he chose to unbutton his britches and follow his manhood. He forgot the order of his loyalties, and then, afterwards, he cared not a smidge for sorry'.

When Ann Tripp died at the age of seventy seven in 1877, Willie worked on as a miner, feeding them all like chicks gathered at the farmer's feet. He was as tough as one of John Julian's boots, never one to be nurly, and made light to the very end of his many aches and his creaking bones. He hid his bruises well and, if malice were a rasping wind, he only contained a hatful of it.

Elizabeth Ann became the keeper of his house and they depended upon each other until he died at the end of August 1885, at the age of eighty one. Only then, I expect, did Willie let go of his shovel.

At first, when we met, Elizabeth Ann and I sat down in town, over a cup of weak tea and a slice of cake. I talked to her about the position as my housekeeper. I had no sense of what to expect as I had always been the servant to someone else somewhere else, all my life. There was no doubt that whilst she had enjoyed glimpses of happiness, life had hurt her to the marrow. She had survived the burns, the cuts and the trampling. Whilst her dark eyes had been dulled by the struggle, Willie's guidance had served her well and she had steered her own children through to adulthood. Now they had flown the nest, and she was lonely, like me.

She had wondered where life would take her next. Having spent her life caring for others she now, suddenly, at the age of fifty two, had no one who needed her. She looked like a dove searching for a peaceful perch after a long and fruitless flight.

She also required hope, and work. She could not survive alone without it.

I offered her the chance, and it was quickly settled. Relief swept across her face and she replied that she could start straight away. We made the arrangements as I paid for the tea. She would sleep in the small back room and she could bring the few meagre sticks of furniture she owned and her small bundle of clothing with her. I would pay for food and give her an allowance.

Over the next few weeks Elizabeth Ann looked after me handsomely. She worked her small frame hard and the sparkle came back into her eyes. I had never seen a house so clean or a shirt so spotless. We shared laughter and she did not seem to mind spending her time in my company. We ate well and her tattie stew was the best I had tasted since Mary Ann had died. I began to put on a pinch or two of weight.

The house was soon straight and it was not long before I had to leave my boots at the door and my cap on the hook. But, who is to mind? I did not.

I did mind about Mrs Trezise's opinion that we were carrying on like a couple of spring coneys. I was told that she had been acting like the Town Crier, stopping everyone on the spit between Vyvyan and Trelowarren to announce the news as she saw it. 'Ave you 'eard 'bout that old dog Zebulon Pearce and the washer moll with the spilling bosom? I reckons she's after his African money and is busy pulling the wool'. After a pause to draw breath she had said 'and we all knows what 'ee sees in 'er, don't we?'

What she said was right on the water line. That one could strip paint with her hot ridicule and more than the odd one or two has remarked that she has a nose that you cannot hide behind a bush. No wonder her pecked husband only came home after dark.

The flames were fanned when Elizabeth Ann and I took a trip to Godrevy. Light, the colour of buttercups, shone through a gap in the cloud, illuminating sheep as they bayed and grazed on the hillside above the red river. We sat high on the bluff, looking out across the moody shades of the sea towards a labouring old bucket that scudded across the foam in a hopeful search for one last catch.

That day Elizabeth Ann explained that she had grown fond of me. I was pleased, for I had grown fond of her. Fortified by my reaction to her words she continued 'I want a better arrangement'. I asked her what she meant. 'If we are to carry on, I want to be honest about it and secure. What if you die? I will be cast out again. What then will become of me?'

I thought about this for a moment or two and agreed. She did deserve better. So, I asked for her hand in marriage. She embraced me, thanked me and said 'Yes'.

We went home smiling, ready to tell my family.

On the 4th October 1890 I married Elizabeth Ann at All Saints, Tuckingmill. I said I was sixty five, just the light side of too old to fool a doubtful vicar. Elizabeth Ann was fifty two.

Now, whatever happened to me she, at least, my third lovely wife, would be secure for the rest of her life.

18. Old Ground (Dolcoath)

Not that long after my seventieth birthday, on a Wednesday in September 1893, Elizabeth Ann and I were woken from an afternoon nap by a low rumble. The house shook and the china plates she had bought for the pantry rattled. The jackdaws nesting in the languid trees by the church must have taken flight, their beaks full of indignant squawk.

We both looked sleepily across the creased pillows at each other and wondered what could have happened.

I dressed and took a glance through the nets before going outside into the lane. There I stood, with others, in the shadow of the mighty Dolcoath mine's engine house. Her dull grey windows lay silent under lowered lids. Men scurried about, shouting. Women chattered anxiously, wringing their hands.

What had fate delivered beneath the flowing petticoats of that grand old lady?

Dolcoath was a giant ant heap where a glut of desperate men busied, burrowed and dug below the surface for tin, copper, silver, cobalt and arsenic. Her pumping, winding, air compressing and tin dressing machines heaved and pulsed every day and night, feverishly sucking water and spoils from the ever deeper cold dark rocks below. She was the pride of Camborne, whose families had suckled hungrily upon her for over a century.

Word came that there had been a collapse half a mile under, down at level 412, where the tunnel was forty feet wide. Men could take two hours merely to reach it. This great lode, bigger and richer than any in Cornwall, had drawn tributers and tutmen in, who then riddled the ground with runs as they pursued the evasive glinting veins of fortune. John Julian said no coney would find their way around such a warren as was left behind. Narrow shafts, or winzes, and old levels, had been filled with worthless attle and tin slime rather than be carried up and out to grass.

The stulls at 412, of pitch pine timber, could not support the gathered weight of deads that had been reburied above their heads. A bend in the timbers meant a team of men had to be dispatched to strengthen and repair any breach they came across. They were buried when all the loose ground above was unleashed by the straining wooden supports finally giving way. The earth ran together, at the bottom, where, even at its most industrious John Julian said the darkness was only ever briefly lit by the dim glow of a passing candle.

It was a true disaster. Seven men died, their voices never again to echo through those damp hammered burrows. One survived, Richard Davies, of Troon. He, like John Julian, had spent time as a shoemaker before the need to live on more than fresh air forced him down into the foul airs of the mine. John said that Richard and the others heard a crack, as wood snapped, then silence. This had been a warning, a God send. He had started to run. Then he had felt the blast of warm air as it rushed past him, snuffing out the flickering flame of his candle and plunging him into darkness. Shortly after, he found himself engulfed by thick muddy spoil. But, without knowing how, or why, he had miraculously escaped the snapping jaws of death. Perhaps he had found himself in a priest hole.

I believe his wife was called Grace. I did not know her, or the other wives whose husbands lie still, buried and broken, way below, under the graves of ordinary men nearby at Tuckingmill.

When they all left home that morning, in their rough flannels, water kegs dangling, croust in their bag and spare dips in their pockets, they will all have known the dangers. I hoped that, before leaving at the cusp of dawn, those dear miners had kissed their wives, mistresses and children, as they slept on. For now we know that day was to be their last. Their goodbyes were for one final time. I hope they were able to cherish the soft touch of their families before they strode heartily to the gaping, greedy mouth of the shaft where the spriggans crouched in the shadows for their chance to snatch them away. Little did they know, as the sound of the whim above them faded as they descended, that Dolcoath's sharp teeth would close around them, swallowing them in silence for ever and more.

We are all soon forgotten, like footprints in the sand washed away by the next tide. After a day or so at Dolcoath the cranking began again, the drills fired up and the stamps roared back to life. The hot breath of miners once again formed plumes in the deep caverns as they sunk into the black fathoms below. When you have lost your grip on her, the world just carries on spinning. Put your finger in a bowl of water, then pull your finger out. The size of the hole that is left is the measure of how much you will be missed.

And so it will be for me.

But, at least, I have had a chance to say goodbye. An unshackled wind has not rushed past me and snuffed a strong flame out. I have been able to prepare for Elysium as my dip burnt low to the gutters around its wick.

Now, my water is coming to the boil.

My own life has still passed quickly and, although I feel I have achieved many good things I, like those miners whose names have been forgotten, have travelled unnoticed for more than seventy five years.

But, I do not seek reward just because I have done my best and served those I love. After all, what I have done has been largely for the benefit of my family and for myself. No one else should ever be expected to do that for you. It would have taken my spirit and my pride if another had stepped into my idle shoes and taken up the slack of my reins.

Life, for me, may have been much briefer. My mother, who died sixty years ago, God rest her soul, said to me one day that she had not expected me to live when I was born. I suffered with an early fever and even Thomas, my father, had knelt down to pray. For that reason, Saunders became my middle name. The church record would thus reflect the grief of both parents in years to come and the pedigree of the babe would never be forgotten. All would know from whence the poor scrap had come as well as to where he was bound.

But, I held on, stubbornly. My name and I have been together longer than anyone might have expected. I have been fond of it. I won that first of many tests and I think I became my mother's favourite boy, the one who reminded her most of her father. My brothers all carried my father's stamp. Now, out of them all, I am the only one left. From that rocky secluded inlet at Porthalloe our family had scattered across the globe, carried on a fanning wind like hot sparks from a dry, crackling bonfire.

I hope my brothers all lie somewhere they want to be and that the brambles have not wrapped themselves too tightly around the carved stones that carry their names. I miss them all but we are swept on the tide, some more willing than others. Most of us have no plan in life's ocean current beyond our own survival. Eventually we will all run a ground, it is a question only of where and when.

I can only hope that where I wash up is as beautiful as where I lived as a boy, or those daisy fields near Klipfontein.

Did I tell you that I found my daughter Mary Jane's two orphaned boys? I do not think that I did and I should have done for I was proud of that. I made many enquiries over many months which had at last led me past uncaring chin stroking clerks and poisoned pen pushers to the Union Workhouse at Budock, above the burnished silver bay of Falmouth.

There I saw them for the first time. Albert was eleven years old and little Zeb was nine. Both were sullen and as thin as scarecrows although the clothes on their back were not as good as those you would find in a farmers field. They did not know what to make of me, or my visit, for I was but a stranger to them when I had first called on them unannounced. For three years no one had wanted them and no one had sought them out or given them anything that wasn't brutal. Suddenly, there was a wrinkled old grey whiskered man, in a waistcoat with a row of Peter's shiny buttons and leaning on a walking stick, who had come to vouch for them, put an arm round their shoulders, and rescue their futures.

'Granfer came back from Africa for us' I heard my grandson Zeb say a couple of months later to Mrs

Williams, as he handed a penny over for a treat bag of allsorts at her shop along Dolcoath Road. It makes my heart truly swell.

I had brought them home to live with Elizabeth Ann and I.

Zeb Harvey has had a terrible time of it after his mother, my daughter, died when he was six. He said that for two years he had helped the nurse at the Union infirmary look after the helpless and the aged imbeciles so he felt he was ready for me. I laughed. I am fond of him. I like his spirit, still strong despite always clearing up the mess. Bessie, their elder sister, was so pleased and relieved to see them both.

Albert is unlikely to stay. He says he has been bitten by the sea and he sees it as his way forward. Perhaps, in truth, he has already dreamt of his escape for what is there here for him but a life lived down a mine shaft? I hope he is not too damaged. He is quieter than his younger brother, and angrier. I will help Albert join the Navy when he is old enough and we'll see if that promises a future for him, beyond these shores, after I am gone. Before that I will love him as one of my own for as long as I've got.

They are but three of over thirty grand children I had. Some have died before me, like little Beatrice Julian at the age of ten in 1892 and sweet suffering Mabel Julian at eleven in 1893. Some others now talk of raising children themselves. The money, like butter, spreads thinly over such a big loaf but in some small way I would like to think that I have tried to help them all and, for the most part, I think with God's onward guidance they will turn out well and play their part in this wonderful world of ours.

I have always tried to give on the basis of need, as I saw it. I never set out to give equally for every need is different. Where you plant an apple tree may be different to where you prepare a field of barley. It has led to jealousy, which is regretful. It was never my intention or desire.

In the last three years my health has not been good. Indeed, a pain strikes me now as I write. The fragrant scent of honeysuckle, my grand daughter Bessie's favourite Cornish flower, washes the face of a warm breeze outside in the yard. There is room there for a few other perfumed stems to remind me of my old home and, in a small hot corner, away from frosted licks, my hottentot figs struggle each year to gain a firm foothold.

They remind me of my son William when he first set foot in Port Nolloth. For months he was all at sea.

I suppose Cornwall is too brisk a climate for the figs waxy flower, although even the blizzard here in March 1891 had me with one step on the steamer back to Africa. I was nearly derailed, like Leopard, a sad old rail engine, which had come to rest, snared by a wicked drift of deep virgin snow as it spread thickly across his path during the storm.

As my memories of that beautiful far off place fade, so the cancer on my face grows stronger and bolder. At first it was but a freckle, brown and beautiful, Elizabeth Ann had said. But, it would not leave me and over these last three years has grown angrier by the day. Now it is ugly, the size of a gaping cavernous gunnis and my sore flesh weeps as though mourning all that I will have to leave behind. I have seen a doctor. Apart from the eye and cheek patch, his heavy breath upon my eyebrows was all he gave me. He said, as he clipped his bag shut, that there was nothing more he could do about it. It was just a matter of time, he had explained, and, as the sight in my left eye fades, that I should prepare myself for the end.

The raw piercing pain is the worst thing.

After that, the worst thing is the constant pain.

My face is like a leaf of parchment that has caught fire in the middle. The tongues of flame, like monbretia petals, have licked a hole that has spread outwards from the centre. The edges are also ablaze and the words of my rhyme can no longer be distinguished from the glow of my embers. It has burnt on too far and the inferno will not now ever be extinguished until it has finally claimed me.

As I prepared, I liked to watch the railway at work. It was my life and still runs alongside Dolcoath and nearby across the levels to Roskear. To keep out of the sun and away from the glances of horror from passing people, I go early, when I cannot sleep, and sit by the embankments at Chapel Hill. I look towards Carn Brea and, sometimes, I think I can still see Willie Tripp's ghost firing up his pipe.

The engine drivers have grown accustomed to sounding their whistles when they see me sitting there, nothing more now than an old cage of bones. I wave back as the timber ribbed carriages strain and stretch towards Camborne and then rattle over the mine workings in the valley below.

I always start thinking when I am there, listening to the birdsong and the still of a sunrise. Rusting bolts lie discarded, now worthless nuggets amongst the rab and abandoned heaps of old workings. The ground there has been lacerated, bruised and scarred. But, nature is a fighter. Gorse tries again to take hold on that slope. I am sure that the hidden grip of those prickled roots will one day win again.

And I know that I am not afraid.

Perhaps Mary Ann, and Jane, are waiting for me, like porters for that one passenger who alights at Gwinnear Road. I have that rare ticket at last. It is a one way stub to a place that now slumbers just a couple of clicks down the line.

I will be buried nearby. It will not, after all, be Porthalloe or the little graveyard overlooking the busy estuary at St. Keverne. Elizabeth Ann did not want to settle back there. She has two grand children, Lillie and Ada, who are growing up nearby. They have all become used to bountiful times where we are. So, we have remained, amongst friends and family, in Camborne. Besides, I do not need to be there, back home. As Willie Tripp, my wife's father had explained to me many years ago when he was leaving St. Keverne for the second time 'It was a mistake me coming back. You should never weave on a former web'.

All that matters is that I know where I am from, and that I am proud of where I came from.

I have put my affairs in order. I know my wife, Elizabeth Ann, has been interested in my money. She has grown comfortable with it and some say, including my daughter's family across the road, that she has taken advantage of me. I could picture Mrs Tresize still clacking away on the street corner. 'I told you so, didn't I? I was right all along, wasn't I?'

My family think that Elizabeth Ann will move her daughter's family in with her and spend all the remaining money. 'It will be wasted. There will be nothing left for anyone else' my daughter Elizabeth had muttered to her husband. I know because he told me. 'We think she is nothing but venomous ivy clinging to your bark, adding nothing to the flourish of your tree' he had said, trying to make me see his sense.

It may be true that she has recently acquired a taste for elegant frippery, and she does now often carry a few more feathers and plumes than she was born with. But, Elizabeth Ann has been a gift to me and she has cared for me, loved me and been loyal to me. I believe we rescued each other. She listened when she could have shouted. She was never too busy to hold my hand when I needed it and she has been the one who has been here, coping with the most miserable of views. I could not have asked for more. I have taken time to see and I love what I have seen.

That is all I want to say and it is all I will go on in forming my everlasting opinion, in words.

I count Elizabeth Ann amongst my many true blessings.

Indeed, I extend a grateful thank you to everyone, including those of you who have read my words. We are both almost there.

And what of my possessions, the few that I have?

Well, my boots will go to Zeb Harvey and my belt to Albert Harvey. They were both made by John Julian and, if cared for, they still have several generations left in them. I expect the belt will need a few extra notches put into it to tie itself to Albert's slender frame.

My four wise monkeys will go to my dear grand daughter, Bessie Harvey. I know she will care for them and they will care for her.

My new Porthalloe pebble, gathered from the shoreline on my final visit last summer, will travel with me, when I leave. I carry it always, wherever I go.

My bible, the one my second wife Jane taught me to read, will go to my third daughter, my seventh child, Elizabeth Julian. It carries my name and all the family dates. Whoever holds the fate of its pages in their hands will know that I, too, existed, that I touched, read and understood every precious word, and that when they read the same words, our connection before God will reach out beyond the years in between.

No one will want my hat. It is as tired and bedraggled as I am so I would like it to remain sitting on my head until its yarns and threads fall away and back to earth, much like my own story.

As for my warm elegant black coat, kindly made for me by Mary Ellen and Lilly, two of my son Nicholas's daughters, well, I think I would like to keep that. Wherever I am going I hope it will be cold, rather than hot, and, if it is, I shall need that coat, wrapped safely around my shivering shoulders.

When I look, as I do as much as I can, I do see God, looking down on me. He says he is ready, now, for me, so I am calm. There is pain, and it is exhausting, but I cannot feel it when he sits with me, preparing me. He has one hand resting on the capstan. I hope when he pulls my weary boat out of the water it will be towards heaven.

In a dream, as a distant choir sung, a mist drifted across an unknown harbour, bringing dying echoes of the past. My mother, Margery, was there. She looked no older. I think she was praying with me. Others, who I had not seen for a long time, were gathering. Somewhere, high above, a weather vane swung, creaking madly as it hesitated about which way to point. My good eye, like King Harold's, followed the shaft of its pointed arrow. It was as if the arrow's head could sense a storm. 'Come now, for he is going', the vane's black flame forged cockerel crowed from its stark open beak.

I walked again, in my dream, and I was running my fingers through a lea's lustrous golden ears. They were ready for the reaper's shave, as they swayed drowsily below a thunderous gathering wind. A heavy rain was looming, its drops eager to ruin the promise of one last harvest. Hurry, sir, with the sharpening of your scythe, and send me on my next journey.

It did all sparkle, and look very much like home, at last.

My son John Henry is here now. He has come back from Africa to say his goodbye. I am so proud of him. I need to speak with him and look after him. Besides, I cannot write any more so I'm going to put my pen and blotter down and hold his hand. Most of what I have wanted to say has been said. The balance can wait until I have gone or it will be for others to say.

I shall tell John Henry that he has arrived just in time, for I can see that the sun from my day has gone. Its bronzed glow has now sunk over the far and distant Porthalloe hills, leaving the pebbles at the shoreline to the pitch dark of the night.

Tomorrow is his, and he should rejoice in it, for life is short, even on the longest of those heady, sun filled summer days. I have written a letter for him.

Of course, it may be that life for me is not over. It may be that it is only now, oh beautiful creation, about to begin.

Dew genough. (Goodbye, God be with you).

19. Letter to my future family

There is no photograph of me from which I can take a good admiring look up at you, and you can look back from beyond time at the faded formal black and white pose of an old platelayer.

If there were such a photograph, you might speculate about what ancient traces remain that we can both share.

So, I leave you this letter.

There is a beech tree near Porthalloe in a spot where I used to go with my brother Sam. A long time ago I carved my name into the bark. The tree has since grown fat. Its roots have been exposed, its trunk has swollen, and its branches have twisted – just as I have. The letters I cut have been swallowed by the gnarled bark and now all you can read is the word 'Peace'.

Never mind. I am happy with an apt word like that and I leave this earth with that word carved in my heart.

I hope the ripples from the boulder I tried to throw into the African frog's pond will bring benefit to you all and that the grandchildren of my grandchildren will be proud of me and all of us who have travelled before them.

I have tried and given you the best I could.

I leave you, my blessed friends and family, with a few words I hope you will see as wisdom, picked up by an old man along life's precious but precarious and slipsey path.

I hope that these words will help you to see hope where there has been none and to have faith when the fogs of evil swirl threateningly in front of you and around you.

I have been an example, firmly proven, that in this life the most extraordinary things can be done by the most ordinary of men. I did as much as I was able in the short time I was given. So can you.

I was not a tinner, nor a fisher, but I was a proud Cornishman, nevertheless, true and free. I lived on the edge of an Empire where those with money were always in charge and many folk I knew starved within sight of wealth. I moved unseen and taken for granted, forgotten by those I helped as soon as I was gone. They probably never even knew my name. However, I had the experience and the will to put my body and soul to good wholesome work and it was to be the back bone of my own salvation.

Qualities to treasure, my dear future family, are piety, obedience, integrity and skill. Be industrious, intelligent, sober and orderly. Do not be soured by hard work or depressed by harsh privations. Be proud in your work and of the work you do, whatever it is.

I grew up into a time when people could at last move to a different employment in a different place, despite their standing. Remember that, for it is a hard won freedom and a precious jewel saved from the devil's greedy grip.

I believe that family and education are the most important gifts man can have bestowed upon him. On all but a flour merchant's scales this providence would far out weigh the material values many place above them.

Be tolerant and understanding, for you will meet many different cultures, peoples and views in your life time.

Try not to make use of bad expressions. There are enough words to find a kind one.

Rely on others but depend on yourself.

Give, without the expectation that you may receive.

Do not let anger consume your soul.

Think clearly and reasonably.

Love your spouses, who could all be in so many other places but who have chosen to be there, with you, by your side.

Be wise.

Be passionate and versatile. Many things will change in your life and some of it will count as progress. When I was born we used a candle to see in the night and later in life sometimes a lamp. It was lit by burning the oil of pressed pilchards caught from the wild ocean beyond our window.

Now those with money have invested in a new light. They call it electricity. Tesla's idea may catch on, I don't know.

I was born into a world where few were able to read but all knew God's word. Some day all people will read but few will know God's written word. Try to be different and drink in wise words so that your soul can absorb them.

Try to help others so that they can help themselves and so do the same as you.

Embrace the goodness in the World and use it to benefit the lives of everybody. Do not use it to look down on others.

Try not to have too much of what you want, and not enough of what you need.

All my life my country seems to have been at war with some body. That has sometimes even been against its own people. In your futures there will probably always be a war somewhere in the world. Try to avoid conflict, even when it seeks you out. Why fight your neighbour? For gold? Are you sure that is worth more than a full belly or a dead husband? Why do we always want more? Try to settle for a simple, happy life.

Humble is a word with a rich lining.

I do not pretend to have the answer to the riddle of life's wonderful pattern or the key to the reason why Margaret was never called that but always answered to the name of

Peggy. It can be a muddle but, like a Port Nolloth fog, if you have faith that it will be a good day, the fog will surely burn off and leave you with a clear view.

I hope my dreams have been sown in fertile soil and I hope my apple trees, for that is who you, my family, truly now are, continue to grow and produce sustenance for those around you for many years to come. I may not have become 'King of the path' and John Carlyon saw to that many years ago, but you can be kings of your own destinies, steadfast upon the highest of hills with the very best of views.

I hope I have done enough to be deserving of a place at God's table.

If not, I would be happy with a place in the same room.

In my dreams in the centre of that table there is a small vase which each day holds a different coloured flower. It is freshened daily and the same one has never been seen twice. All around are trees, plants, animals and insects. There are too many to count or summarise but all have their frailties and their admirable qualities. All do deserve their place.

I have taken some daisy seeds from the scapes beyond Port Nolloth that I told you about. I have planted them in the fields surrounding the cot at Roskorwell where I spent much of my childhood. Should they come through and bloom I hope the sun shines on them as it did on me.

All I ask of you, my dear family, is that you put some of those daisies on my grave one day. Plant them in the earth above my cold, crumbling and silent bones. When their stalks grow in summer and their white and yellow petals embrace the breezy sun, think of me as I, in spirit, will think of you. Look up to the heavens, like the golden centres of those daisies do, and let your faces be bathed in warm light. Stand and feel the power of the stars and the force of the world. Let it surge through every sinew until you can sense the tingle at the very tips of your outstretched fingers.

Be thankful for each day.

Be the best you can be.

Be happy.

Do not, as the poet Sir Walter Scott once wrote, die 'Unwept, unhonored, and unsung'.

Zebulon Saunders Pearce. 1823 – 1898

Acknowledgements in no particular order

St Keverne Local History Society

Patrick Richard Carstens: Port Nolloth (The making of a South African Seaport)

Richard Thomas Hall and the Little Railway of Namaqualand by Graham L D Ross (A paper prepared for The Heritage Foundation of Transnet Limited in July 1998)

Cornish Hedges Library

Soft Words Butter No Parsnips (The Collected Wisdom of Nellie Gambles) Edited by Patrick and Mary Gambles

Cornish Dialect by Les Merton

Hayle, West Cornwall and Helston Railways by G H Anthony

God